The Esau Convergence

BOOK TWO of THE ESAU CONTINUUM

by

J. C. Lynne

Ngano Press
PO BOX 524
BERTHOUD CO 80513-0524
www.nganopress.com

Revision 1.3

Trade Paperback:
ISBN-10: 1940421020
ISBN-13: 978-1-940421-02-5

eBook:
ISBN-10: 1940421039
ISBN-13: 978-1-940421-03-2

Cover art by David Aimerito
Edited by Jennifer Top

NGANO

PRESS

PREFACE

Hello again or for the first time! It's always a risk choosing a new author to read and I thank you for spending your precious time with my books. If you enjoyed my story there's nothing more valuable than spreading the good word. A few minutes on Amazon or Goodreads to let people know what you think is welcome and irreplaceable. Nothing sells books like you!

I'm indebted to Sarah Elizabeth Lacher for her incredible insight and recommendations on the science in this book. I'm so fortunate to know such amazing brains! Again, I must thank my cousin and cover artist, David Aimerito for the inspiration for this story. Without his unique eye, Sebastian might still be missing.

You can find me on Facebook. I love to see those likes on my page. Feel free to follow me on Twitter and of course, check out my website to see what's going on with The Beard and our family! I love to hear from folks about my work.

http://jclynne.com
http://twitter.com/jclynnenow
http://facebook.com/jclynnenow

JC Lynne
November, 2015

"Every child comes with the message that God is not yet discouraged of man."

— Rabindranath Tagore, Bengali polymath

PROLOGUE

The little girl sat on the floor and placed the wooden blocks with care. Silence surrounded her. She had turned on a little light, illuminating a haloed space on the floor where she worked. The blocks grew into a castle. She turned each block over and over in her chubby hand before choosing its placement. Pausing, she admired the turrets and the walls of her little fortress. Darkness hovered around the edge of her luminous kingdom. She liked the early morning quiet. No one prodding or poking. Her nose wrinkled at the thought of what the day might bring. An awareness tickled the back of her neck. The tiny hairs on her arms perked to attention. She swept her arm through the wooden palace sending blocks across the floor with a clatter and peered into the murkiness on the other side of the glass.

Light bloomed, brightening the laboratory. The little girl saw Dr. Carol exposed under the fluorescent lights. She disliked Dr. Carol. The woman's eyes never smiled. Nadja looked at Dr. Carol without expression. She saw the doctor's eyes narrow. The girl turned her back and began placing the blocks in neat piles in the wooden box. She only played when she was alone. The blocks stowed away and pushed back to their place on the bottom shelf, Nadja chose a picture book from the top shelf. She settled into a bean bag near the books and began turning pages. Dr. Carol wouldn't bring her breakfast. In her peripheral vision, Nadja saw the woman spin and go to her office. She kept a little smile inside.

Other staff began trickling into the laboratory. Nadja didn't know all of their names though it was the same people over and over. She didn't see Dr. Carol, but she knew by the shifting grind of the cameras in the corners of her space the doctor would be watching. Someone was always watching. Dr. Toby approached her room with her breakfast tray. Dr. Toby tried to be kind. He told silly jokes in the hopes of coaxing her smile.

"What's up, Buttercup?" Dr. Toby radiated a bright grin. He set the food tray down to swipe his security card. A light chirp sounded the lock release and he pushed the door open with his back, balancing the tray in both hands. "This morning's selection includes fresh strawberries, my famous egg scramble with some blueberry toast and some sliced melon."

Nadja rolled her eyes.

"You doubt my famous egg scramble?" He opened his eyes wide with insulted outrage. "I'll tell you, I cracked and scrambled these eggs with my own two hands for you, little miss."

Nadja didn't smile, but she allowed a tiny bit of amusement to show.

"Ah, now that's more like it." He pushed a button and stepped back to let a small table drop from the wall.

Nadja watched while he set the plates on the table with exaggerated ceremony.

Dr. Toby looked up to make eye contact with her. "Come, come, little bird. Breakfast first, then Dr. Ellen will take you to shower and dress." He pulled a small chair out for her.

An explosion blew Nadja to her back. The glass panels of her room shattered into the space. A thousand tinkling shards blasted into the wall over her head. She peered through the smoke to see Dr. Toby lying on his side; glass splinters glittered in his skin. His eyes were blank and thin trails of blood crept along his face toward the floor. Her attention turned to the soft pops coming through the haze from the lab side of her empty windows. She burrowed back, slipping under her bed through the field of glass and watching the shadowed figures wind through the smoke. She didn't make a sound.

CHAPTER ONE

Vancouver
2015

Sebastian strode through the busy Vancouver International Airport. He carried his leather overnight satchel with purpose. Alonzo had ordered a car for him. He sailed through customs and wound his way through the main terminal. Out of habit, he scanned the crowd moving around him like fish in a current. He'd allowed his thoughts to distract him from his surroundings once. The lesson had been expensive. He surveyed the crowd and allowed his practiced senses to work. His thoughts tangled around the reason for his trip. *What're you going to say? Do you know what you're doing?* He spotted the doors to passenger pickup. Miguel Torres would be waiting for him.

A face in the crowd registered. He slowed, doing a double take. A ghost leaned against a pillar with a cocky grin on its face, a face dead and buried years ago. Sebastian Cole stopped, his thoughts swirling.

The ghost strode toward him, lanky ease in his tread.

A cold quick stab took Sebastian by surprise. Whipping his hand around, he caught the wrist of his assailant. He applied pressure and heard a satisfying snap. The man fell to his knees clutching his arm to his chest. A hypo dropped out of his hand and clattered to the floor. Security officers surrounded

Sebastian with their weapons drawn. He swore under his breath and glared at the corpse. "You bastard." His vision blurred.

The specter's smug grin slipped into darkness. "Cole, long time no see."

Sebastian stumbled. He shook his head to clear his vision. "You're going to pay."

"I doubt it."

Sebastian blacked out.

****

"Mr. Jackson, I'm not an alarmist, but the last time Cordelia got caught up in your business she ended up in a coma."

Cordelia opened her mouth to speak, but her father put a hand up. "Even if it's an improvement, but you've changed."

Cordelia's nonna snorted, but stifled it when Cordelia glared at her.

Enzo Fiore patted Cordelia's hand. "You're not hiding anymore. You're using your gift more than ever. You spend time in the shop talking to folks. You brought Busto home. You're confident in a way I've never seen. It's all good. They're professionals, why do they need you?"

Anthony Jackson cleared his throat. "Mr. Fiore, Cordelia's talents are useful. Her participation in the case we worked in Rome proved invaluable, and we're more likely to find Sebastian with her help. Cordelia is far from helpless. Not only is she a gifted psychic, because of you she's a strong fighter. She's an asset."

Cordelia smiled. Anthony disliked facing angry fathers. *How many have stared him down?* "Enzo, give Anthony a break. It's true I've changed. I'm not holding back. If I can help find him I have to try." She spoke past her father's frown. "I'm going to England. You can bluster and moan, but I'm capable of taking care of myself, and Global Sureties has plenty of people on staff who can handle anything I can't."

Lucia Fiore slapped her hands down on the table. "Good, end of discussion. Now let's eat." She stood up. "Anthony … or Tony?" She didn't wait for a response. "Tony, pull on the end of the table to open up the leaves. Cordelia, you're setting. Enzo, call Carlo and tell him we're eating if he wants to join us." She clapped her hands. "I'll open a bottle of wine and make sure dinner's ready."

Her father looked as though he wanted to say something else. "Okay, Ma." He glared at Anthony. "You'll make sure she's safe." Without waiting for a response, he went to the kitchen to call his brother.

"Whew," Anthony said, pulling the table out to its full length.

Cordelia laughed. "When was the last time you faced someone's father?"

"Jeez, 1995? Jessica Roberts's debutante ball. Her father almost had me arrested."

Cordelia tilted her head. "Arrested?"

"Jessica is white," Anthony said. He took the silverware out of Cordelia's hand to help set. He lowered his already baritone voice. "Don't get me wrong, son, I'm not prejudiced. Hell, your father's a member of my club, but it's not appropriate for you to accompany my daughter to her cotillion. What would people say?"

"Really? In 1995? What an asshole." Cordelia folded the napkins.

"Eh," Anthony said. "Not like it's much different now."

Cordelia shot him a surprised look. "Surely it's a little different. The US voted for a black president."

Lucia brought a bottle of wine from the kitchen. "Here, Tony, open this." She walked back into the kitchen.

Anthony shook his head. "Your grandmother's a piece of work."

"Not much rattles her." Cordelia handed him a wine key.

"I like her." He set the open bottle on the table. "President Obama didn't change things. There are a lot of people out there who've amped up their prejudice. You don't know what it's like to walk into a store and have clerks hover to make sure you're not stealing anything."

Cordelia pulled the wine glasses out of her nonna's hutch. "I can't even imagine what that's like."

"It is what it is. Some things change, some things are slow to change, and some things never change." He looked over the table. "I like your grand-mother's china."

"Not sure I'd call it china but I've always liked it." She pulled out a water pitcher.

"It looks like Maiolica. Do you know how old it is?"

Lucia answered as she walked back into the dining room carrying a covered serving dish. "It's been handed down for generations, one of Enzo's professor friends thinks it might even be from the late fifteenth century. He was appalled we ate off of them. I said, 'What good are dishes you can't use?' He hasn't come back for dinner since. Cordelia, run and grab the salad."

Anthony picked up a plate to take a close look. "I don't know. The design is less ornate than some I've seen. It's terrific, but it's probably lead-glazed." He put the plate down.

"Yep, hasn't killed anyone in my family yet. How do you know so much about dishes?" She walked to the hutch to pull out serving spoons.

"Yeah, it seems a little out of your depth," Cordelia said, putting the salad bowl on the table.

Anthony wasn't embarrassed. "My grandmother's a stickler for things, particularly china. She's proud of her full set of Nippon china. The family my great-grandmother worked as a nanny for gave it to her. She raised three generations of them. It's white and green with a border of daisies. I can't remember the particular name, but I know the china dates to the 1920s. My grandmother values the history of things."

"It's good to know," Lucia said. She gestured to herself. "Old things have the best stories."

Cordelia rolled her eyes. "Do you want me to bring the bread out?"

Her nonna waved her away. "No, pour the wine. Sit. I'll get the bread and see what's taking those boys of mine so long."

Anthony pulled out a chair for Cordelia. "She reminds me of my grandmother. I wouldn't cross either one."

Cordelia heard fondness in his voice matching the warmth of his thoughts. "Don't even think of it. She'd put the whammy on anyone who did."

"The whammy?" he asked, moving to sit across from her.

Cordelia tapped her head. "You know my thing? Well, it includes whammies. Curses. It works too. In college, I dated this football player. He dumped me right after I slept with him. I wasn't heartbroken or anything, but Nonna put the whammy on him and the coach moved him from first-string starter to third-string backup." She shrugged. "I've never used it myself. Too worried it might work."

He took the glass of wine she held out. "Well, I've seen your brain at work, so I don't doubt the whammy. Besides, my grandmother isn't above cursing someone. She calls it the evil eye."

"Here's to grandmothers." Cordelia raised her glass.

Anthony touched his glass to hers. "Grandmothers."

"And don't forget it," Lucia said, plopping the bread down on the table. "Where's my wine?"

****

Sebastian woke up in the back of a moving van. He swallowed down light nausea, a residual from the sedative. From his angle on the floor, he saw two sets of boots. He remained motionless; pretending to be unconscious. His metabolism burned off the drug faster than his captors intended. The van's engine changed pitch as the vehicle slowed. Sebastian waited, holding his rage to a low boil. *Take your time.*

The van turned left and continued to reduce speed. Sebastian paced his breath, unwilling to tip off his guards. As the van braked to a stop, the two guards stood and adjusted their weapons. They moved to lift him. Sebastian went limp. They shifted their balance to brace for his bulk. As they stepped toward the back doors, Sebastian planted his feet and drew the two men in toward each other. Startled and unsteady, the guard on the left tried to grab Sebastian around the waist. Ignoring the struggling guard on the right, Sebastian wrapped his arms around the left guard and lifted his feet off of the floor. He swung the guard's feet overhead and used him to knock out the other man. Both guards fell into a heap as Sebastian kicked the back doors open, flinging them into another guard outside of the van.

Sebastian leapt out. He drove a right hook into a man rushing to contain him. Another assailant ran from the front of the van with his gun drawn. Sebastian charged him, striking the man's gun hand at the wrist. Grabbing hold of the trigger well, Sebastian continued his momentum to grab the collar of the attacker's jacket and threw him to the ground. He felt the electrode darts of a taser sting his back. He crashed to his hands and knees at the jolt of electricity. Shaking his head, he adjusted his grip on the pistol and planted a foot forward to gain his feet. Aiming the gun as he spun around, Sebastian shifted his weight to one knee. He pointed the gun at the sound of applause.

CHAPTER TWO

Afghanistan
2006

"I'm not asking your permission," Lorena said, her rifle tucked against her shoulder. The barrel rested on a tripod. A digital readout on the screen near her provided the wind direction, velocity, and the air temperature. She kept her eye to her scope.

"You know he's an ass."

"Fucking hell, Sebastian. Could we talk about this later?" she hissed between gritted teeth. "You're supposed to be covering my back, not lecturing me."

Sebastian sat three feet away from her. Tucked behind a boulder, he focused his gaze on the rear approach. "I am covering you."

She put her hand up; her target moved into sight.

He went quiet.

Lorena took a deep breath in and let it out with a low, slow hiss. At the bottom of her breath, she pulled the trigger with measured motion. The rifle recoiled into her shoulder pad. "Let's go." She packed her gear in less than two minutes.

Sebastian took point, checking their retreat through the small ravine. Too far away for any shot to be effective, the distant reports of gunfire echoed across the landscape. He heard Lorena's steps behind him. Without rushing, he moved toward the rendezvous point where Thomas waited with a beat-up Honda Civic. Getting through the terrain was easy. The sun still hung below noon but the heat killed. *God, it's going to be a scorcher.* He paused at a turn in the ravine until he saw Lorena move into position behind him.

Two more miles and they spotted Thomas leaning against a car so dirty it blended in with the ground. He climbed into the driver's seat as soon as he spied them.

"Shotgun," Lorena said. She opened the hatchback and placed her case in the back.

"Shit, Lorena, how am I supposed to fit in the back of this tin can?"

She drew herself to her full six feet. "And I'm going to fit any better? You lose."

Thomas leaned out the window. "Children, children, could we move this along? I know we should have a clear path outta here, but I'd like to get moving just in case."

Lorena held the door open for Sebastian. "After you."

He grumbled as he folded himself into the tiny backseat. "This sucks."

"Yeah, don't it," Lorena said, slamming the passenger door twice before it latched. "This is a real peach, Thomas."

Thomas slammed the gearshift into first. The engine sputtered and the little car lurched forward. "Better hope the road is clear cuz this thing won't get away from anything chasing us."

Sebastian kicked the back of Lorena's seat. "He's an ass."

Lorena flipped him the bird.

"We're talking about Haager, I presume," Thomas said.

"Hell on toast. The whole unit knows? What've you guys got against him? He's been a Wolf for three years. You trust him with the job."

"He's a player. He's a hound when it comes to women. You've seen him. He may be someone I'll work with, but I don't think he's a guy to marry." Sebastian stretched out as much as he could in the backseat. He kicked the back of her seat again. "You're one of us. He's passing through. Bottom line, he's not good enough for you."

Lorena looked at Thomas. "You haven't said much."

He shrugged. "Not much to say. Do I think you should marry him? Nope. Do I think you're gonna do what you want? Yep. You're the number one shot in the world. He's what? Number six?" He shook his head.

"That's your argument? He's only the sixth best shot?" She rolled her eyes.

Sebastian jumped in. "He's lazy, arrogant, and not good enough."

"You're both full of shit." She folded her arms.

There's no talking her out of it. He closed his eyes and tried to relax in the cramped backseat.

Silence filled the car the rest of the way back to the base. After clearing the security gate, Thomas pulled the little rust bucket around to the back of the motor pool.

The man in question came trotting from the direction of the briefing hangar. "Hey, you goons took long enough." He leaned against the Civic. "You get 'em, babe?"

"You need to ask?" Lorena said, throwing her equipment pack at him. She lifted her gun case out of the car.

"We've got a briefing. You're late. Hawthorne's waiting and he's not happy."

Sebastian groaned as he disengaged his rangy frame from the back of the Honda. "When's Hawthorne ever happy?"

"You going to be all right?" Thomas watched Sebastian stretching side to side.

He waved him off with a flash of his middle finger.

Haager slung his arm around Lorena. "This one's big. We're all going in."

Sebastian grunted. "Hmm."

"Scary bad guys with big scary bugs," Haager said over his shoulder as he and Lorena started walking.

Thomas sighed. "Biologicals. Shite, I hate biologicals."

"Yeah, why can't we kill each other civilized?" Sebastian punched him in the shoulder.

Jeremy Hawthorne's voice boomed through the metal hangar with little effort. "The intelligence survey reports twelve insurgents are in residence in the building while up to five more come and go with little warning." He frowned over the map. "We have up to twenty moving targets to deal with at any given moment. This group has biological agents. Info is confirmed through several different sources. Shaw." The commander's stony eyes looked up to find his supply officer.

"Sir."

"We'll need a full array of antibiotics and epinephrine in the event of exposure. Masks, in this case, are too restrictive to vision and won't do anything to protect against an agent absorbed through the skin. You all know the routine."

Lt. Orozco grinned. "Hold your breath and grab your ass." The thick exaggeration of his natural L.A. street accent inspired some chuckles.

"Or grab someone else's ass!" Lt. Smith leered, making a good-natured grab at Lorena's rear end.

Haager stepped forward, danger in his face. "You should stick with Davidson's ass, Smith. Lorena's is taken."

Hawthorne's cool, stony voice broke over the jokes. "Reports show the biological agents are kept here." His beefy finger rested at the center of the diagram. The unit focused without further comment. Hawthorne continued. "Cole, you and Shaw'll come in from the southwest along this line of overgrowth. The street lights along this road are broken so there's good cover. Haager and Gellat'll be positioned west and east. There's a low building on the northwest corner of this empty lot." Hawthorne looked at Haager. "You'll position here." His finger slid across the diagram. "Gellat, you here. There are two guards walking the perimeter. Each of you will eliminate a guard then make your way to the second floor to provide cover."

The briefing continued until each of the team knew the plan without error. The Wolves broke up to grab some chow before getting to bed. An 0200 assault time meant up at 0000 hours to make their target drop. Sebastian stopped his commanding officer as the rest of the group headed to mess.

"Sir, about Gellat?"

Hawthorne put his beefy hand up. "I'm not her father. They're not breaking any fraternization regulations. I can't order her to dump him on the basis he's an asshole. She's a grown woman. She's no dummy. She'll figure it out on her own. Understood?"

Sebastian kept his face blank. "Understood."

"Go eat and get some rest. We've got a busy night."

****

Marcus Haager leaned against the hood of a black Porsche Panamera clapping his hands. "Good show, Cole. You always were one of the best."

Sebastian narrowed his eyes and stood. "Tell your man behind me to stand down."

Haager looked surprised, but he waved off his man. "You don't want to shoot me."

"Really? I'm running through the list of reasons. It's pretty long."

"You're not done with Vivienne Carlson."

Sebastian reflected a moment. Haager and his lackeys didn't know about his nature or they would've been more prepared. His involvement with Carlson's takedown wasn't a secret. Haager could be fishing. He thought about Vancouver and Cordelia. He didn't know how the situation would play out, but he was working on letting go of Vivienne Carlson and her science. He took a deep breath. He also couldn't be sure Haager didn't know something. Ian had discovered gaps in Carlson's research, which they'd taken from the laboratories at Biogenesis and Carlson's personal lab. He dropped his aim. "Okay, go."

Haager visibly relaxed. "I'm CIA. We monitored Carlson's work. We managed to plant a mole who fed us information."

Sebastian tamped down his rage and disgust. "You farmed her research to weaponize." He clenched the pistol.

Haager put his hands up and approached Sebastian with caution. "Not my call. I moved the information upstream. Several years ago, Carlson moved to human subjects. She genetically modified human DNA so she could create a human with an amped up immune system."

"Yeah, I know," Sebastian said, not impressed.

"Not only immunization, but genetic manipulation of embryonic DNA. She tried to create a superhuman race," Haager said.

Sebastian frowned. Nothing they'd found in Carlson's research indicated gestation of embryos. She had been shocked to learn her insertion changed Sebastian. Her focus had been harvesting stem cells for gene therapy.

"I know she thought about in vitro gene therapy for conditions like Down's or spina bifida, but nothing we found indicated she planned to gestate embryos full term."

"We found the cloned embryos." Haager's eyes narrowed. "She used the DNA of a human subject to insert into embryos scrubbed of their own DNA. She created viable embryos. She planned to clone a human being."

"You have proof?" Sebastian's thoughts spun.

Haager shrugged. "Why so many embryos if she wasn't going to fully gestate them? Our guy managed to smuggle some of the embryos out of the lab."

Sebastian ground his teeth. Haager and the rest of the idiots working with him believed Carlson planned on creating clones. What did they do? They tried to beat her to it. Haager didn't know the full extent of Sebastian's role. He felt sick to his stomach. Pushing back the blood haze creeping into his eyes, he swung a powerful left hook clipping Haager square in the jaw. The resurrected flew off of his feet and landed full force on the ground. A handful of security surrounded Sebastian, weapons drawn. He stood motionless while Haager, rubbing his jaw, allowed his men to lift him to his feet.

"Damn, was a time you wouldn't have caught me off guard. Never thought you'd cheap shot a guy."

Sebastian narrowed his eyes, willing his internal heat to a simmer rather than a rolling boil. "Cheap guy, cheap shot. Times change."

"People usually don't," Haager remarked, feeling his teeth with his tongue. "I think you loosened a couple of my teeth."

"Soft diet for a couple weeks, good as new."

Haager motioned the security team to holster their weapons. "We need to take this discussion inside."

Sebastian crossed his arms. "Give me one good reason."

Haager's nerves showed in a telltale twitch of his neck.

Sebastian snorted.

"What?" Haager demanded.

"You're right. People don't change." He brushed his neck with his finger. "Still nervous?"

"Fuck you, Cole. This is official. It pisses me off, but I need your help. You can help willingly or not."

The men surrounding Sebastian closed some space.

"Think you can, eh?" Sebastian shifted his weight and widened his stance. His entire body radiated tension.

The security unit surrounding him started shuffling their feet and fidgeting.

Haager waved them back. "Fine, have it your way. Be a dick. You'll be leaving Carlson's clone in the hands of someone worse than me."

"You stole the embryos and gestated them. They've been stolen from you and you're asking me to help you? You might regret it."

The Lazarus man turned back with a winning smile. "Don't count on it."

CHAPTER THREE

Busto rode in the Rover with his head and front paws on the console between Cordelia and Anthony. A soft, constant drizzle fogged the countryside along the road to the Cole estate outside of North Walsham. One of the Global Sureties jets carried them into Norwich International Airport. The puppy did well on the plane and slept the majority of the time. They had an hour layover in Montreal for fuel and to change pilots. Gerald recalled everyone to the estate to keep security tight. Seamus traveled to Rome to pick up Thomas and Rachna. Sebastian might have been the only target, but no one wanted to take any chances.

"We're all meeting up at the estate. Alonzo's working with some of our contacts to get the security footage from Vancouver International. He'll pipe it to the estate so we can try to figure out what happened." He gave her a sideways glance. "Didn't think you were serious about bringing the dog."

Cordelia stroked Busto's head. "I'm always serious." She watched the woods blur through the window. "I don't think I'll be able to determine anything from a video."

He shook his head. "No, not from the video. We know he landed. Sebastian has worked with a lot of people. Some not exactly upstanding members of society. He could've been caught in some kind of a power struggle or taken by someone with a grudge. You might get another flash like you did last time."

"My insights are stronger after … Slovenia." Cordelia read Anthony's discomfort about the genetic manipulation loud and clear. "But I haven't had any flashes similar to Sperlonga." She picked up his unease with Sebastian's second nature. "If you feel uncomfortable about all of this, why do you work with them?"

She sensed his struggle to organize his thoughts and put up a light screen around her mind. Something she'd learned to do recently when she didn't want to hear people's thoughts. *Should've put it up sooner to give him some privacy.*

After a long pause, he answered, "I respect Sebastian and the others. Hell, Seamus is my friend. I know Sebastian changed Thomas and Lorena by accident, but I don't understand Seamus's decision. Carlson's science became madness. To be human is to be vulnerable, to be mortal."

Cordelia resisted the urge to peek at his thoughts. She reached up to brush the scar at the base of her neck. "They're vulnerable. You haven't forgotten Lorena," she said, sadness creeping at the edge of her thoughts.

"No, I haven't," he said, "but outside of a bullet to the brain, I've seen Seamus and Sebastian heal from killing wounds."

"I might not have evolved the way the others have, but I'm different too," she reminded him.

"You're human," he asserted, his voice flat.

"You don't think Sebastian and the others are human?"

He stared at the road ahead of them. "Seamus told me you couldn't read them clearly. He said something about existing outside of the strands of fate." He glanced at her.

Cordelia nodded. "I did, but it's a theory. I don't understand what I could do before, and now that things are growing stronger I'm still clueless. If you say they're not human then I'm not, by strict definition, either."

"You've seen them. You feel the energy they radiate. I worked a job in India a few years ago. In the forest, I ran into a tiger. A one in a million chance, they're endangered and few live in the wild. I froze, entranced and terrified at the same time." He looked at her. "Not much scares me but when the tiger looked at me, I felt an intrinsic, irrational urge to run. Something primal written in my biology."

"What'd you do?" Cordelia asked.

"I took control and remained stock still, but I'll never forget the threat exuding from the cat. It looked at me deciding whether I'd be good eating. I stayed rooted for a long time after it left, to be sure."

She saw his hands clenched on the steering wheel. "Couldn't you have killed it if it had attacked?"

"I'm not sure if I would've had time. The thing is, even when they're not shifted, the others have the same aura. They're predators. I trust all of them with my life and Seamus ..." He shook his head with a smile. "You know how he is."

Cordelia gave a light laugh. "Yeah, I do."

Anthony's face grew stony. "They're the good guys, but they're something other than human."

"Are there levels of humanity? Different stages of evolution are acceptable? I know some people you'd consider normal who have far less humanity than Sebastian." She looked out across the hills. "We've been forced to evolve. I say *we*, Anthony, because I feel the change in me."

"You don't seem different to me. I don't know, I'm torn. I don't believe in God, you know. I spent my entire childhood bracing against those Sunday school lessons. A lot in this world reinforces my atheism. I understand the science of evolution. What Carlson did to you—" He paused. "It was not natural evolution. It was folly. Pure manmade recklessness."

"I'm all right because I don't change into a seven-foot tall monster?" She raised her eyebrows at him. "Unfair. You're prejudiced against the others because they become physically different? I'd say pot and kettle." She raised her hands to his look of doubt. "Okay, the shifting aside, you said it, they're good people. Does it matter if they change into something else? I've known monsters." She thought of Vivienne Carlson. "They're not monsters."

"A part of me thinks it's irrelevant, no matter what I think in terms of morals or integrity. They're a different species." Cordelia waved her hand at him. He sighed. "You're a different species. I don't have it all sorted."

"You work with them. You respect them."

He shrugged. "It's complicated."

Cordelia laughed a little. "That's a mouthful."

Arriving at the Cole estate, Busto jumped out of the SUV. Tail wagging, he lumbered from one side of the drive to the other. He paused to pee and then ran, nose to the ground to another spot. Cordelia called him. "Busto, come."

Arthur Lindsay stepped out to greet her. "Let him be. He won't hurt anything." He hugged her.

Busto quit his ranging to bark at Lindsay.

"Busto, sit." The dog settled his hulk but chuffed. Cordelia rolled her eyes at the dog. "You have no idea what trouble he can get into."

"He won't have a chance once Elsa sees him. She adopted some feral kittens. There's a little goat following her everywhere. We've had to chase it out of the house twice. One more creature isn't going to make a difference though Reynolds might not agree." He held a hand out to Anthony. "Tony, we're having lunch on the terrace since the weather cleared. Alonzo's on his way with the video footage."

Anthony shook his hand. "I contacted a colleague with access to the facial recognition software. She's going to run the video and see if she can't narrow down Sebastian's movements." He glanced at Cordelia with a strange look.

She thought about dropping her guard to see what it meant.

"Well, we have time to eat. Nothing to be done until then." Lindsay dropped a hand to let the bulldog sniff him. Busto didn't break his sit but decided Lindsay smelled good and slavered over his palm with his long tongue. The author looped his arm through Cordelia's. "Reynolds'll have your bags in your room by now. Ian's in the barn. Let's swing by and remind him it's time for tea."

"I'm going to the office to make a couple of calls. I'll meet you on the terrace." Anthony went into the grand house.

"Busto, come." Cordelia smiled. She enjoyed the Cole estate. "Can't get Ian to stop working, eh?"

"He's been poring over Carlson's files. There are gaps and some of the files were corrupted, but he's determined to get a handle on the research. How'd Anthony do with Busto?" The dog ran ahead of them rushing from bush to tree to bush. Her companion smiled at the wiggling, wagging tail.

"Fine. He doesn't like dogs?" The roof of the barn came into view.

Lindsay laughed. "I think Anthony's fondness for pets has been taxed by Seamus."

"You're awful," Cordelia said, laughing.

"It's true." He shrugged.

Cordelia saw Busto run for the stalls. He caught the scent of the horses and other animals. "Busto, come." The dog whined but obeyed. "Busto, with me." His droopy eyes looked at her, but he stayed in step with her. "Good heel."

Lindsay opened the same door Cordelia had stumbled through a few months ago. "He can come in. Ian lets Elsa and her kittens roam around."

The man in question looked up from his computers, eyes bright when he saw Cordelia step into the lab. "Halloo, gorgeous." He crossed the space between them to hug her. "Oh, who's this?" He bent to let Busto sniff his hand. No huffing or woofing from the dog, only a lolling tongue.

"He's decided we're among friends. This is Busto."

Ian grinned and scratched behind both of Busto's ears. The dog's eyes rolled in delight. "Good Busto. What a burly chap! Aren't you wonderful?" He crooned and moved his fingers under Busto's chin. "He's marvelous. When did you get him?"

"Several weeks ago. He's five months old, but he's learning."

Cordelia.

Cordelia looked around for the creature whose thoughts touched her. "Elsa?"

Ian stood to wave his hand toward the open stall doors. "She's outside watching over her kittens." He looked at her. "She's been waiting for you."

"Really?" She reached out with her mind. *Elsa.*

The large russet chimera moved into sight. A genetically engineered animal created by Vivienne Carlson, she had human DNA along with orangutan, mountain gorillas, and jaguar. Distinguishing any particular trait except for her eyes would be impossible. Elsa's mahogany eyes stared out from her hominid features. Cordelia imagined her face reflected early human ancestors.

Busto approached Elsa with care. He didn't make any noise as he walked up to her foot. He licked her toes.

Busto.

Cordelia smiled and answered out loud. "Yes, he's Busto."

Elsa looked up and gestured with her hands. She folded her right thumb into her palm and wiggled it over her left palm toward her body. *Busto.*

Cordelia looked at Ian.

"Elsa's learning American Sign Language. She's named Busto. A wiggling letter B. She's decided that's his sign."

Cordelia mimicked the sign. "Busto. He's definitely a wiggle butt."

I'm glad at seeing you.

Cordelia looked into Elsa's eyes. *You're well?*

Yes. Elsa placed a heavy hand on Ian's shoulder. *I like him even though he's not red.*

Cordelia laughed. "Seamus is hard to resist."

Lindsay snorted.

I like Busto. I'll take him outside. The kittens will like him too. Without waiting for an answer, Elsa turned to walk out into the arena with the wiggler in tow.

"I'll never get him back," Cordelia said.

Lindsay laughed. "I told you. Let's go enjoy our tea. As soon as Alonzo arrives with the footage, we'll be rushed."

"What's going on?" Cordelia asked. "Outside of the fact Sebastian's missing, Anthony avoided answering my questions."

Ian took Lindsay's hand and they walked out of the barn toward the house. "He didn't give you any answers to your questions because we don't have any. Sebastian left Rome on a ticket for Vancouver. He arranged for a car. We thought he'd come to his senses."

Cordelia grunted.

"It's a lot to hope for, I admit, but he did fly to Vancouver." He gave her a smile.

"Okay." She conceded. "He got on the plane, which means he arrived, but I haven't seen him."

They climbed the stairs to the large main terrace. Reynolds served tea and lunch on the table. He nodded to Cordelia. "Ms. Fiore. Your things are in your room. I've served a rather large tea. I didn't know if you'd eaten on the plane."

"Thank you, Reynolds, you're very thoughtful. I'm starving." Reynolds held her chair out.

Lindsay added to the narrative. "That's what Alonzo is working on. He's trying to get access to the security films from Vancouver International. Thomas and Rachna are on their way from Rome. Seamus is with them."

Worry shadowed her excitement to see her friends. "You think everyone could be a target?"

Ian patted her hand. "We're covering all of the bases. Until we find out what happened to Sebastian, we're flying blind."

CHAPTER FOUR

"I need to make a call. My people will be looking for me," Sebastian said, following Haager toward the unassuming house.

Haager shook his head. "Sorry, for now we need this under the radar." He opened the front door. "It wouldn't do to tip off anyone to what we're doing."

Sebastian shook his head and rolled his eyes. Drama queen. "If you think the people you're looking for are watching me, I guarantee they'll catch on as soon as my team starts searching." A thought occurred to him. "Do you even know who you're looking for?"

Haager's back stiffened.

"Ho ho. You've no idea who you're after." Sebastian whistled. "Shit never changes with you, does it?"

"Look, I'll give you a full briefing. I have a team at your disposal. You're the one who took Vivienne Carlson out, so you'd have the best line on what we've got. We've sold the idea upstream." He stepped into the house.

Sebastian tried to keep the smug look off of his face. "A phone call would keep my team off of it. Your call. We told Lorena you weren't good enough."

Haager asked, "How is she?"

Sebastian took a moment to control his rage. "You dropped off the grid and never looked back? You're still an asshole." He stood on the porch debating whether he could walk away from Haager and his bait.

"They don't give you much choice. You're dead. There isn't a lot of discussion about it." Haager ran a hand through his hair.

Sebastian crossed his arms, not letting Haager off of the hook. "You're trying to play a player. You forget, I worked the life. I know exactly how it can go. You could've recruited Lorena."

Haager looked at him. "Maybe you got to her first."

Sebastian snorted. Haager never bothered a second thought for Lorena. "You didn't deserve her."

"Seriously, how is she?"

"Dead." Sebastian didn't flinch. The thought of Lorena ached and Sebastian suppressed the urge to punch him again.

Haager blanched. "How?"

"Not going there with you, Haager. You claim to need my help. Okay, I'll listen to your pitch, but you get one shot and then ..." He trailed off.

"And then?" Haager asked.

"I'll consider not killing you," he said.

The house served as a makeshift base ops. Haager led Sebastian into what used to be a formal dining room. One end of the large eight-seat table was divided into three computer stations. Two men and a woman sat before terminals. The other end of the table was buried under files and maps.

"Travis is looking for any sign of offers or auctions of high-tech medical research," Haager said, gesturing to the young man at the end of the table. He gave Sebastian a tilt of the head. "Aitken is digging into people who have a history of peddling black market med tech or biotech." The short-haired woman glanced at Sebastian then turned her eyes back to her screen. "Roberts is tracking air traffic." The last man, older than the others, gave Sebastian a nod. "He's looking for flight plans filed around the time of the break-in."

Sebastian looked at the files stacked on the other end of the table. Aware of several others around the house, he asked, "How many people are working this?"

"These three working the tech end. Four others are running the normal criminal angles. I did have eight on security, but after your run-in with my team, I'll be lucky to have four uninjured. You didn't have to bust them into pieces." Haager moved into the kitchen. "Coffee or something to drink?"

"Yeah, coffee. You didn't have to bag and tag me. Where am I anyway?" He took the mug Haager offered. In what used to be a den, several of the men Sebastian tangled with received first aid.

"Virginia. The original lab is a few miles from here. I thought you might need to see it, but all of our research materials are accessible from these terminals."

Sebastian looked back at the tech squad. "You gestated the clones to term. How many are there?"

"We smuggled three out of Carlson's lab in cryo, only two successfully implanted and only one gestated to term, born three years ago."

Sebastian stared at his coffee. *A bloody nightmare.*

"We named her Nadja. Our researchers have been raising her in a controlled environment." Haager continued on, clueless to Sebastian's reticence. "We have video of various stages of her development. The files containing her medical records were scrubbed. The doctors diagnosed her with selective mutism. They couldn't find anything developmentally wrong with her." He looked at Sebastian.

"Carlson's files indicated a male test subject. How'd you end up with a girl?" Sebastian tried to stay focused on the basics. *I might be sick.*

"Our researchers decided to muck with the XY chromosome. They thought girls would be more tractable research subjects." Haager gestured toward the family room. Another set of tables with computers took up the space.

Sebastian coughed. *Never been my experience.* "The breach at the lab?"

"Two weeks ago, a team with flash bombs and light arms broke into the lab. They downloaded all of the files, scrubbed the machines, and took the girl. The entire staff eliminated," Haager said.

"You have any line on where they have the clone?" Sebastian sipped his coffee.

"Not currently. We're combing through data and trying to narrow down the path of transit." Haager looked at his former team member. "I thought you might know who would be interested in the research."

"You mean because people cooperate with me rather than an upstanding covert operative like you?" He sneered over his mug.

Haager cleared his throat. "You can insult me all you want. I need to find the girl."

"Good to know, cuz I don't think I'll ever get tired of insulting you." Sebastian swallowed the last of his coffee. "It's a bad idea not to notify my team."

"Not authorized." Haager shook his head.

Sebastian shrugged. "On your head."

Sebastian sat sipping the terrible coffee while Haager hovered over his tech team's shoulders. Sebastian caught the kid named Travis rolling his eyes a couple of times and chuckled into his mug. "Does Bishop know you've tapped me?"

Haager looked up and nodded. "It was his idea. We're running out of time on this one."

Sebastian barked a laugh. "He authorized illegal medical experiments. Bishop's flapping in the breeze rushing to salvage the project and his career. Watch yourself, Bishop's only concern is Bishop."

"You know, he did what he could," Haager said seriously. "Your retrieval was a clusterfuck. Hawthorne dead and then you and your team AWOL. Bishop could've hung you out to dry, but he kept the agency off your back."

Sebastian put his mug down and crossed his arms. "I know exactly what Bishop tried to do to help me. You think I don't have my own contacts? Bishop's always viewed me as an obstacle to his aspirations. You might think for a minute why Hawthorne didn't choose him for the Black Wolves team in the first place. I know who he's worked for and what he's done in the meantime. Don't kid yourself, Bishop would love to bury me. With Hawthorne's job available and me in the running for it, he needed me out of the way." He looked at Haager. "Didn't work out so well for him in the end considering where he's working now, did it?"

"He's heading up a high-level security operation," Haager threw back.

"Not for the NSA, and now who is he tapping to help him clean up his mess?" He didn't bother to keep his contempt in check. "This is a bloody shambles and Bishop's looking at damage control. He'll try to shift this on you or more likely me to save himself."

Haager frowned. "This is about containment."

Thunder rumbled across Sebastian's face. "Containment," he said. Anger and disdain filled his voice.

From the dining area, Haager's young tech wizard Travis spoke up. "I think I've found where they've holed up."

Haager bent to look over his shoulder again. "What makes you think so?"

"Transit receipts, the uptick in staffing, and medical equipment already on site," the young computer guy said, shooting an exasperated look at Sebastian.

This is a kid who knows worthless when he sees it.

"Get me schematics and security schedules," he ordered Aitken. "Roberts, give me access to any security cameras or ATM cameras in the area." He looked at Sebastian, satisfied. "Your team couldn't do any better."

"Whatever makes you sleep better at night," Sebastian said.

"I'll get the rest of the crew rounded up and we'll get going." Haager turned on his heel to leave the room.

Travis asked in a low voice. "He always this much of a douche?" His fellow tech people stifled laughs.

"Always," Sebastian said.

CHAPTER FIVE

Cole Estate

Thomas and Rachna arrived an hour after lunch. Cordelia embraced the Indian woman, noticing her healthy glow. She stepped back to take a good look. "You look terrific. How are you feeling?"

"The flight proved a bit challenging, but, for the most part, my nausea is limited to the morning. Ian assures me it'll ease up in a week or two." Rachna smiled. *I haven't told Thomas about the baby being a boy yet.*

Cordelia picked up her friend's thought without trouble. Meeting Rachna's eyes, she gave her a quick wink. "When is the bebe due?"

Rachna patted her tummy. "Maybe October."

Turning to Thomas, Cordelia smiled. "And how is Daddy holding up?"

The shaggy-headed Englishman beamed. "I'm ecstatic. I feel I should be asking you how you're feeling."

"Oh, you know, levitating and bending spoons with my mind." She gave a cavalier wave of her hand. Cordelia asked, "Anthony said Seamus flew with you?"

"Somebody asking about me?" the rakish ginger asked as he entered the drawing room. He threw his arms around Cordelia in a bear hug. "You miss my humor and charm?"

She laughed, catching her breath after his squeeze. "Oh yes, you're irresistible."

"I had a chat with Tony. He's tapped someone to help us with the footage from the airport. She's due to arrive any minute and then we'll move forward. Alonzo's convinced the Canadian government to send us the security videos, but it's a lot of data. All of this waiting around is driving me mad."

Lindsay arrived with Reynolds in tow carrying a tray of tea. "I thought Rachna could use some repast." He crossed the room to place a kiss on her cheek. "Gerald has requested Thomas and Seamus's presence in his office."

Thomas asked Seamus, "Who'd Tony get to help?"

Cordelia noticed the quick glance Seamus gave her before answering. "Mai Li."

Rachna took a seat on the couch and looked askance at Seamus. "Really?" She shot Cordelia a glance too.

A cough from Thomas sent Cordelia's suspicion off the charts. "Okay, this is ridiculous. You're all looking at me as though I'm going to implode. Anthony acted oddly earlier. What's going on?" Cordelia said.

Seamus cleared his throat. "Ahem, Gao Mai Li is a security operative we've bumped into now and again."

Taking a cup of tea from Reynolds, Thomas added, "We met her while we were still in the Black Wolves. She used to be an MSS operative, but now she's an independent contractor. She's able to access some high-tech resources faster than we could. We don't ask how."

"Well, she and Sebastian …" Lindsay started.

Once again, Rachna's thoughts tumbled into clarity in Cordelia's mind. "Seriously? You're all worried about one of Sebastian's exes?" Cordelia rolled her eyes. "Listen, I'm not sure what's going on between Sebastian and me, but we're both grownups. I'm here to help find him. After we do, I've no idea what will happen. Don't walk around on pins and needles because of me."

Lindsay chuckled. "Of course, you're right." He sat next to Rachna with his own cup.

Reynolds politely reminded the group, "Sir Cole is waiting."

Seamus grabbed a biscuit from the tray, earning a slight frown from Reynolds as the butler left the room. "Right, let's go, Thomas."

The younger butler James entered the foyer and announced, "Ms. Gao Mai Li."

Cordelia turned and steeled herself to act as mature as she claimed. She'd never felt inadequate in her life until she laid eyes on this graceful, tiny woman. *Not even Rachna is that beautiful.*

"MacGolgan." The music of Mai Li's voice danced through the room.

Seamus crossed the room, hand extended. "Mai, thanks for coming."

Mai Li's hand disappeared in Seamus's large one. "Of course, I'm anxious to help." She turned to Thomas. "It's been a while, Shaw."

Cordelia saw Thomas blush a little. She looked at Rachna, who had covered a chuckle with her hand. Thomas quickly turned to his wife. "You remember my wife Rachna?"

"I do." Mai Li's voice poured honey into the room. She gave Lindsay the briefest of nods. "Mr. Lindsay."

"Ms. Gao." The typically warm author returned her nod with the barest of chills.

It took every ounce of self-control Cordelia had to keep out of Lindsay's mind. Her curiosity piqued. *What could she have done to cause Lindsay's ire?*

The pause in the room grew awkward. Mai Li turned to Cordelia. "I'm Gao Mai Li." She glided to offer Cordelia a handshake.

"Oh, Mai Li, I'm sorry. This is Cordelia Fiore," Thomas said. "Cordelia's a freelance consultant for Global Sureties. Cordelia, this is Gao Mai Li."

"Ah, another free agent. Do they give you any more warning than they give me?" Mai Li asked.

Cordelia shook her hand. Hit by a flash of insight, she kept her face a mask. "Not really." She offered a rueful look. "Seamus said you could help with the airport footage."

"Yes, in fact, I'd better get to it. The sooner we upload the footage into the BIS, the sooner we'll have a lead on Sebastian." She moved past Cordelia toward the study. "MacGolgan, you coming?"

The plucky Irishman nodded. "Yep."

"BIS?" Cordelia asked.

"Biometric Identification System. Fancy tag for facial recognition," Thomas said. "That'll take at least an hour if not longer." He looked at Cordelia. "We'll call you as soon as we find him."

Mai Li's interest in Cordelia sparked on her face, but she said nothing as she floated from the room with Seamus and Thomas in her wake.

"Holy shit!" Cordelia burst out. "You could've warned me. She's unreal. I didn't think women like that existed outside of fanboy fantasies. Jesus, even I think she's hot."

Rachna chuckled. "Hmmm, could I have said anything that wouldn't spin you into a funk? I'll admit, I find her overwhelming sometimes."

"I think I'll go curl up in my room and die." Cordelia brushed her hair out of her face.

"You're a beautiful woman Cordelia," Lindsay said with a reassuring tone.

"When I first met you, Rachna, I felt homely. Everything about you is serene grace. Me? My nose is too big. My eyes are disproportionate. I'm too tall by half. I recovered because you're a spectacular person and I'll be honest, you're married to Thomas. If someone had said, this stunning woman used to be Sebastian's lover … might've been different. That woman …" She took a breath. "I'm out of my league."

"You sensed something when she touched you," Rachna said, looking intense.

Cordelia startled at the change in Rachna's demeanor. "I didn't scan her. I thought it would be childish, but I thought I caught some overflow. I felt Sebastian. She feels proprietary about him. She's hiding something, but that's a big pool." She thought a minute and turned to Lindsay. "You don't trust her?"

Lindsay leaned forward to refill his cup. "Gao Mai Li has helped Sebastian and Thomas in the past, but she doesn't know about their nature. I think she'd try to use it to her advantage. Lorena didn't like her much. She used to say she had a gut feeling and that's always been enough for me."

The short stab of pain at the mention of Lorena's name didn't hurt Cordelia as much as it had in the recent past. "I'll take a closer look. If Lorena didn't trust her, I consider it the gold standard. Seamus mentioned she played a lot of different angles. Why would they trust her?" Her conscience pinched her as her imp mocked. *You mean Sebastian, not they. Jealous much? It wasn't jealousy. Oh ho ho, keep on saying it and you might begin to believe it.*

"Your guess is as good as mine," Rachna said. "Typically, I would say Sebastian's impervious to sex appeal in a woman, but look at her. You watch Thomas when we're all in the same room. He tries to hide it, but he doesn't look her in the eye." Rachna smiled at the thought. "Can you blame him?"

Cordelia set her mouth into a determined line. "I'll find out what she's up to."

Rachna noted her grim face. "It wouldn't hurt to know what happened between her and Sebastian, either."

Cordelia puffed a loose strand of hair out of her eyes. "I don't think I want to know. I might pale by comparison."

Rachna gave a light laugh and Lindsay joined her.

Cordelia chuckled, but she resolved to dig deep into Gao Mai Li's thoughts. *Maybe not too deep.*

Rachna begged jet lag and disappeared to her room after a light snack.

"You know, don't you?" Lindsay asked after the expectant Rachna left.

Cordelia sipped her tea. "Don't know what you're talking about."

Lindsay chuffed. "Fine, keep it a secret."

"How can I tell you something she hasn't told Thomas yet?" Cordelia scolded the author.

"Oh ho! Would it be unethical to place bets?" he asked in a wicked tone.

Cordelia rolled her eyes. "What is it with you people and bets?"

Lindsay sat straight and gave her a serious look. "Keeps things interesting."

"As if life around here isn't interesting enough?" She sighed.

Reynolds walked into the drawing room. "Ms. Fiore, Sir Cole would like you to join them in his office."

Cordelia stood up and looked at Lindsay. "Here we go."

****

"Well, bugger me, it's Haager!" Thomas swore.

Mai Li asked. "Who?"

Cordelia read the Chinese operative's thoughts and narrowed her eyes.

Thomas turned to pace around the library. "He was a Black Wolf. He's supposed to be dead."

"He's not now is he?" Seamus said, looking confused.

Gerald Cole spoke up. "You didn't work within the government, my boy. They can make things happen if it's in their favor. I imagine someone tapped him to work black ops. A nasty business, little oversight and too much power."

"And a serious lack of intelligence if they thought Haager was a good resource," Thomas said, glaring at the face on the screen.

"Okay." Cordelia broke in. "Haager has him. Can we track where they took him?"

Mai Li nodded at Cordelia. "Already thought of that. They made it look like a medical emergency." She pointed to the screen. "See here, they load him on a gurney and take him out of the airport." She clicked a different video file. "I picked Haager up in the South Terminal, no sight of Sebastian, but my guess would be ...."

Cordelia cut her off. "A seaplane."

"Yes." Mai Li nodded. "Afraid it's all I can do as far as the BIS is concerned. Tracking flights out of South Terminal, I'm not sure if I can help."

Anthony, who'd been quiet the entire time, spoke up. "No need, Mai. We can do it in-house."

"Jarske," Alonzo agreed. "I'll call him."

"Paul Jarske?" Mai Li asked. "You've got Jarske?"

"Yes," Anthony said. "I'd appreciate it if you considered the information confidential."

Cordelia clenched her fists. Mai Li radiated avarice. The woman's thoughts whirled in her head.

Seamus muttered, "Jarske's a nutter."

Cordelia faced Mai Li. "You know Haager." Marcus Haager. She picked the name out of the Chinese woman's brain.

Seamus and Anthony scrutinized the beauty.

"That's ridiculous," Mai Li said. She squared her shoulder and glared at Cordelia, wondering.

Cordelia advanced on the woman. "She knew Haager was trolling for Sebastian. He contacted her for information."

"Mai?" Seamus asked. He radiated a halo of energy. Cordelia felt an answering pulse of her anger.

"I didn't." Mai Li clung to her faltering position.

"You did some checking." Cordelia moved closer to her. "You sent feelers out."

Anthony stepped in line with her, cornering Mai Li.

"I wasn't sure at first, but your interest in Jarske made it obvious." Cordelia tilted her head, listening to the noise in Mai Li's head. "You didn't warn anyone. Always playing the best advantage. Keeping your options open."

"Mai Li?" Anthony asked, his face a stern reflection of his thoughts.

Gerald seemed resigned. Cordelia looked into the patrician man. *He's spent too much time with MI-6.* Cordelia turned back to look Mai Li in the eye. "Don't bother denying it."

The Chinese woman narrowed her eyes. Apprehension flitted across her face, replaced by calculation. "I've worked with Marcus. Asking questions about Sebastian wasn't illegal last time I checked. I had no idea I needed to warn anyone."

Anthony grunted. "A heads-up would've been professional courtesy. Where's Haager now?"

"It's not like we have permanent addresses." Mai Li glanced around the room. "Most of us."

Seamus moved to loom over the diminutive figure. "Where would you start looking?"

Mai Li wouldn't be cowed. "No idea. He needs me, he calls."

Anthony glanced at Cordelia. She heard his thought loud and clear.

Mai Li shifted her stance to a defensive position. She looked at Cordelia, ready for a fight. "Try something."

"With pleasure." Cordelia moved forward eager.

Gerald slapped a hand on the desk. "Enough!"

The energy in the room deflated.

"Mai Li, unfortunately, we'll need all of the information you have on Haager. Jobs, contacts, the works. You can volunteer the information, and it would go a little way to restoring our relationship. No one in this room denies a part of our job is deception." He looked around. "However, professional ... ethics demands certain inquiries need to be communicated." He rubbed his eyes. "You're no angel, we understand, but this is a breach of principles. It's cliché, but honor among thieves and all. You've racked up a debt, my dear, and you'll pay it off."

Mai Li pressed her lips together.

Cordelia read her resistance on her face and in her thoughts. "She's not going for it."

Mai Li glared at her.

Cordelia laughed. "One good reason."

"Young woman, make no mistake I've no problem doing this the hard way," Gerald said, a grim look on his face.

Gerald's calm resignation convinced Mai Li. "Fine," Mai Li conceded. "I'll give you what I know."

Cordelia made a note. *Never underestimate him.*

CHAPTER SIX

"You did fine in Slovenia," Anthony said, sliding on his safety glasses.

"Luck and adrenaline aren't something on which I like to rely," Cordelia said, looking at the Bersa Thunder 40. The gun reminded her of Lorena.

Anthony looked at her. "You have other skills. You're not helpless. Did you forget Rome?"

"No, but it's not always hand to hand." She looked at him.

"Okay." He gave her a pair of ear plugs. His own hung around his neck attached to a cord. "Lorena showed you how to load and release the magazine on this thing."

She nodded, a lump in her throat preventing her from speaking about Lorena.

He continued. "You want to keep your elbows soft and your shoulders rolled forward." He holstered his gun. "Practice your draw over and over. If you build the habit," he said as he drew his gun, "you won't have to think about it." He holstered it again. He put out his arms and bent his elbows a bit. "Rolling the shoulders and softening your elbows transfers the recoil into your back muscles. That'll eliminate the upswing of your gun on recoil."

She picked up the gun from the counter. "Like this?"

Anthony moved her arms a bit. "Think about hugging a tree. It sounds silly, but it puts your elbows at the right angle." He pushed her arms down so the gun aimed at the floor. "Let's work on your grip too. Put the gun down.

43

The clip is out and the safety is on, but aim the gun down or holster it when you're moving around the range."

"Okay." He pulled his own gun. "Place the grip all of the way into your palm, pointer finger parallel to the gun and thumb pointed forward. Place the palm of the other hand on the grip, finger and thumb the same." He holstered his gun. "You try."

Cordelia gripped her gun.

"Good, not too tight. Keep your hand firm, but not tense. Time to shoot some targets. Once you get used to the grip and the rolled shoulders, your aiming'll improve. Earplugs in, glasses on."

Cordelia set up to shoot the target.

Anthony placed his own earplugs and stepped behind Cordelia. He moved close to her and placed his hands on her elbows.

She stiffened, surprised at the warmth of his hands.

"Relax. Soften your elbows. Aim with both eyes open, breath out and squeeze the trigger." He spoke into her ear loud enough to hear over the plugs.

Cordelia fired. The recoil pushed her into Anthony. Her shot hit to the left and high in the shoulder.

"Not bad. It'll stop someone. Try again."

She fired, hitting closer to center. The recoil moved her into Anthony again, sun-warmed granite against her back. *He smells like coffee and rich leather.*

"Again." His breath warmed the skin of her neck.

She fired, hitting the target inside of the nine ring.

"Better." His voice resonated in her ear. "Again."

Cordelia fired three more shots. Each one inside of the nine ring.

"Okay, not bad." Anthony stepped back, evaluating her target. He removed his earplugs. "More practice. Seamus can run you through how to handle your gun in motion. You'll be a good shot."

Without effort, Cordelia slipped into Anthony's head as she removed her own plugs. Admiration laced with sexual attraction slammed into her. He thought of the warmth of her temple against his cheek. Heat flushed up her neck as she yanked back into her own space.

No fool, Anthony noticed the shift in the atmosphere. Not a sign of his true feelings was readable on his face. "You okay?" He took a step toward her.

"I'm fine. Revved up maybe." She looked him in the eye for an uncomfortable beat.

He cleared his throat. "It's definitely a rush." He didn't break eye contact.

Cordelia felt heat shimmering around him. *You're crazy. Anthony's a good man. Splendid to look at, all calm water where Sebastian churned, a rip tide.* He balanced Seamus's over-the-top personality with cool, measured humor. *And Sebastian? Sebastian isn't here. He came to see you. What does that mean? We've had some moments, but is it enough?*

Anthony moved toward her imperceptibly. "Cord—"

The door to the firing range burst open. Seamus's shadow enclosed them. "We've got a line on Haager." It took him an instant to read the tension in the room. "Christ on a bike."

Anthony shot his partner a look and punched him in the arm on his way out the door.

Seamus shot Cordelia a devilish grin. "Well, this is arseways from Sunday."

She sighed. "Fuck off, MacColgan."

He chuckled tailing her to the main house.

Elsa intercepted them on the path. Busto wiggled his butt at her feet. She stroked Seamus's arm with affection and signed a curled *g*. Seamus patted her stroking hand.

Cordelia smiled at the simian's rumbling purr and chuckled as she picked up Elsa's thought. "Ginger? Pretty Ginger?" Her chuckle launched into a full-blown laugh.

"Ian thinks he's funny, teaching her to call me Ginger." The tall Irishman exuded irritation and good humor. "Hard to be mad at her, she's quite sweet."

Elsa walked with them, one hand resting on Seamus's tall shoulder and one hand curled around Cordelia's hand. *Friends are nice.*

"Yes, friends are lovely." Cordelia agreed aloud for Seamus's benefit. "I can only imagine how lonely you must've been."

No more. These people are kind. This place is wonderful. Elsa's liquid gaze traveled along the grounds. She sighed.

Cordelia squeezed her hand. "You're happy."

You'll find him. Elsa returned the gentle pressure.

The woman stopped, bringing the little band to a halt. She dropped her hand and looked intently at Elsa. *How do you know?*

Elsa shrugged. *I know what you know.*

The enigmatic answer didn't make sense. *What do you mean?*

"Hey, I'm getting weird vibes." Seamus watched the two of them. "I'm literally getting vibes." He waved in the air between Elsa and Cordelia. "Look, I've got goose pimples. I can almost see the energy moving between you. You're communicating mind to mind?"

"You can tell?" Cordelia tried to process. Somehow Elsa tuned into her precognition and something shifted to allow Seamus awareness of their silent communication.

Seamus held out his arm. "The hairs are standing on end." He frowned and then brightened. "This is so cool!"

Elsa placed a hand on Seamus's arm and took Cordelia's hand again. *Family. Touch him.*

Cordelia placed a hand on Seamus, closing the circle, and winced with the strength of Elsa's push. The simian amplified the energy of her thoughts. *Family.*

"I can almost hear that!" The Irishman's eyes grew wide. "It's …." He leaned closer. "It's an echo of a whisper, but—" He looked at Cordelia. "I can feel both of you."

How about this? Cordelia didn't have much practice trying to send her thoughts to anyone. *Hell, I spend most of my time trying to close people out.*

Seamus stood, eyes closed. Cordelia almost laughed when he turned his head to aim his ear toward her. "That was you." He opened his eyes with a gleam. "I can tell." He processed a minute and then jumped in the air, releasing their grip on him. He danced and shouted. "It's kind of a picture. You putting a wall up. Holy cripes!"

He grabbed both of Cordelia's hands and spun her round. Busto barked and jumped near their feet. Elsa stood serenely, radiating satisfaction.

"I'm going to fall." Cordelia tried to put the brakes on and nearly tripped over Busto.

Giddy and bright-eyed, Seamus released her and wrapped his arms around Elsa. It wasn't far for him to tip his head to place his forehead against her russet brow ridge. Meeting eye to eye, he smiled. "Family. We're all the same. Don't you get it, Cord?"

Thoughts clicked into Cordelia's brain faster than she could track. She remembered the deeper rumbling between Thomas and Sebastian when she first met them. The times she thought there was something passing between

Lorena and the others. Something intuitive. How often they moved as though they knew each other's thoughts? Elsa's knowledge of their presence at the lab in Slovenia.

"Fucking hell, Seamus. You all have been doing this the whole time. I wrote it off as familiarity, but it's the DNA." She slapped her head. "We have the same communication structures. Mine is amplified by my abilities, which allows me to connect directly to Elsa."

"Ian's going to shit the brick." He headed toward the house laughing.

CHAPTER SEVEN

Virginia

Sebastian evaluated the building from their hilltop position. "Intelligence?"

"Two stories, lab's in the basement and standard security setup. Three night guards. One at the front desk, one monitoring the security feeds, and one walks the rounds. They come on at seven and rotate through the duties. Visual motion detectors along both floors deactivated in sequence as the guard makes his rounds. Offices have multi-digit keypads. Outside locks are electromagnetic, accessed with key fobs. There's one bank of elevators behind the security desk and another freight elevator at the back of the building is key operated. The guard walks the halls, makes a full round once every ninety minutes."

"You think the clone is in the basement labs." Sebastian's tone said everything about his confidence in the plan.

Haager pulled a set of blueprints out and spread them on the hood of his car. His finger marked the area, throwing shadows from the small LED flashlight in his other hand. "Travis'll patch the outside security feed while interrupting the signals from the building's motion detectors. Three of my team'll come in from the roof and secure the guard if he's there. The rest of us will go through the front door and secure the two remaining guards. That'll give Travis access to the security room, here." He pointed to a room behind the lobby desk. "Three men will secure the first floor while Travis overrides the security locks on the freight elevator and we'll have access to the basement labs."

Sebastian kept his gaze even. He'd be damned if he admitted the plan didn't sound terrible. "When are we going in?"

Haager looked at his watch. "It's twenty-one thirty. We'll start at forty-five. One of the guards'll be walking the floor."

Sebastian tamped down the urge to growl at the Black Wolves watch on Haager's wrist. "Let's go now."

Travis popped the junction box. "Okay, we're patched."

They moved down to the building.

Haager gave the order. "Go, go, go."

One of the roof crew pried the elevator maintenance door open while another checked their line anchors. He nodded. They slid down the shaft dripping down the line, inky drops of oil swallowed by the dark of the space. Reaching the second-floor doors, the leader inserted the clamps of the pry jack and opened them.

The point man slid through feet first, his soft thudded landing echoed by the others. A brief click released their harnesses from the lines. Guns ready, two men took point with one rearguard. Footfalls absorbed by the carpet, they moved to secure the floor. Their leader spoke softly into the comm unit. "We're in." Not interested in the offices, the glass framed sentries received only cursory glances.

"Let's go." Haager motioned his men and Sebastian.

They moved to the back of the building to access the main electrical box. After a few minutes, Travis nodded. "Front door's open." He trailed the four armed men with his laptop bag.

Without hesitation, Sebastian and the others took a four-point formation moving around to the front of the building. Zero confidence in Haager, Sebastian took the front right corner. *Let him go in first.*

Sebastian and the man next to him yanked the doors open. Haager and his other man strode forward, guns aimed. The security guard behind the desk stood surprised.

"Hands off your weapon." Haager moved forward while his man went around the desk to secure the guard.

Travis hurried to the door of the security room. He dug in his bag for a handheld tablet attached to a magnetic card. He swiped the door lock and started working to break the lock code.

The other three men of Haager's team split to sweep the first-floor halls for the last guard on their way to the freight elevator. On the second floor, the three men looped around toward the bank of regular elevators.

****

On the second floor, Mai Li stepped out of a doorway unarmed.

The three men stopped, disbelief freezing them for a beat.

"Looking for someone?" she purred.

Guns aimed. The two front guards moved forward a step. The rearguard turned to cover both his companions and any approach from the rear.

Mai Li raised her hands and turned her back. "I'm unarmed."

The lead guard glanced at his men. Moving forward, he slung his TEC-9 to the side by its strap. Reaching Mai Li, he frisked her top to bottom. Before his hands left her, two of the office doors opened. Anthony and Thomas stepped out behind the rearguard and the middleman. Mai Li grabbed one of the lead's wrists and in a graceful dance, twirled around taking his arm with her. A distinct pop announced the dislocation of his shoulder. Mai Li tangled his pistol strap around his neck as he fell to his knees. The other two men went down in a blink.

Anthony zip-tied the two men closest while Thomas moved to help Mai Li. He spoke to the others via the tiny comm piece in his ear. "Second floor is clear. We're heading down." He took one of the comm units from the trussed up team. Using the blandest American accent he could manage, he pushed the button. "Second floor secure."

Haager's voice answered. "Roger."

Mai Li, none too gently, gagged the men before she trailed Anthony and Thomas down the hall.

"We're in the elevator." Anthony transmitted.

Mai Li moved to stand between the two men. "What? No music?"

Thomas chuckled as the doors slid shut.

****

Haager's second-floor team checked in floor secure as his group stepped into the freight elevator for the basement. "Roger."

Sebastian's mouth grew tight.

Haager looked at him. "Ready?"

"Seriously?" The taller man fell silent and kept his eyes forward.

"You two." Haager motioned to the two men in front of them. "Break out to either side and sweep the basement. There shouldn't be anyone down here. We'll come out right behind you."

The slow moving elevator grumbled the entire way down, an old giant hassled by the effort. The descent was interminable until the large doors opened, the giant's mouth yawning from exertion.

Sebastian kept his stance loose and watched the two-point men step out. A blur of movement from either side of the elevator disarmed both men and had them on the ground. Taking advantage of Haager's dismay, Sebastian launched his elbow into Haager's diaphragm. He kicked away his weapon and trained his own gun at the man's head.

Seamus and Cordelia poked their heads into the elevator.

"You good?" Seamus asked as the corner of his mouth crooked up.

"Dandy. Anything?"

"Nope. Place was empty before we arrived," Seamus said.

Sebastian looked down at Haager. The downed man gasped for breath. "Should've let me call my team."

****

The two teams marshaled at Haager's safe house. Sebastian hopped out of the SUV with Haager close behind. A Mercedes Sprinter van, Thomas at the wheel, pulled into the circular drive. Anthony tailed him, helming a Suburban.

Seamus stepped out of the van, catastrophe clouding his face. Cordelia stepped out right behind him.

Sebastian closed the space between them ignoring Seamus's silent warning. Stunned to see Cordelia pop into the elevator, he hadn't said anything. They'd blown out of the building without stopping, he hadn't been able to talk to Thomas or the others. *Damn, she looks fabulous.* Before he could say anything, Gao Mai Li floated out of the SUV. Sebastian's brain vapor locked. He looked at Mai Li for a full minute puzzling the situation. He reached out for Cordelia, who stood within arms' length, but Mai Li glided into the space, pecking him on the cheek with intimacy.

"Cole." She breathed into his ear.

"Mai." He returned with familiar ease, then he caught the look on Cordelia's face. He recoiled from Mai Li. *Bugger it all.*

Thomas approached, hand outstretched. "You barmy prat, good to see you."

Sebastian took his hand. "Took you long enough."

Thomas pulled the taller man into a bear hug. "Had to find a moment of opportunity."

"Your American accent needs work." He cuffed his friend on the shoulder with affection.

"What're we going to do with this wanker?" Seamus clapped his two compatriots on the back with a nod toward Haager.

Haager's face recovered from his apoplectic rage at being overtaken by Sebastian's group. He kept silent, his embarrassment of coming up short choking him. The clone had been moved.

"Nothing." Sebastian studied Haager. "Yet." He saw Anthony shooting a quick glance at Cordelia as he approached. Cordelia wouldn't miss Mai's presumption. Of course, Cordelia could read her. *Shite, there's no winning.* He looked at Anthony. "Jarske?"

Anthony waved at the van.

Paul Jarske stepped out. "Hey, boss." He ran his fingers through shoulder-length, sandy waves softened by gray streaks that matched his silver beard. "Took me a blink after we got the rundown on Haager from Mai." He shoved his hands into the deep pockets of his robe-like sweater. "Once we found his trail the pieces came together, easy peasy." He shrugged.

Sebastian nodded his approval. "Good job, Jarske."

"That's all well and good," Haager commented. "Your team blew our chance to recover anything."

Anthony balked. "Whatever your target, the building was cleaned out before we set up. They saw you coming. We had to wait for you to show."

Sebastian saw Cordelia's brow furrow. She wanted to tell him something.

He shot her a look, willing her silent. She returned his look sharply and pressed her lips closed.

"I'd prefer to have this discussion inside." Haager gestured to the house.

"After you," Sebastian said. He kept his distance from Mai, sending Anthony a questioning look.

Anthony shook his head. Too much to go into now.

Shit and shinola.

They followed Haager through the door.

****

"Let me get this straight," Thomas said, his anger plastered on his face. "The CIA knew what Carlson pursued, but rather than stop her, decided to see what they could farm from her lab?" He looked at Sebastian, who stood, stone.

Cordelia struggled with the tension in the room. The three shifters broadcast strongly without their connection, even Anthony struggled to keep his cool. The hum Cordelia had felt around Sebastian before, now pulsed at a deeper resonance. Her chest felt heavy under the vibration he radiated. There hadn't been an opportunity for her to speak with him alone. She read his confusion towards Mai Li. *Glad I don't have to tell him the woman sold him like a market-day fish.*

Sebastian camouflaged his undercurrent of rage. Anthony stood impassively, but his thoughts swirled. Cordelia avoided delving into his mind. The moment she had slipped on the firing range shook her. Perplexed by her feelings, she wanted to talk to Sebastian. He came to see her in Vancouver.

She struggled with vexation. Sebastian's mind spun in a tempest. She couldn't get a read on any one thing. Anthony wrestled with his feelings, but his respect for Sebastian dominated. *What a fucking mess.*

Haager shrugged off the accusation. "Decisions above my pay grade. Be self-righteous, you followed orders."

"I trusted the man giving the orders," Thomas said, his disdain for Haager apparent. He turned to Sebastian. "Want to give us the rundown?"

Sebastian looked at his team. Cordelia noted he avoided eye contact with Mai Li. *Oh jeez, we aren't fifteen here.* She held back a sigh.

"In addition to farming the research, the CIA took three of the embryos Carlson had fertilized for stem cells."

Cordelia saw Haager roll his eyes. A quick scan made clear Haager's belief Carlson planned on gestating the embryos to term. She shuddered. She agreed with Sebastian on this count. Vivienne had no intentions to gestate those embryos to term. Though, she did want Sebastian desperately. Could she have?

A murmur traveled through Sebastian's team. Thomas swore aloud.

"Yeah, doesn't take much imagination," Sebastian said, voice flat.

Anthony pressed his lips together. Cordelia couldn't ignore his wave of distaste. "How many to term?"

"Only one survived. A three-year-old female." Sebastian clipped each word.

"How'd they manage with a male test subject?" Seamus asked, without any hint he knew the identity of the test subject. His displeasure rolled over her. *I don't blame him.*

Haager answered. "A tweak with the chromosomes. Scientists thought girls would be more cooperative subjects."

The Irishman sniggered. "None of them women, I'll bet."

Cordelia agreed but resisted a snicker of her own.

"The clone was taken from the CIA lab two weeks ago. Haager kept coming up dry, so he brought me in." Sebastian kept his rage invisible. Cordelia cleared her throat of the amped up pressure he broadcast.

"Polite way to put it." Thomas voiced everyone's thoughts.

"We're in it now," Sebastian stated. "We'll deal with the particulars after we find the clone."

Haager stepped forward. "We're keeping lines on the chatter in underground biotech circles. My tech team's cross-checking any mention of the research parameters."

Sebastian put his hand up. He looked at Anthony. "Alonzo set you up locally?"

"Yep, we've taken digs in Norfolk. He's at the estate working with your dad. Andre's at the London office."

"We'll head to Norfolk to settle in. I need a shower and a meal. We can coordinate with them at the house. I also need to talk to Ian."

Haager frowned. "You're not taking over this operation."

Sebastian ignored him. "Tony, get everyone loaded up. I'll ride with you and Thomas."

Anthony nodded. "On it, boss."

Sebastian laid a hand on Cordelia's shoulder sending a shockwave down her spine. She felt the grip of premonition take hold. She clamped her mouth, reluctant to speak in front of Haager. Looking at Sebastian with wide eyes, she hoped he recognized the fervor on her face. Without hesitation he leaned into her, placing his mouth on hers. The strategic block transmuted his real passion without warning. Ignoring the looks from their team and Haager, Cordelia welcomed his arms around her. She pressed into his heat. She let desire wash over the impulse to trumpet the portent looming in her mind.

The room stood silent until Thomas cleared his throat, pulling Cordelia back into reality. The urge to speak under control, she disengaged from Sebastian.

He stared at her a moment, then collected himself. "I'll be a minute with Haager."

Avoiding Anthony's face and ignoring Mai Li's eyes, Cordelia walked out of the safe house, spine erect and gaze trained forward. She didn't look at Seamus when she dug her elbow into his ribs to stop his chortle.

****

"You could always pick 'em. Trouble is, you could never keep 'em." Haager leered.

The crack from Sebastian's fist echoed in the room. Haager went ass over backwards for the third time in as many days. Sebastian's fury emanated nuclear cold. "One, talk to your men. I'll wager Cordelia left a couple with broken bones. Two, mention your thoughts on any one of my team again and you'll be sucking your meals through a straw. Three, I am taking over this operation. You're welcome to tag along when I give the go-ahead. If Jarske thinks your tech team is viable, he'll deal with them directly. This was a clusterfuck. How you managed to stay in the ranks this long is a mystery to me. Understand one thing: the CIA no longer has jurisdiction or claim on the clone. People with more power than you owe me." He turned to leave. "Oh, when you call, tell Bishop to watch his ass. He's on my radar now."

CHAPTER EIGHT

Alonzo's done it again. Cordelia looked at the dove-gray shingled house Alonzo arranged for the team. Norfolk provided the quintessential beach house. The double front doors greeted them with cheer in robin's egg blue. The wide wraparound porch charmed with bright white Adirondack chairs. Nesting on a stretch of sand south of Virginia Beach, the generous porch and enormous upper deck offered unfettered views of the Atlantic. Eight bedrooms and seven bathrooms assured the team's comfort and Cordelia's relief at not having to share a room with Mai Li.

The drive to Norfolk had been silent. Mai Li rode in the suburban with Anthony, offering Cordelia a reprieve from the effort to keep their thoughts out of her head. She understood Sebastian's kiss as a tactic to keep Haager from hearing the impending prophecy she received. It wouldn't do to have to explain her abilities or her real role with the team. As much as he intended to camouflage, the kiss sparked something. Being separated hadn't diminished the yearning between them. She thought about Anthony's silent attraction. She didn't deny she'd felt an answering attraction. *Nothing's ever easy, especially with this bunch.*

The sun gleamed clarion and brilliant in the sky, but the early summer breezes scampered onto shore with a light chill. Jarske hopped out to figure out how to move the access from the van's equipment into the house. She followed without looking at Sebastian. Without a word to anyone, she opened the back doors and fished out her suitcase.

She heard Anthony talking to Sebastian behind her. "The house is stocked. As soon as Jarske gets the sat gear up and running, we'll patch in the estate and the London office."

"Good. Is there a bag for me? I don't know what happened to my luggage in Vancouver."

"No problem. Alonzo managed to recover your bags. Haager's sloppy." Cordelia noted the disdain in Anthony's voice.

"Always was," Sebastian agreed.

Seamus opened both of the front doors ahead of her. "Welcome my dear, I don't know about you, but I'd like a shower and a beer."

"I thought you all were hardened mercenaries." She lowered her voice imitating Sebastian. "I remember a time when we were pinned down in some jungle seven days without a shower or a toilet."

He shrugged. "I've spent my fair share of time with a group of stinking, unwashed soldiers. Just means I know how to enjoy life's luxuries. And a hot shower ranks up there in the top five. Among other things." His eyes twinkled with unspoken reference to Sebastian's kiss.

She sighed. "Ditto. One word, Seamus. One and I'll shoot you."

"I heal quick," he returned with humor.

"I'll pick someplace painful, you gammy idiot."

Seamus laughed. "Oh ho, you'll make me homesick with that kind of talk."

Cordelia smiled. "Wanted to be sure you understood." She breezed past his chuckle to find a room and a shower.

Cordelia let the scalding water run over her head. She tried to push thoughts of Sebastian, the clone, and Mai Li out of her brain. With a little luck, they might find a lead on the girl in the next twenty-four hours. *Is it wrong of me to wish it might take a bit longer?* The house wooed and the beach enticed her. The hum and buzz of the other people in the house drifted along with the steam in the shower. She couldn't read everything from Sebastian, but Mai Li didn't cause her worry. *What about Anthony?* She pushed Anthony out of her head. Too much going on to deal with any of this, no sense in wasting energy on something she couldn't control. Find the little girl and then maybe there'd be time to sort out their deal.

She stepped out of the shower picking up a distinct pattern. *Seriously?* She wrung her hair out with a towel. She slipped on a thick robe and unholstered the Bersa that was resting on the counter. Both Anthony and Seamus stressed keeping it within hands reach at all times. Using her big toe, she opened the bathroom door wide, aiming the gun at Mai Li.

"Damn, no surprising you." The Chinese woman leaned back on Cordelia's bed with a saucy look.

Cordelia didn't hesitate to pry. She dove deep into the woman's mind. Mai Li thought to startle her and her irritation at her failed plan simmered. Cordelia remained quiet with the gun level. The woman worried about someone named General Wong. Given the images in her head, Mai Li had a right to be worried. She had played Sebastian false. Cordelia didn't care.

"I'm trying to figure you," Mai Li said. She stood up and walked to the glass doors overlooking the beach. "You're not a professional. I've never heard of you, but Sebastian doesn't bother with people who can't handle things." She looked back over her shoulder.

Cordelia saw the questions swirling in Mai Li's mind. What did she mean to Sebastian? How did Cordelia know about her? Could Mai Li find an advantage? Cordelia kept her gaze even. "I don't have answers for you."

"You're wondering a tiny bit what I meant to him?" Mai grasped at straws. Sebastian's kiss bothered the woman. Mai Li didn't love Sebastian, but her ego demanded a certain claim on him. In a weak position and lacking confidence, she gambled Cordelia would be the chink.

Cordelia let a big smile bloom on her face. She enjoyed the anger flareup in the woman's mind, even if it didn't reach her face. "You're desperate."

At this, Mai Li couldn't keep her anger contained. "What do you know? Sebastian won't do anything to me."

Cordelia thought about the Sebastian Mai Li had known. *Nope.* The old Sebastian probably wouldn't turn her over to the general she betrayed. This Sebastian, transformed, would. *You love this kind of man?* Cordelia pushed the thought away. Wasn't Cord a similar creature? She didn't feel sorry for Mai Li. *Monsters made for each other. Was Anthony right?* "Let me know how that works out for you." She lowered her weapon. "Right now, get out."

Mai Li meandered toward the door. She wouldn't let Cordelia see her anxiety. "He doesn't love anyone. He won't love you." The statement was her last assault.

Cordelia grunted. "He already does." She shut the door close on Mai Li's heels. Flipping the lock, she flopped down on the bed. She felt Mai Li stiffen. Sebastian stood in the hall. *Fuck it all.* She flung her arm over her eyes.

****

It took Jarske an hour to run cables into the house to hook up their satellite equipment to the flat screen television in the great room. The time allowed everyone to grab a room and shower. After pulling an all-nighter, the group felt more than jet lagged. Someone moved in the kitchen. Sebastian heard the blissful noises of a steamer going as he ruffled his wet hair with a towel. Thank goodness. He pulled on a pair of jeans and a long-sleeved linen shirt. The temperature warmed. The sun was sitting past its apex.

He descended the stairs to the kitchen to see Thomas deft and nimble at the espresso machine. Cordelia hooked her feet around a stool at the island counter. Her hair lay damp and heavy in a braid down her back. She sipped a cappuccino with a blissful look on her face. He noticed some slight smudges under her eyes. Seamus pounded down the stairs behind him.

"Oy, anyone claimed the one in your hand yet?" His disheveled, crimson mane tumbled ear length.

Thomas grinned. "Nope. It's yours. Coffee, Sebastian?"

Cordelia glanced at him, composed.

"Absolutely. Is Jarske done?"

Anthony entered from the deck. "Yep, we hooked up the last cables. Alonzo and Andre are waiting on their end." He nodded at Cordelia and settled on the stool next to her. "Thomas, line me up with one too?"

"Coffee all around. Where's Mai Li?" Thomas kept pokerfaced.

"In her room. Jarske's wired it up. We'll know if she's up to anything," Anthony said.

Sebastian took his coffee mug, puzzled. "What she's up to?"

"It's like this, boss—" Seamus started. Anthony threw a balled up napkin at him. "What?" He glared back. "She sold us out. You want to tell me how we can put that delicately?"

"She sold us out? How?" Sebastian didn't blink. He looked at Cordelia, who kept her gaze on her coffee.

Thomas spoke up. "Haager grabbed you based on info he bought from Mai Li. He put a call out for intelligence. She used her familiarity with us to get details from the London office. No one thought twice about it."

"Hell, we brought her in to help," Anthony grumbled.

Sebastian let his thoughts settle before saying anything. "It's the world we operate in." He shrugged.

Seamus spoke up. "We wouldn't have done it."

"No, and we work with plenty of people who'd eliminate Mai Li if they knew she was doing this kind of business." He looked around at the group. "We'll hang on to her until we're done and then we'll cut her loose. Word's probably already out. She might be retiring early." He sipped his coffee. It didn't bother him. He and Mai Li had been over for a long time. Was there ever really a beginning? He looked at Cordelia. "So what do you have?"

Cordelia's face colored. "Hope, fear, and choices. Your humanity hangs in the balance."

"That makes total sense!" Seamus slapped his forehead.

"Really?" Cordelia looked for something to throw at him. Sebastian saw his own confusion mirrored on her face. "Would you like to explain it?"

Seamus piped in his two cents. "Not the hope-fear thing, the kiss. Now I get the kiss." He looked around. "Tell me I wasn't the only one wondering if Sebastian had dropped his basket?"

Thomas coughed back a laugh. "No. You weren't."

"You kissed Cordelia to keep Haager from knowing what she can do," Anthony said. Sebastian thought he saw something behind Anthony's eyes, but it disappeared.

Cordelia's blush crept down her chest. "I wouldn't have been able to stop."

"That's all you have? Hope, fear, and choices?" Sebastian let his frustration bubble out. "We might as well use a magic eight ball."

"Hey, she gave us Mai Li, which led us to Haager faster than we would've on our own. Mai Li couldn't tip him off. So some of the information is vague? The last one played out," Anthony reminded.

"Thanks, Anthony," Cordelia said. Sebastian didn't miss the venomous look she gave him. "Next time you go missing, I'll let you stay missing." She took her coffee and stepped out onto the patio.

"Way to go." Seamus snorted and followed her out.

Thomas patted Sebastian on the shoulder. "Sometimes I think you're getting the hang of things and then—"

"When did you think that? The last woman I had a relationship with sold me out to a person I loathe. Cordelia kidnapped by a mad scientist who tortured and experimented on her. This is why I don't get involved."

"In your defense, you and Mai Li weren't much of an item. It was a mutual 'This isn't going to work' kind of thing. You didn't know Mai Li sold you out until Cordelia read her mind so I don't know if it counts." Thomas sipped his coffee, sanguine.

"You and your friggin' optimism. Did you think that would help?" Sebastian asked.

Thomas shrugged. "Meh."

Anthony choked back a sip of coffee. "We should go link up with Alonzo and Andre."

"We need to move faster." Sebastian stood up. "The clone has to be destroyed along with all of the files. The longer it takes, the more chance we lose control of the information."

He looked at the faces of his silent men. "What did you think we were going to do?"

****

"We're pulling in the feeds from Haager's tech team. Jarske has Izzy and Clementine evaluating the data." Andre's smooth tenor matched his serene features.

Cordelia couldn't help admiring Andre's beauty. She felt dowdy after being up most of the night and all of the morning souped up on caffeine. Andre's porcelain skin and too-full lips fit his high cheekbones. She had managed a shower. Self-conscious about her black fatigues compared to Andre's pressed shirt and crisp slacks, she stopped her hands from smoothing her clothing. *You're just grumpy, in general. Don't blame Andre. This is all on you, baby.*

Alonzo appeared on a different screen. "As soon as Jarske finds a locale, I'll make travel arrangements. In the meantime, groceries are being delivered for the next couple of days."

Sebastian's disgruntled impatience radiated. "Hopefully it won't take long."

Everyone felt his mood. She felt Seamus wince.

"Even so, I'll need at least six hours to make travel arrangements. That puts you in the house until tomorrow afternoon minimum." Alonzo didn't show any concern over Sebastian's tension.

He's probably used to it by now.

Andre spoke. "Ian received Carson's complete files from Haager. He thought to join us, but...."

"He's working," Sebastian finished.

"Exactly. We hit a cache of new files. I'm compiling a contact list for Vivienne's experiments. Once that's done, I'll add it to the leads I'm following related to the research she sold. We may come across names of people who've been following her work. Cloning and stem cell research are at the forefront of the underground medical market," Andre said.

"I'll talk to Ian tomorrow. Good work. It's all on Jarske and his team. We wait." Sebastian ended the video feed. "We're all beat. Jarske has security set up. Let's get some rest before dinner."

Anthony stood up. "I'll cook."

Seamus groaned.

"What're you complaining about, you overstuffed leprechaun? I'm a good cook."

"Sometimes, my friend, I want a plain burger. You're going to fancy it up with caramelized onions and a balsamic glaze."

Cordelia's stomach growled. "If you add a crumble of gorgonzola, I'd run away with you." The words popped out before she thought.

Anthony's face remained mild, but the sparks snapped in his mind. "Consider it done." He turned to Seamus. "You can stuff it and go hungry, Mr. Ketchup and Mustard Only."

Seamus grinned. "How's that taste with a balsamic glaze?" The two men continued their culinary debate up the stairs.

"I suppose we should let Mai Li out of isolation?" Thomas looked at Sebastian. Cordelia sensed his hostility toward the woman.

Sebastian shrugged. He didn't try to hide his antipathy. "Bugger all, there's no good way to handle this. I don't much like having her loose, but we can't keep her prisoner."

Cordelia piped in. "She's agreed to restrictions. Outside of what Jarske has set up, I don't see how letting her have the run of the house is avoidable."

"Jarske's good but so's Mai Li. We'll all have to keep our guard up," Thomas said, thinking about their shifting and Cordelia's abilities. "I'm going to call Rachna and then I'm going to collapse." He left the room.

Cordelia knew Sebastian wanted to talk, but her foul mood wouldn't be helpful. "Look, this cloning business has you out of whack. Believe me, it's unsettling for all of us. You're not the only one with a stake in this. Try to remember." She headed to her room without giving him the chance to reply. She knew he stewed without looking back at him.

****

Sebastian knocked on Mai Li's door.

She opened it and leaned against the jamb. "Have I been reprieved?"

"Not funny." He kept his face blank.

"You can come in." She moved to the side, opening the door wide.

He took a step back. "We've agreed you have the run of the house as long as you don't attempt to contact Haager or any of your people. We'll control the information Haager receives."

"You overestimate me, Sebastian. You've got Jarske blocking my tech in or out. What can I do?" Mai batted her eyes.

"On this end, you can work with the team as long as you follow orders. You've proven helpful, though an inside asset."

"I play nice, I get to go along? Gee whiz, thanks." She shot him a hostile look.

Sebastian made his voice cold. "I knew a long time ago the kind of person you are. I'm under no illusions." He locked her gaze with his. "You compromise this operation and I'll turn you over to Wong. I'm sure he'll be happy to see you."

He noticed a brief hitch in her pulse. Her eyes dilated, but she didn't miss a beat. "You wouldn't."

"Without a second thought." He let his anger show in his eyes.

Mai looked at him without blinking. "You've changed."

"You've no idea." Sebastian turned to walk to his room. "The kitchen's open if you want something and Anthony's cooking dinner."

CHAPTER NINE

"We've found an auction going down in Hong Kong." Jarske looked pleased.

"When?" Sebastian's casual lean against the wall didn't fool Cordelia.

"Next week. Invite only," Jarske said.

Sebastian ran his fingers through his hair. "Any confirmation the clone'll be there?"

Jarske shook his head. "The chit chat's discreet. This isn't your run of the mill arms auction, but I'm betting she's on the menu."

Thomas broke into the conversation. "Hong Kong is Wong's territory. Plan?"

Cordelia watched Sebastian's impassive face; his thoughts churned.

"Jarske, check around with our contacts. Let's see if we can identify the bidders. Try to verify the clone is there." Sebastian turned to Thomas. "You work with Alonzo and Andre. Find accommodations and get the groundwork going for our trip. You may have to negotiate with Wong, but let's give a polite heads-up and see if he's in a good mood. We'll need a second team undercover."

Thomas's sly smile mirrored the mischief in his mind.

They're all crazy. Cordelia knew a bit about Wong from poking into Mai Li's head. Her crimson wave of fear accompanied by some graphic images gave Cordelia pause. "What's with this general?"

"Wong's the biggest worm in Hong Kong." Seamus winked at her.

Cordelia shot him a blank look. "And?"

Sebastian went to the fridge and grabbed a beer. The hiss of the church key popping off the lid punctuated his answer. "General Wong," he paused, looking at her, "is the current head Dragon of Hong Kong." He sipped his beer.

Pouring his beer over his head would feel amazing. Her thought must've been focused because he startled. She shook her head and waved her hand for him to continue.

"General Wong is the Triad boss. He runs the largest syndicate in Hong Kong. Any criminal element and some legitimate businesses need his blessing and his organization to operate. He's a brutal son of a bitch, but he's the guy who needs to approve an auction like this one. If he's not the one holding it."

Seamus spoke up. "Toss me one of those, will ya?" He nodded at the beer. "Wong's in charge of everything going into or out of Hong Kong. We don't usually deal with him, but it doesn't hurt our operations if he knows we're coming." He took the bottle Sebastian handed him.

The refreshing hiss of the cap stirred up her taste buds. She nodded at Thomas's silent offer to give her one.

"We don't pay him tribute and he's never asked. He's too savvy for that, but we'd be idiots to think he wouldn't be aware of our presence." Thomas opened two bottles and handed one to Cordelia.

"If Wong's the one hosting this auction, won't it be impossible for us to get in without being recognized?" Cordelia took a deep draw of the beer. The smoky tang of the barbecue wafted in from the back porch. Her stomach grumbled, riled up by the spice of Anthony's cooking.

Seamus started to lay the table. "Depending on the guest list, we may be able to substitute one of our guys. Either we can buy the girl straight out or have our inside man help us breach security."

"If this is Wong's auction, won't he be put out if we steal the girl?" Cordelia thought about Mai Li's fear.

Sebastian's look of approval banked her irritation. His respect for her thought process irritated her. *Stop it. Stop what?* Her imp asked. *I don't care if he appreciates my brain. Yeah, right.*

"Damn straight, but we could track the buyer and find a way to retrieve the clone outside of Wong's possession." Sebastian pulled a giant bowl of salad out of the fridge and put it on the table. He looked at Thomas. "Grab the dressing, would you?"

Thomas took two bottles of dressing to the table. He read the label. "Simple Italian and Ranch. Fancy."

Seamus rolled his eyes, breaking three baguettes into pieces with his hands. "You expected the Ritz?"

"There are knives in the kitchen," Anthony hissed as he carried a heaping tray of ribs in from the porch. "Barbarian."

"Prat," Seamus returned, winking at Cordelia again. She felt his satisfaction and tried not to laugh. Seamus loved to goad his partner.

Jarske pulled a few more beers out of the fridge and sat down. Cordelia echoed his anticipation and moved to the table.

They all paused as Mai Li stepped into the room. Cordelia pulled her awareness tight into her head. The rumbling and roiling from her friends became too much. She gave Mai Li credit. The Chinese woman glided to the table without a misstep.

"Sebastian invited me to dinner." Her gaze traveled around the room.

Cordelia didn't dare look to see if the traitor hid anything more. She didn't need her extra awareness to feel the waves of disdain reverberating around the room.

Anthony, with cordial aplomb, moved to pull out Mai Li's chair. "Of course."

Cordelia thought of Anthony's grandmother. She felt his gaze and mirrored his small smile.

Seamus dug into the platter of ribs. "This is getting cold."

The tension eased and the rest of the group sat down. Plates rattled, food traveled, more jokes were told, and for the moment, what lay ahead of them was suppressed.

Cordelia leaned toward Sebastian. "We forgot about Haager."

"I didn't." He tore into a rib.

****

The house darkened. The rhythmic pulse of the sea washed over Seamus and Anthony's quiet bickering while they clinked and rattled their way to a clean kitchen. Jarske dozed on the couch, the soft glow of computer screens casting shadows on his features. He refused a bedroom preferring to keep close to his equipment. His drives hummed and clicked running their tireless security programs, ready to alert him to any breach. Upstairs, lulled by the wonderful food and the ebb and flow of the waves, Cordelia slept sound. Despite his exhaustion, Sebastian couldn't get his mind quiet. He lay in bed, hands linked over his head, and stared at the ceiling.

****

In one of the upstairs rooms a curtain opened, exposing three-quarters of the window. Mai Li slid a table lamp from the left to the right and then closed the curtain.

A car, three blocks from the house, pulled away without headlights.

****

Sebastian woke to the fog hugging the beach and misting the windows. It cast a silvery haze across the horizon. Waves sounded, invisible, behind the moist curtain. The unnatural silence of predawn hung over the sand. Sebastian pulled a sweater over his head as he padded down the stairs. A waft of the smoky, rich scent of coffee met him as his feet left the last step. *Someone else couldn't sleep either.* He took a cup from its seat on the open shelves and tipped the carafe. Steam drifted up as the dark umber liquid tumbled into his mug. He took a careful sip as he stepped out to the back door into the morning.

"Couldn't sleep either?" Cordelia spoke low and rough from sleep. She sat in one of the bright Adirondacks, feet on the seat, knees up, a soft blanket wrapped serape-style against the wee-hour chill.

Sebastian sat on the arm of her chair. "No, jet lag."

The corner of her mouth twitched. "Okay."

He knew her ability to read him grew stronger. Something was different between them. *Why bother?*

"Indeed." She smiled.

He took a sip of coffee. "You could keep out."

Cordelia leaned her weight toward him, her elbow over his thigh. "Little late."

The warmth of her body shot through him, a quiver of lightning. Tangible threads of her thoughts whispered and wove around him. The fog danced with dappled light as the sun started its climb and warmed with probing rays. They sat quiet, drinking coffee.

"I still don't know what to say." He placed his hand on the base of her neck under the mahogany tangle of her hair. He felt the scar mirroring his own. "There's no time."

She chuckled.

"What?" He gazed into the murk, willing it to dissolve.

The fog smothered her sigh. "Have you wondered if we'll ever have time? You don't lead a bucolic, uneventful kind of life and I, by circumstance, don't think my life is destined to be boring. If we don't make time, I don't know."

He worked his fingers into the knots under her skin. His thoughts simmered.

"Mmmmm," she murmured.

"Mai Li—" he started.

She cut him off. "Nope. Not starting my day off with her. Can't trust her, but you know already."

"You know what I said to her." He didn't ask.

"Yep and she's afraid, but she also thinks she's clever. More shrewd than any of us." She leaned her head on his arm.

He moved his hand to her shoulder, welcoming her weight. A thought crystallized. "We'll see. Anthony… "

She sat up to wrap her arms around her knees.

The nip of dew hastened into the gap between them. Sebastian pressed his lips together with regret. "I wouldn't blame you."

"Hell and crumpets, Sebastian. I'm struggling to figure out us without dealing with someone else." She put her hand up. "Don't start with the 'he's better for me' tripe. I'm not denying I have mixed feelings about Anthony.

Shit, if I had stayed out of his mind, I wouldn't even have thought about it. But this, you and me." She gestured. "It's big."

He pulled her to her feet with a sigh. "Yeah, I know."

Jarske burst out of the house. "I've got a line on who is attending the auction."

Sebastian felt Cordelia's flush of frustration. He sighed. "Thanks, Jarske." He looked at Cordelia. "No time."

She looked like she might throw her coffee in his face. He stepped back a bit.

"You keep telling yourself that, Mr. Cole." She marched past both men. "Hardheaded," he heard her murmur on her way inside.

****

The little girl lay unconscious; an IV dripped fluids into a vein in her hand. The lights darkened. Beep, beep, beep. The monitors chimed out her vital signs. Líu Qīngyún watched from the hallway. That little thing gave his men quite a fight. Two with broken noses and almost all of them with bites, scratches, and bruises. A tranquilizer dart had been necessary. It wouldn't do for his valuable merchandise to be damaged. This auction would seal his position with the Triad. No more would he be middle management. Biotech would become the import of the future. He had balked at first. The talk of stem cell harvesting and medical cloning seemed out of his league, but his source assured him of big money.

He began to research the potential of biotech as a new black market. Sure, there had been organ harvesting and pharmaceutical markets, but this new technology proved colossal. Harvest stem cells or create cells wiped of DNA and grow your own organs. Not limited to transplants, but skin cells, tissue regeneration, and the potential for extended life span. Money would be no object. The one thing he could count on, the wealthy's desire for immortality. It would start with this girl.

"Gōngtóu?" A middle-aged doctor, balding and paunchy in the middle, bowed.

He returned a slight bow.

"Her vitals are strong, but I do have some concerns about the time we need to keep her unconscious. It's not healthy." He fidgeted with his stethoscope.

Líu Qīngyún didn't offer comfort. Better to have the fear of his subordinates. "It's a necessary risk. She might damage herself if we wake her. I'll have details of the bids within the next forty-eight hours. Once those arrive, we'll arrange the location. We can revisit wakening her. That will be fine." It wasn't a question.

The physician cleared his throat. "Yes, yes. Fine."

Líu Qīngyún ignored the man's retreat. He stared at the girl in the bed and tried to divine some hint of her extraordinary traits. He had read in the files retrieved with the girl that the researchers planned on testing her regenerative qualities. She had been remarkably healthy and though exposed to several different illnesses, she had shown immunity resistance to all of them. His curiosity would have to wait.

CHAPTER TEN

Opening the door, Jarske led Sebastian back into the house. "The Nigerian's got an invite."

"Okay," Sebastian said, thinking. "That's good news. Get Alonzo on the line and let's make plans to get everyone on the move."

"You going to see the Nigerian?" the older man asked.

"Yeah, have Alonzo make arrangements ASAP. I'll head out with Anthony and the rest of you can follow." Sebastian ran his fingers through his hair.

"Will do, boss." Jarske went to contact Alonzo.

We've caught a break. Sebastian took the stairs two at a time to his room to throw his things into a bag. "Finally."

"Talking to yourself is a dangerous sign," Cordelia said.

He turned to look at her leaning against the doorframe. Hair still rumpled and standing barefoot in her pajamas, the sight of her pleased him. "A sign of genius, you mean."

She rolled her eyes. "You're heading out."

Stepping closer, he took hold of her hands. "Yeah, I'll take Anthony and see if the Nigerian will help us."

He felt her gaze measuring him. "The man is a criminal."

"Yes. I told you I wasn't the good guy." He didn't recoil or flinch. For a brief second, he fancied he felt her fingertips brush his temple, but looking down her hands remained warm within his.

"He's your friend," Cordelia said. Her knowing tone sent a shiver through him.

"That's creepy sometimes," he said, his tone light and joking.

She puffed out a breath. Leaning in, she spoke in a whisper. "Rumor has it you're a bit terrifying yourself."

Recognizing her teasing mood, he still couldn't refrain from stiffening a bit. He released her hands and returned to packing. "Made for each other, I suppose."

She sighed. "Can dish it out, eh Cole? Sometime or another we're going to have this out and you're going to have to get over yourself."

Sebastian whirled around defensive to catch a glimpse of her disappearing down the hall. Over her shoulder, he heard her call out, "Fly away home Sebastian, but you gotta lighten up."

****

Cordelia watched Anthony and Sebastian tear off for the airport with a fresh mug of coffee. Her eyelids hung heavy after two days with little sleep. *And a few too many beers last night.* She felt Seamus walk out the front porch before she heard him.

"Damn," he said, the cheer in his voice matching the brightness in his thoughts. "I won't be able to sneak up on you again."

"Like you could before," Cordelia quipped, taking another precious sip of coffee.

Seamus sidled up and bumped her shoulder. "At least now I can tell what you're thinking."

She looked at him over her nose. "What am I thinking now?"

"You're going to tell me to bugger off." He grinned.

"That took a lot of talent." She rolled her eyes. "Is there any breakfast?"

Seamus linked arms with her. "I may not be able to tell exactly what you're thinking, but I've known my fair share of late-night binges. I can see you're a bit worse for the wine."

Beer, just a little foggy from the beer.

"Look," he said and put an arm out, "when you're pushing out with your mind, the hair on my arms stands on end."

Cordelia smiled. "You're crazy and I need more coffee."

As they moved toward the front door, a black Porsche Panamera sped into the drive.

Thomas stepped out onto the porch. "We expecting company for breakfast?"

Cordelia caught Haager's thoughts before he even stepped out of the car. "He's in a mood."

"When isn't he?" Thomas said, turning to go back into the house without looking at Haager. "Come on, I put together some food."

Seamus led Cordelia into the house and said, "Good, I'm starving."

Haager bounded up the steps behind them. "I haven't heard from your team and now Sebastian's taking off?"

Thomas glanced at Cordelia and she heard his mental question clearly. *Mai Li?* She pushed into Haager's thoughts pursing her lips at the things she saw. She gave Thomas a quick nod.

The shaggy-headed Englishman shook his head.

No one answered Haager as they moved through the house into the kitchen.

"Is anyone going to explain what's going on?" Haager demanded, trailing them.

Cordelia smiled at Jarske already sitting at the table with a coffee and a plate of fruit. "Breakfast should be a familiar concept," she said lightly, going to the pot of coffee to refresh her mug. She looked at Jarske with gratitude seeing the French press started with more. "You're a prince." He blushed and looked into his mug.

Seamus continued the joke. "You see, we have several pastries here." He sat down and waved his hand over a tray. "I prefer cheese Danish, but without those, I'm happy to munch on a croissant." He picked up a croissant and tore it open.

Cordelia felt Thomas struggling to keep his laughter inside. He sat down. "You're welcome to join us."

Haager huffed his breath. Cordelia read his mind spinning with fury. He couldn't pick a response. She held the pot up. "Anyone like a top-off?"

Jarske raised his hand. "I'd take some, Cordelia," he said.

Haager doesn't know which way is up. Serves him right.

Ignoring Haager's temper, Cordelia brushed past him to pour Jarske fresh coffee. She returned the carafe to the counter and sat next to Seamus. As though on cue, the three of them turned to stare at Haager standing in silent indignation.

Thomas asked, "Was there something you wanted, Haager?"

This would be funnier if my head weren't so heavy.

Haager's mind burned with ire. He finally decided to act. Slamming his hand on the table, he demanded, "Where's Sebastian? He said he would keep my team in the loop."

"Clearly it was unnecessary," Thomas said, his voice going cold.

"Look, so I kept an eye on things." Haager puffed up. "What's going on?"

"Sebastian left for London to touch base with a colleague," Thomas said. He sipped his coffee and glanced at Seamus.

"We're trying to get a line on any auctions where the girl might be on the docket," Seamus added. His mild look didn't hide his violent thoughts from Cordelia.

The more I'm around this guy, the more I agree with him.

"So you're all sitting around waiting?" Haager asked.

Thomas leaned back in his chair. "No, we're all headed to London in a few hours to regroup at our offices. We'll contact you when we know more," he said.

Haager's body stiffened at the dismissal.

"Run along," Seamus added, shooing the man with a hand.

Cordelia let loose the chuckle she had been holding.

Haager glared at her, but she shot him a venomous look in return, pushing the force of her mind at him. She surprised herself with the act, but Haager started fidgeting and broke eye contact, affected by her effort. *Very cool.*

The former Black Wolf tried to regain an air of potency.

Thomas said, "And we'll leave Mai with you. If we think you should know something, we'll tell you."

Haager stormed out of the house without another word.

Seamus turned to Cordelia. "Bloody goose pimples." He lifted his arm to show her. "I wish I could do that."

****

Haager returned to his team apoplectic. He slammed the door behind him and shouted to Travis. "Get Bishop on the line." He paced around the table with a dark look.

Travis kept his eyes on his screen. "It'll take a minute." He patched in Bishop's call.

Haager's phone chirped. He looked at Travis.

"All clear. We're patched through several IPs."

He took the call. "Haager."

"No kidding." Bishop's slick voice pierced through the ear piece. "Status."

"They moved the clone. Sebastian's team tracked him down and spooked our targets."

Travis kept his eyes on his screen, managing the routing of the call, but his mouth quirked.

Bishop snorted. "Sebastian doesn't spook anyone. I take it he's closed you out."

"Yes." Haager's mouth twisted with the bitterness. "He's agreed to keep me in the loop."

"Fine." Bishop clipped his words. "He has better resources than we do and I can handle him after we deal with the clone."

"Yes, sir." Haager's face matched his sour mood. He nodded at Travis.

Travis disconnected the call as Haager stalked out of the room. Bishop had a checkered reputation. Haager had shown his incompetence in more than one way. The hacker didn't think either of the men were worth much. After a moment's thought, he pulled up his personal algorithm software. A few keystrokes later, he pushed the button.

****

Jarske's phone beeped. He said looking up from the screen, "Alonzo's on the line."

"Oh good." Thomas stood up. "Plan in motion."

They moved into the living room where Jarske had the video call on his computer. "The camera frame focuses here." He showed them where to stand so Alonzo could see them.

Alonzo smiled. "Good morning. Sebastian's meeting is scheduled. He and Anthony will wait for you in London. I have a plane ready to go in Norfolk as soon as you can pack up and get there."

Thomas sighed. "I'd say about a half an hour to load up and another half an hour give or take the drive to Norfolk. Jarske?"

Jarske nodded. "I can do that."

"A man named Bishop is setting Sebastian up," Cordelia spoke out.

"I thought you picked something up," Thomas said.

"As tiny as his brain is, I'm not impressed," Seamus added.

Cordelia laughed. "No details. I don't think Bishop thinks much more of Haager than we do, but he's making plans. Who is he?"

"Ahem." Jarske cleared his throat. "I have information that makes sense now." He typed a few keystrokes. "I picked this up on the surveillance from Haager's feed."

Thomas leaned over his shoulder. "Never underestimate the power of idiocy." He looked up at Cordelia. "Bishop works in the science intelligence section of the CIA. We've crossed paths with him in our Black Wolves operations and our NSA days. He's a right wanker."

Seamus snorted. "He's worked his way up the chain shifting his ineptitude onto other people and he's no fan of ours."

"Particularly Sebastian. I picked that much up from Haager," Cordelia said. "I have the feeling it's personal." She looked at Thomas.

"Bishop was Hawthorne's number two before his assignment to Marines Special Ops. Hawthorne handpicked the Black Wolves but didn't bring Bishop over with him. Some question about misconduct in the initial operations in Afghanistan. Hawthorne didn't have him officially charged, but Bishop's military career ended."

"Makes sense that the CIA would pick up someone like him." Contempt filled Seamus's voice. "I ran into him when I was in Somalia with the Fiannóglaigh. The CIA was running black ops to stabilize the Transitional Federal Government. At least, that's what we suspected. There were a lot of shady deals going on in the aftermath of the Indian Ocean Earthquake. Bishop's name popped up in certain circles."

"Given his track record and what I know of him," Thomas looked again at the computer screen, "it doesn't surprise me he's running Haager. Mai Li's involvement makes more sense. Bishop knew her. The fact someone in his camp is having second thoughts doesn't surprise me either." He ruffled his curly hair. "Cordelia, can you tell if this thing is a setup?"

She shook her head. "I can't be certain. Mai Li is involved, but without contact with Bishop I have no idea. Haager thinks the situation is real but would Bishop play his team false?"

"No question," Thomas said.

"Want me to make the connection?" Jarske asked.

"Yeah, we'll act like it's a trap, but if this is on the level—" Thomas looked up with a twinkle. "I love being one step ahead in the game." He looked at Alonzo on the screen. "Let Sebastian know about Bishop though I doubt it'll be much of a surprise."

Alonzo smiled grandly. "Forewarned is forearmed. Ping me when you've arrived at the airport." The screen went blank.

CHAPTER ELEVEN

"This is big." The Nigerian's resonant voice complemented the smoky polish of the eighteen-year-old Laphroaig.

"I wouldn't ask otherwise." Sebastian swirled his glass.

Nwora sipped his scotch and leaned forward. "I'm wondering what you're saving me."

"I might be shorting you." Sebastian nodded when Nwora offered the bottle. He held out his glass for a refill.

The Nigerian chuckled. "You don't interfere with my business. If it's on your radar, you're saving me from a shit storm."

"I can't tell you specifics." Sebastian rested his elbows on his knees. "I can say you don't want to be anywhere near the fallout."

"It sounds like you should duck and cover yourself." His obsidian eyes studied the honeyed glow of scotch as it swirled around the crystal.

"Believe me, I'd like nothing better. This entire thing's bollixed and there's no easy way out."

Nwora's eyes focused on the faraway. "A holy man might say this is your Àyànmô, your destiny. You chose this path because you're an Orisha, an evolved spirit, a vizier of the divine source of All."

Sebastian snorted this time. "You've never struck me as a spiritual man, Nwora."

His friend turned his ebony gaze to meet Sebastian's equally black eyes. "Oremi, where you're concerned, I've postulated and surmised. I've meditated and consulted the Babaaláwo. It's undeniable your Orí-Inu's strong. You hate what you've become, but you strive to transcend. How can I question tangible proof of Olódùmarè?"

"You're making me out to be something I'm not. Transcendence? Bullshit. I'm trying to keep my feet, except the landscape keeps shifting." He tipped the last of his scotch and rested his glass on the table. He looked at Nwora with a twinkle in his eye. "You going straight then?"

The Nigerian's laugh rumbled, a cannonade bombarded across the room. "Oh ho, I recognize righteousness when I see it, doesn't mean I'm walking the path."

"Dodgy git. Shall I say a prayer for your soul?" Sebastian asked.

"I've got the Babaaláwo invoking prayers for me, but a quick word from you couldn't hurt. You may have a more direct line." Nwora wiggled his eyebrows and then grew serious. "I do, however, have a favor in return."

Sebastian sighed. "No kidding."

****

Líu Qīngyún sat at his regular table near the back of Mott 32. He relished the wafting scent of his barbecue Iberico pork with Yellow Mountain honey, a restaurant specialty. He loved the warm, reserved atmosphere. No crowding of tables with white linens and turnstiles here. No gaudy red-fringed lanterns or tinny music weighing down the atmosphere. He sipped the Château Cheval Blanc, enjoying the perfect balance with the pork. He celebrated.

His phone buzzed, rattling on the table near his elbow. "Hóu."

"Boss, we've heard from our operative. The CIA knows about the auction but thinks it's Wong's deal. They're sending a group to Hong Kong. Do we change plans?"

Líu Qīngyún drummed his fingers on the edge of the table. "No, are you able to keep contact?"

"Yes, but should Wong figure out-"

"Enough. Wong has no idea what's happening. He won't until it's too late." Líu Qīngyún thought for a moment. "Move the clone to the new location. As the buyers arrive, be sure to tail them in case the CIA tries to be clever." He took another sip of wine. "Get a message to our agent. I want to know where the CIA will be."

"Xiān shēng."

Líu Qīngyún took a bite of his pork, savoring the tender meat and delicate flavors. He signaled his waiter.

"Yes?" The young man bowed.

"Another glass of the Château Cheval." He waved the man away.

****

Cordelia began to see spots. Andre had dragged her all over London to build the perfect wardrobe for her. The minute the plane landed, Andre herded her into the back of an S-class Mercedes. She envied the rest of the group on their way to Sebastian's Georgian house in Bloomsbury for food and naps. Traveling undercover as Nwora Oni's mistress grew more complicated by the minute. *Why did I agree to do this?*

"Hurry, Cordelia, we've one more stop before we're done." Andre spurred her along with a motion of his hand.

She thought about the load of bags and packages headed back to Sebastian's. Surely they didn't need anything else. The Nigerian agreed to allow Anthony to impersonate him at the auction in Hong Kong. A favor for Sebastian. Anthony worked with Oni's personal concierge to perfect his look. Andre towed Cordelia along in his wake. "Andre, I'm exhausted."

The slender and elegant Slovenian took her hand. "You never know when you have a date with destiny. And it's best to be as pretty as possible for destiny."

"You made that up," she accused, stopping in her tracks.

He shook his head. "Nope, Coco Chanel. You'll like this next place."

Cordelia easily read his sense of mischief. Her stomach growled. "There better be food."

Andre hummed a little tune. "I can arrange that."

****

Sebastian leaned against his brother's desk, arms crossed. He waited, along with his father and Thomas, for Ian to join them. He glanced at his watch. Cordelia and Andre would be back at the house soon. Nwora had called a few minutes ago to let him know Anthony was ready to go. Acquiring the clone was imperative.

"Stop worrying," Sir Gerald said.

Sebastian sighed. "I'm not."

Sir Gerald snorted. "You've looked at your watch three times in ten minutes."

"Dad, if we don't get the clone—"

His father put up a hand. "We'll get her. If not at the auction, wherever she ends up."

"It's not that simple," Sebastian argued.

"It is that simple. You have a good plan and good people to implement it." Gerald leaned back into the tobacco leather of the wing-backed chair. "Fretting won't change anything."

Thomas turned from perusing Ian's bookshelves. "But he's damn good at it."

Sebastian rolled his eyes. "Ha ha. You're not as cavalier as you make out."

"Cavalier?" He thought a minute. "I'll take it. I agree getting the girl is critical. I have more confidence in our plan than you do." Thomas sat opposite Sebastian's father. "Sir Gerald, how did you raise such a fusspot?"

"I've no idea, Thomas, no idea." Gerald leaned into his hand, a gleam in his eye.

Ian entered the study, interrupting Sebastian's rejoinder. "Sorry, waiting for the last results." He looked at his brother's sour face. "You're still bothering about the auction?"

Sebastian threw his hands up. "All right. Sod it! Let the whole thing go up in flames, why don't we?"

"What did I say?" Ian asked, tossing the files in his hand to his desk.

Gerald chuckled. "Nothing, son, what have you found?"

Ian dropped into his chair. "There were a lot of holes in the files we accessed when we recovered you." He gestured toward Sebastian. "When we breached Carlson's compound in Slovenia an automatic fail-safe began a file scrub, but we managed to stop it before we lost everything. I've been able to piece together some of the research and procedures developed in the DNA sequencing."

"What about the files Haager provided?" Thomas asked.

Ian leaned back into his hands. "Those files are specific to the cloning process. The embryos were cloned from your DNA after the complete insertion. The embryos were cloned as a way to harvest the newly modified stem cells. Carlson's staff used those cells to recreate your results. We know how that worked out."

Sebastian frowned. "What about Cordelia?"

"I've been working with my staff on Cordelia's DNA. She's an anomaly," Ian said.

"That doesn't sound good," Gerald said.

Ian waved his hands. "So far I'm only seeing regeneration in Cordelia. I'm confident she's in no danger of the deterioration evident in the man who attacked you in Rome. Also, Elsa is completely healthy aside from Carlson's goal of rapid tissue regeneration; she carries all of the stronger genetic markers that you have." He gestured toward Sebastian and Thomas. "The other factor to consider is her incomplete insertion. It's impossible to say what the final outcome will be, but right now, she's fine. Better than fine, she's growing stronger. Her bone density is increasing and while I haven't tested her, I believe she'll be developing heightened physical senses akin to yours. Her psychic talents are also heightened, which means she's able to detect your ruddy tosh."

Sebastian glowered at his brother's wink. "Do you have enough information from the files to determine any characteristics of the clone?" he asked sharply.

His brother ignored his tone. "No, it was clear in Carlson's notes she had no intention of gestating the embryos to term. Without tissue samples and blood work, I can only infer. We inherited Dad's antibodies from Arthur Carlson's original immunization experiments, but I can't say for certain she will have the same antibodies. She also wasn't exposed to the biotoxin."

Gerald leaned forward. "Your working theory is the interaction between the dormant biotoxin and Carlson's recombinant DNA cocktail is what resulted in Sebastian's transformation."

"Epigenetics has opened the study of the inheritance of genetic traits gained from environmental factors. Ian and I have your immune resistance. It would stand to reason my clone would also have it," Sebastian said.

"Epigenetics is an interesting new field." Ian walked to the bar and poured himself a cup of coffee from a carafe. Leaning against the counter, he took a sip. "The research Haager provided shows she has higher than age-level cognitive skills though she doesn't speak. Based on her scores, I'm guessing it's voluntary rather than developmental."

Gerald said, "Despite his track record with women, Sebastian's always been a sharp one."

Thomas snorted and busied himself with pouring more coffee.

"Thanks, Dad," Sebastian snapped.

Ian took a seat near his father. "I thought about it, but without the data from his childhood development it's impossible to compare the curve. Also, she has his re-engineered DNA, not his normal DNA." He looked at Sebastian. "I'd say she's more on track with your current level of cognitive and physical response times though I'd attributed your amplified physical strength and speed to your change. Your bone density is greater, muscle mass is more substantial, and, of course, your tissue regeneration is accelerated. I'm eager to examine her."

"Maybe on par with how Cordelia is changing?" Thomas asked.

Ian shrugged. "Without observation and testing, we won't know. What I am sure of is it won't take a uniquely intelligent individual to backward-engineer the genetic changes and that means farming out her cells. Right now, she's chattel priced on the hoof."

"No bloody wiggle room," Sebastian growled.

"Let's head back to your house. I need refreshment and then I'm heading back to the estate. Arthur is complaining that his only company is Elsa and the puppy." Ian chuckled.

Gerald stood and stretched. "You know he's loving it."

****

Cordelia and Andre returned to Sebastian's house just as the Coles and Thomas arrived. She picked up Sebastian's irritation without even trying. He growled a bit and stormed off into the house. She moved closer to Sir Gerald. "Has he been like that all morning?"

The cheerful patriarch smiled. "Worse. How was your excursion?"

"Shopping?" Cordelia puffed a stray hair out of her face. "I think I'd rather have spent the day dealing with Sebastian's mood."

"Ah, you're a rare creature, Cordelia. Make sure he doesn't run you off." Sir Gerald patted her hand. "I'm going to take a nap before dinner. You'll excuse me?"

She nodded. "I need one after Andre's gauntlet."

Ian stopped her. "I'd like to take some vitals and draw blood."

"Oy, fine. You come stick me while Andre unloads. I'll take poking and prodding over shopping any day."

Andre directed the delivery of more boxes to her upstairs rooms. "I'm such a tyrant."

Cordelia placed her hands on Andre's shoulders. "You're lovely. Shopping, not so much."

He shooed her up the stairs with Ian in tow.

"Did you talk to him about it yet?" Cordelia asked Ian, watching Andre unpack shopping parcels with eyed practice.

Ian's fingers rested on her wrist. He placed his stethoscope in his ears. "No. If you haven't noticed, he's a wreck." He shushed her response listening to her heart.

Andre pulled out the luggage Nwora Oni sent over. He started arranging her wardrobe for placement. "He's managing it pretty well, but I've noticed a tad more … electricity, since Virginia."

Cordelia sighed. "First a clone. What's he going to think about sharing his thoughts?"

"Well, he's already accustomed to it." Ian jotted the last of her vitals. "He knows you're growing stronger."

"He doesn't know he's been connected to Thomas and Seamus this entire time." Cordelia squeezed the pressure bandage where Ian drew blood. "Seamus is right, isn't he? This stronger affinity is genetic?"

Ian shrugged. "I wasn't keeping track. Like you, I'd assumed it to be familiarity, discipline." He stood and stretched. "I did do some research after we talked. Electric eels and Mormyrid fish alternate the wavelength and frequency of electric current to transmit information. Elephants use low frequency, infrasound to communicate across long distances. What we're talking about could be a variant of this kind of physical communication rather than psychic."

"It isn't enough I'm able to read minds and tell the future, but now I'm using subsonic super communing?" She threw her hands in the air. "How do you explain Elsa?"

"I'm saying it's possible the two things are distinct abilities. One linked to the genetic component you all share and another increasing your presentiment. You're still not reading Sebastian or the others more clearly than you do regular humans."

Andre spoke over his shoulder as he packed. "Is it subconscious though?"

"What do you mean?" Ian asked, intrigued.

"You have a strong affinity for Seamus. I've seen you cut off his comments before he says them." The lithe, young man told Cordelia. "Perhaps the rapport you share is more conducive, whereas the tension between you and Sebastian constricts the flow of the connection."

Cordelia threw a skirt at him.

"No wrinkles," he admonished, smoothing out the fabric. "It's a theory."

Ian grabbed his case. "It's not a bad one." He put a hand up at Cordelia's snort. "You've developed a screen allowing you to silence people's thoughts. Who's to say you haven't done the same to Sebastian?"

She thought about it. "Not like he's hard to read without using my abilities." Switching topics, she felt Ian's concern. "You're worried about his reaction to this girl."

"I don't need to tell you how he feels about his change. Thomas, Seamus, and now you-it weighs on him. A clone." He stared into the room. "How would any of us feel if we were asked to look ourselves in the eye?" He shook his head. "I'm worried my brother is projecting all of his self-loathing onto this little girl. She's a victim as much as any of you are."

Andre voiced the question hanging in both Cordelia's and Ian's head. "Is he going to see it that way?"

CHAPTER TWELVE

Hong Kong

General Wong sipped his tea and gazed out at the azure swells of Clear Water Bay. Eleonora expected their mornings to begin with a bit of peace and quiet. The soft breeze chaperoned the crisp tang of the sea and ruffled the edges of *The Standard* and the *Wall Street Journal* stacked, patient, at his elbow. Habit dictated his observance of the sun's morning sacrament. He waited for the first tentative flickers of light to diffuse the predawn sky with the devotion of the ecclesiastic. After spending years in a Chinese work camp, deep in the claustrophobic jungles of Fujian province, he woke some nights in a panicked sweat. Eleonora would soothe him with cool compresses and Hungarian lullabies. He reveled in the open horizon of the South China Sea.

A soft, porcelain hand interrupted his quiet meditation. "Szerelmem, what a lovely morning." Eleonora placed a delicate kiss on his cheek then settled into her chair across from him. "Shall I have Bao-Zhi start breakfast?"

He never tired of hearing her Hungarian-flavored Cantonese. He liked the way her granite voice curled around the tonal syllables in silky slurs. "Yes, I don't have anything until this afternoon."

She rested her elegant manicure over his gnarled oak of a hand and rang a little bell in the other. "Tell me about the sunrise this morning."

Wong folded her creamy hand between his. "Radiant. Did you sleep well?"

"Mmmmm." She turned to their young houseman. "Dishi, would you ask Bao-Zhi to prepare a light breakfast? Some poached eggs with his lovely cheddar sauce and a side of toasted ficelle, maybe a tomato salad. What do you think, Bǎo bèi?" She tickled her fingers against the palm of his hand.

"I think you'll make me fat and you're mixing your Chinese again." He smiled at her Mandarin endearment.

Her luscious mouth pouted an exquisite O. "Oh shosh." She turned back to Dishi. "And a pain du chocolate if we have some."

The diminutive young man bobbed and nodded his way back into the house. "Hai, hai."

"Tea?" He lifted the pot from the low flame.

"Please." Eleonora brushed her fingers back and forth along his pulse. "Busy schedule this afternoon?"

He tipped the pot over her cup with care. "Some development meetings for the new building. Líu Qīngyún later in the day."

"Again? You mark me, Jian. That man's up to something. I don't trust him." She took a tentative sip of tea.

The General chuckled. "Is your crystal ball talking or you?"

She waved her hand. "Make fun, but watch your back."

"How do you think I've remained alive all of these years?" He reached for *The Standard* and unfolded its pages. "Don't worry, your lifestyle is secure no matter what happens to me."

Eleonora planted her slipper into his shin with smart force.

He let loose a grunt and pulled his gaze from the paper to his mistress.

"You know that's not my concern, you goat." Her hand swooped down through the front page of The Standard. "He's hungry, that one. Loyalty has no room with his kind of ambition."

"He who sacrifices his conscience to ambition burns a painting to obtain the ashes. Believe me, Lou Po. I'm watching him." General Wong shook out his paper to scan the news.

Eleonora picked his glasses up from the table. "It might be better if you used these."

Without looking up, Wong took his glasses from her and slid them on. "He who scatters has much."

"If you have butter on your head, don't go out into the sun." Her eyes twinkled with humor.

"That's not Confucius," he said, without looking up. He didn't need to see her beautiful mouth to know it was crooked into a droll smile.

Dishi returned with a plate of pain au chocolate and a crisp, linen envelope. He placed the plate in the middle of the table and offered the letter to the General with a little bow.

"News?" she asked, leaning forward with curiosity.

General Wong's face remained blank while he peered through his glasses, low on his nose.

"Has misfortune arrived on horseback?" Eleonora prodded.

"Hmmm, I don't think so." He looked out at the sea. "A fool despises good counsel, but a wise man takes it."

"More Confucius, Bǎo bèi?" She leaned forward, curious.

"It seems the morning for it. Sebastian Cole is coming to Hong Kong." He looked at the letter again, trying to divine more from the ink on the page.

Eleonora clapped her hands. "I'll put together a dinner."

"Let's wait and see how business goes first," he said. He glanced at her with a small smile. "He's bringing me a gift."

"I know that look, General." She folded her hands in her lap. "Nem zörög a haraszt, ha a szél nem fújja. *The bushes don't rattle if there's no wind.*"

"Yes, my beloved. And finally the wind has shifted." He handed her the letter.

She placed her hand over her mouth. "Oh, dear."

****

Cordelia had never been to Hong Kong. Nothing could prepare her for the rattle and hum of the city. Manhattan, London, Rome. The thrumming energy of Hong Kong surpassed them all. She loved it. Skyscrapers alight with neon dimmed the stars. Never afraid of heights, she resisted looking up after a glance at the sublime elevations sent her eyes spinning. The sidewalks bustled with people of all ilk. The sheer numbers of people moving in migratory throngs eliminated the need for her to shield. The murmuring buzz that the crowds transmitted drifted through the corridors of the city with little impact on her mind. The volume of sound drowned out any other noises that might be a bother.

Anthony stepped out of the Rolls Royce on her heels. The gold-rimmed Gucci sunglasses reflected the glossy exterior of the hotel in their violet lenses. He took her elbow as two bell boys moved to carry the luggage. After the shooting range, she diligently kept out of his head. Trevor Crosse placed several pieces of Rimowa luggage on the sidewalk.

The concierge stepped through the large glass doors. "Mr. Oni, welcome to the W Hong Kong. Our Extreme Wow suite is set up and stocked per your directions. The rest of the floor has been readied for your group. Please follow me; my staff will take your bags." He jerked his head and hissed at the two boys. "Go get a luggage cart."

"Thank you. My man will take the two smaller pieces." He waved a regal hand at Crosse. "Please get my other staff settled." He gestured to the SUV parked behind the Rolls.

Devyn Park, Adam Morely, Daniel Barth, and Ujah Ikoku stepped out to the curb. Cordelia had met Park a couple of times. She had been on the raid in Slovenia. Ujah Ikoku, the Nigerian's nephew, was a new addition to Global Sureties. Sebastian didn't say, but Cordelia's curiosity piqued. *Why would the Nigerian want his nephew to be a part of Sebastian's group?* She did know the young man's excitement and desire to do well bubbled over. He put on a serious mien as they surrounded Anthony, but she had seen his bright, engaging grin upon introduction.

Andre stepped out from the hotel lobby. "Things are arranged, Mr. Oni. I would suggest that Park and Morely clear the room and the floor before we go up. Perhaps a drink in the bar?"

The concierge made a strangled noise. "Our security is without blemish."

Anthony, playing his part, looked at him, glacial and aloof. "My people will do a sweep." He gestured to Barth and Ikoku. "Tour the bar, gentlemen. We'll be along." He turned to Trevor. "We're taking a drink in the lounge." He moved Cordelia with purpose into the hotel with Trevor taking rear guard.

Andre gestured to the concierge. "The bags can go to the rooms. I believe you received a shipment of Krug Clos d'Ambonnay?"

The concierge nodded.

"Make sure a bottle is at our table." He left the frantic concierge directing bell boys and shouting orders to the valets.

The black and purple furnishings of the Woo Bar flushed of pink neon. Barth and Ikoku cleared a table with a view of the skyline out the lofty windows. They shadowed the table, two daunting bookends. Anthony and Cordelia lounged on a sofa, sipping champagne and nibbling crostini with roasted carrot harissa and crème fraîche. Andre sat across from them, notebook open to their calendar for the week. Between the intimidation factor of their bodyguards and the combined bling sparkling on Anthony and Cordelia, the group drew notice from the bar's hip patrons.

"I'm going to send our host a thank you note. This champagne is life-changing." Cordelia kept her voice low and her face impassive.

Anthony, only sipping lightly, had to agree. "I have good taste."

"Without question, sir." Andre tipped his flute toward his boss. He shifted gears as the sommelier approached. "I'll have the chef in at ten for a light breakfast, and then we're expected at Gagosian gallery for a showing and lunch. We've an invitation to the Fringe Club—" He pretended to drop his voice when he noticed the sommelier. "Yes?"

"I would like to freshen the ice in the bucket. Is there anything else you'd like to eat?" The poor man stammered under the frosty gazes from Barth and Ikoku.

Andre looked at Anthony for confirmation. At his slight nod, he answered the man. "I've heard from our people upstairs. The rooms are ready. Have a selection of light dishes sent up with another bottle of the Krug and have the rest of this bottle brought up with fresh ice." He folded a fifty dollar bill American into the man's sweaty palm. At an invisible signal, the three at the table stood and followed Barth out with Ikoko bringing up the rear. A murmur from the crowd followed the entourage as they left the lounge. They crossed the lobby with equal grandeur and stepped into a waiting elevator.

The doors closed. "Whew, who knew being glamorous and fabulous took so much energy." Cordelia let out a heavy breath.

Barth sniggered a bit and shouldered Anthony. "I'm having a hard time keeping my hands off you."

"Struggle," Anthony said, keeping his face stoic. "We're in the trenches. Characters people."

Andre moved forward to the doors. "He's right. Eyes everywhere."

Cordelia pulled up to her full height and linked her arm with Anthony's. "Showtime."

The doors opened on the penthouse floor. The concierge waited with Park. "The suite and the other rooms are clear, sir."

"Good. Room service is bringing up some dinner." Anthony glanced at Andre and moved past the concierge without a look.

Andre moved into the space. "Thank you. Please double-check our plans with the chef for the morning and leave the morning concierge notes on our requests." He pressed another folded bill into another sweaty palm.

"Yes, sir. Thank you, sir. I'll be sure and do that." The little man hurried to the elevator.

Park closed the double doors behind their entire group. "Swept for bugs and Jarske's little toys are putting out the static."

"Bags are clear and in our rooms." Morely pulled the drapes against the towering, glittering skyline.

Cordelia dropped to the sofa and kicked off her red-soled shoes. "Oy, I should get hazard pay for wearing those heels." She looked at Andre. "I'm not sure I'll make it a week."

Andre slipped off his jacket and sank down beside her. "You did great." He patted her knee. "And you." He waved a hand and bowed to Anthony. "You pulled off the perfect amount of cool indifference." He pressed his fingers to his lips. "Muah! Magnifique."

"I figured out how to channel my character," Anthony said, sliding off the sunglasses with relief.

"How?" Cordelia asked, rubbing her foot.

Anthony peeled his leather jacket off and draped it over a chair. "Simple. I act like Sebastian."

Everyone except Ujah exploded with laughter; even Andre chuckled. Ujah looked a bit confused by this joke at the expense of his new employer.

Cordelia wiped a tear from her eye and tried to settle her giggles. "Oh, that's perfect." She saw Ujah's bewilderment. "Don't worry, Ujah. A few more weeks and you'll get it. You wait."

Her comments sent the rest of them into another fit of mirth.

"Where's that champagne?" Cordelia demanded. "I'd like another drink."

****

The dim light helped her remain still. Counting the beeps of her slowed heart rate helped maintain the rhythm. She built intricate towers in her mind with imaginary blocks. The IV drip staved off hunger, but she missed the sensation of eating. She dared not give any sign of being awake. Five days. She'd counted the number of times someone had checked on her. Blood pressure, temperature, pulse. Familiar routines carried over from the lab.

She listened to whispered conversations. Something important was happening in two days. A chance to slip away. Putting her blocks into a different nook of her mind, she turned her attention to the room around her. The first scrabble, though unsuccessful, did offer her an opportunity to get an idea of her surroundings. Her break into the hallway made it clear this wouldn't be the place to try an escape.

Two days. She kept tight control of her heartbeat. *Nice. Steady. Pace.*

CHAPTER THIRTEEN

Cordelia groaned. The blackout curtains made it impossible to guess the time. Jet lag and champagne complicated her grogginess. Gravity played a joke on her body. She lay, body heavy, her eyes closed. A warm flush of desire pushed against her sluggish brain. *Shit!* Gravity wasn't pressing down on her. Anthony's arm looped across her ribs. His unconscious hunger, loosed from his normal discipline, intruded into her head. Cordelia froze for a moment, trying to gather her wits. *Coffee. I need coffee.* She worked to recall the night.

A few bottles of champagne, a lot of Sebastian-mocking, and a collapse into the huge bed. *No, nothing happened. I'm positive. Am I positive? Yes.* She tried to trace the moment she managed to climb into her pj's. Things were fuzzy. She jerked to lucidity at the soft swish of the bedroom door. She braved a cracked lid and saw Andre float into the room.

Andre gave her a discreet nod.

"Help," she mouthed with a glance at Anthony's inert form.

An impish smile played across Andre's mouth as he gently lifted Anthony's beefy arm.

Cordelia rolled her eyes at him but slithered feet first out of the bed, a fish sliding out of a bucket. She dreaded waking the unconscious man.

Anthony turned to his other side and began a rasping snore.

Andre took Cordelia's hands and helped her stand. He led her out of the bedroom holding her hand like an errant child.

"Whew!" she exploded as they moved into the kitchen. "Don't look so amused." She placed her hand on her cheek. "How much did we drink last night?"

"Plenty," Andre said. He motioned to the chef. "Coffee first." Moving a chair at the table, he motioned Cordelia to sit. "I'll admit I don't feel especially crisp this morning either."

Cordelia slumped into the chair. Keeping her voice low, she leaned in. "I vaguely remember telling—" She had to think for a minute. "Nwora it would be a silly waste of an enormous bed to sleep on the floor."

Andre pursed his lips to keep his chuckle smothered. "Yes, it's quite a large bed." He leaned into his hand, fingers pressed against his lips.

She scowled. "Do not laugh."

The arrival of the coffee cut the rest of her comment short.

"Ahh." Andre sighed into his cup holding it, a treasure, with both hands. "I think we agree last night never happened."

Through a haze, Cordelia remembered Anthony strutting around the room trying to outdo Park and Barth's Sebastian imitations. "Oh yeah, taking it to the grave." She clinked his coffee cup. "What's the agenda today?"

"Gallery viewing and lunch. Hopefully, we'll get information about the auction and dinner with the principles." Andre settled into his chair. "I'll rouse the troops and have the chef get breakfast ready. I think some grease will be in order all the way around."

Cordelia stood with her coffee. "I'm for a shower. You'll wake him?"

Andre didn't bother to keep his chuckle reined. "Yes."

She headed back toward the master bedroom.

"Celia," Andre called out her false name.

It took her a minute, but she stopped and looked back.

"To the grave." He grinned.

"Phhhhth!" She went into the bedroom.

****

The penthouse took up almost the entire floor. Sitting in the kitchen with a cup of coffee, Sebastian gazed over the city toward the W hotel. The light rain tapped a rhythm on the sliding glass doors that opened to the outdoor patio. Jarske had pulled one of the tables over to the bank of windows to the left of the patio doors. He had made the coffee and pulled up surveillance links and begun hooking up comm links.

Haager had arrived a few minutes before, still showing signs of jet lag. Without a word, he poured a coffee and leaned against the counter. "Up and running yet?"

Sebastian already regretted giving him access to their operations. He tamped down his disdain. "Getting there. Your team ready?"

Haager nodded over a sip of coffee. "Yeah, I have a two-man team waiting outside of the hotel and a team working electronic surveillance at another location."

"Good." He kept his disdain hidden behind a blank face. "Crosse came back late after they settled into the room. Things are in place."

Jarske came into the kitchen to fill his mug. "I have Haager's team linked up." He looked at Sebastian for a full beat. He swished the coffee pot at Sebastian. "Better make another pot."

"I'll get right on that," Sebastian snorted.

"Get on what?" Thomas asked, running his fingers through his unruly curls as he trudged from one of the back bedrooms.

"Watching you make coffee," Sebastian sniped.

Haager moved to peer over Jarske's shoulder. "Do you have a team on them?"

"I get stage fright," Jarske deadpanned, a blank look on his face.

Haager moved to sit on the sofa, looking put out.

Sebastian chuckled at Haager's petulance. "Who's outside, Jarske?"

"I tapped Leung and Mau. They're reliable and they know the city." Jarske tapped the computer screen to his right. "I've linked our system to the GPS links in their phones and they have comm links."

Thomas bustled around the kitchen. "You know, they have a chef over there."

"You'd have to be a notorious criminal." Seamus's brogue broke in with humor, his crimson curls still damp from a shower. "Are you taking orders?" He slid onto a stool at the counter next to Sebastian.

"No, but I'm happy to give you one." Thomas slid a coffee mug across the counter.

Seamus chuckled.

Conversation stopped as Mai Li walked from the hall, her look flat. "Seriously?"

Seamus opened his mouth, but Sebastian put a hand up. "Enough."

"What's the plan?" Haager leaned an elbow on the couch.

Jarske answered from the computers without looking back. "They're going to Gagosian gallery for a luncheon. Someone from the auction is supposed to make contact there. We'll know time and location, though with all of the chatter, I'd guess it'll be soon."

"So they'll keep up their little charade through the auction," Haager said.

"We'll either be able to purchase the clone outright or we'll know who the winning bidder is. Either way, we won't be making any noise in Wong's territory. We don't know if he's behind this sale." Sebastian stood up. "Mai Li, you're on lockdown. It was a bitch getting you into Hong Kong. I won't have everyone at risk if one of Wong's informants catches sight of you."

Thomas threw him a set of keys with a nod.

Haager stood up. "Where are you going?"

"To pay my respects," Sebastian said.

****

I've become one of those women in a gangster film. She resisted the urge to tug at the very short hem of the geometric black and white dress Andre laid out for the gallery thing. The dress killed with a little peplum waist and a drop back. In a small blessing, he had placed a pair of cushions into the toe box of the peep-toe Louboutin heels. *I might survive this yet.*

Andre slipped in to check on her. "Everything okay in here?" He smoothed a stray hair in her sleek ponytail. It had taken the hairdresser thirty minutes to blow it straight under Andre's keen direction.

"I know a lot of women would really enjoy this, but I feel like a sham." She sighed with a little wiggle. She willed her hands to remain at her side, but her fingers pulled her ponytail making sure it covered her scar.

"Well, I know some shams who'd give their left arm to look as fabulous as you do." He held out an elbow. "Don't worry, it doesn't show. You have so much hair. How do you Americans say it? Giddy up?"

She laughed. "Something like that."

They stepped out of the bedroom. The low-level conversation stopped. Anthony stood. Barth and Morely both gaped, mouths open. Ujah stared with solemn admiration and even Park's eyebrows rose a notch. She broke the silence with a long whistle.

Cordelia blushed crimson but laughed with a look of thanks.

Barth opened up a small case. "Everyone gets one of these." He made the rounds. "These are the comm links. Each one has a GPS chip so we're covered there. Nwora and Celia also have additional GPS chips. C," he gestured to the simple bow belt at Cordelia's waste, "yours is there, and Nwora," he touched a hand to Anthony's cuff link, "yours is there."

"You think we'll need them?" Cordelia asked, touching her belt.

Park stepped in. "After Slovenia, we're not taking any chances." She looked with meaning at Cordelia.

Cord nodded. It had been luck Vivienne Carlson hadn't scanned her for any implanted chips. *Luck or madness.* Even then, it had taken Andre's help to speed the cavalry. They dealt with calculating and intelligent criminals on this job. They may take her comm link, but she would keep her clothes. *I hope.*

Barth spoke up. "The additional chips are passive. We're able to scan them, but they won't trigger any security scanners."

Ujah stepped forward with another case for Anthony. "My uncle sent this as a luck gift." He revealed a Sig Sauer P226X-Six Scandic. The semi-automatic pistol rested against blue velvet; its gold accents and polished birch grip plates gleamed. "It's his signature weapon. He thought it would be a nice touch."

Now Cordelia understood Lorena's appreciation for guns. More than a gun, this pistol exuded deadly, artistic grace.

Anthony placed the gun in his burnished Spanish leather holster with respect. He nodded at Ujah. "I'll be sure to thank him when we're done here."

Andre moved behind him and helped him with his jacket. Anthony waved his hand to settle into his imperious character. "Let's go."

****

Sebastian ordered a scotch at the open bar. He sipped and scanned the crowd. "See them yet?" he asked Thomas.

His friend leaned an elbow on a tall table, a plate of hors d'oeuvres at hand. "Nope, but they'll be hard to miss."

Crosse chimed in over their comm links from the penthouse. "They've arrived."

"In the south elevator," Jarske informed them.

The gallery luncheon gleamed with wealth and privilege. Sebastian scanned the room. These people represented the hip and cultured of Hong Kong. Among the high society names, low-level gangsters and celebrities mingled with clinks of glasses and enthusiastic discussion of the artwork.

Haager cut in over the comm link. "My guys didn't see Wong anywhere."

Sebastian ground his teeth. "This isn't his kind of crowd. Keep off the comm." He glared at Thomas.

The cheerful Englishman shrugged. He nodded his head. "Here they come."

Conversation in the coterie began to stir as the Nigerian and his entourage exited the elevators.

Thomas whistled low. "Blimey, she cleans up well."

"Seamus, keep eyes on them." Sebastian ignored Thomas's grin.

"Righty-oh, won't be a problem. Did you see that dress?" The Irishman's humor was clear in his tone from his position across the room.

"Mac." Sebastian's voice froze.

"Yessir," Seamus replied, all business.

Sebastian shot Thomas a warning look.

He put his hands up. "I didn't pick the dress." He chuckled.

Without humor, the head of Global Sureties drew their attention back to the group. "The gallery owners approached them. Focus, please."

****

"Mr. Oni, I'm Suen Jianyu." He gave a little bow. "I'm honored by your presence."

Cordelia peeked into the gallery owner's head. She gave Anthony's arm two quick squeezes. Even amid the pidgin mix of English and Cantonese in the man's mind, she knew this wasn't their contact.

"Your kind invitation made for a pleasant afternoon's excursion. This is C." He introduced Cordelia. "My companion, Celia Wright."

The slight, well-dressed man bowed deeply over her hand. "Ms. Wright. I'm enchanted."

"Thank you, Mr. Suen. I was so glad to receive your invitation. Nwora can get caught up in business and he forgets the delights Hong Kong offers." Cordelia gestured at the various pieces of art. "If you don't mind showing me the work?" She looked at Anthony. "You wouldn't mind, Nwora?"

Suen's eyes bulged a bit. Cordelia smiled at his mismatched thoughts blazing his avarice at Nwora Oni's mistress shopping his gallery. "It's my pleasure."

Anthony nodded. "Of course." He glanced at Ujah and Park, who moved to shadow Cordelia.

She slid from Anthony's arm to Andre's arm. "Lead on, Mr. Suen." Cordelia only half listened to the gallery owner's explanation of each piece and artist. Her awareness floated through the room. She picked up the three familiar hums and avoided making eye contact with Sebastian. His thoughts burned in her direction.

Andre leaned in with a soft whisper. "Can't take his eyes off of you."

Cordelia shook his comment off. "Working here."

"Any luck?" he asked, waving down a server for a couple of flutes of champagne.

"Really?" She squinted at the glass through a still cloudy head.

Mr. Suen took his own glass. "To beauty in all of its forms."

"Hair of the dog," Andre whispered, a glint in his eye.

"Such a gracious host, I think we'll find Nwora. Will lunch be served soon?" She took a sip at Andre's urging.

The svelte Chinese man looked at his watch, suddenly frantic. "Oh my, I've forgotten my other guests." He gave her an apologetic look. "Such delightful distraction. Excuse me." He bowed and hurried away giving brisk orders to the servers.

"Some of this stuff is awful," Park commented, moving in tighter toward Cordelia and Andre.

"The wealthy can afford bad taste." Andre smiled. "Did you find anything significant?" He looked at Cordelia.

Frustrated, she took another drink. "Funny thing, I don't speak Chinese."

Her companions looked at her quizzically.

"Andre, what language are you thinking in?" she asked.

The handsome, lithe man laughed but thought a second. "English?"

"And if you were speaking Slovene?" she prodded.

His look amused her. "Let me see." He took a minute. "Slovene, maybe a little English."

Park caught on with a chuckle, but Ujah's confusion appeared on his face and in his thoughts.

Cordelia looked at him. "People think in their native language. I don't speak Chinese. The most I can get are impressions of emotions."

The tall woman spoke into the comm. "You get that?"

In her ear, Cordelia heard Sebastian's deep voice. "Yeah, we're working without the extra edge. Head back to Anthony."

"Okey doke." Park waved her arm. "After you, Ms. Wright."

Cordelia turned toward where she last had sight of Anthony but stumbled as a short, stocky man ran into her, spilling her champagne on her dress.

Ujah and Park snapped into action, moving Cordelia behind them.

"Oh, apologies." The man bowed and spoke heavily accented English. "I didn't look." He flustered under the tough scrutiny of her bodyguards and backed away with more bows.

"Let's get some water on it," Andre said, spurring the group to move to the restrooms.

Park and Cordelia went into the lavish washroom.

"Wow, some digs," Park complimented, watching Cordelia dab at her dress with a damp towel.

"Leave it to me to spill something on this dress." She scowled.

Park chuckled. "Not technically your fault and looks like you're getting it." She leaned in a little. "You have a smudge."

Cordelia looked in the mirror. "Great." She fished around in her purse for a tissue and pulled out a thick, creamy envelope. "Looks like I did get it."

"Well, all right," Park said, looking pleased. She activated her comm. "Contact."

CHAPTER FOURTEEN

"Meet up with Anthony and we'll clear out. We'll convene at street level." Cordelia felt Sebastian's hum moving through the crowd as his words accessed her ear piece.

"Roger," Park replied, gesturing to Andre and Ujah as she and Cordelia left the restroom.

Anthony piped in. "I'll meet you at the door."

Cordelia's little group was waylaid by the gallery owner. "You're not leaving?" Mr. Suen's voice contained a hint of panic.

"Oh, Mr. Suen, I had a little accident." Cordelia gestured to the damp spot on her dress. "I'm afraid I need to deal with this."

The little man bobbed his head in despair. "Of course, of course." He pressed a catalog into her hands as Anthony approached. "If you'd like anything, feel free to contact me."

"Thank you," she managed as Anthony stepped in to usher her out the door.

"Mr. Suen, thank you for your hospitality," he rumbled, sliding his arm around Cordelia's waist.

The group entered the elevator. Anthony looked at Cordelia. "You got it?"

"Yeah, had to spill champagne to do it." She started to pull the envelope from her purse.

Andre put his hand out to stop her. "Not here."

"He's right," Park agreed. "We'll figure out our next move at the hotel."

The elevator doors opened to the lobby and Cordelia saw Sebastian, Thomas, and Seamus waiting on the street.

Their group moved to the curb and Andre gave the valet their car ticket. The valet took off at a run and a second valet pulled up with Sebastian's car.

As Sebastian walked around the front to the driver's side, two dark SUVs slowed in front of the building.

Cordelia, picking up an immediate sense of danger, shouted, "Get down!" She dropped to the ground without looking to see if anyone else paid heed.

Bullets hailed at them from the vehicles. She peeked out to see her warning, thankfully, had inspired immediate response. Ujah, nearest to her, dropped to one knee while pulling out his gun. He shielded her on the ground, looking for the threat. Sebastian, directly in the line of fire, had to drop to the ground while glass from shattered windows showered him. Park was able to fire a few answering rounds before ducking completely behind the valet station. Anthony, standing closest to the street, took a round in the shoulder and flew backward into the splintering glass of the building. He fired several rounds.

People on the street screamed and ran in circles. The offending vehicles disappeared with speed. Sirens blazed and smoke cleared. Ujah offered her his hand. She stood up. "Ujah!" She examined his shoulder. "You're shot."

The young Nigerian holstered his weapon and glanced down at his arm. "A crease. Are you hit?" He scanned her up and down.

She shook her head. "No. My knees might be sore later, but not shot." She looked around frantically remembering Andre. "Andre?"

Ujah motioned her to stay put. "Let me." He moved toward Thomas and Seamus, who were both brushing off glass shards with furious looks on their faces.

Cordelia cringed at the deep, rumbling waves of anger boiling off of them. She turned to see Park pushing herself up on the remnants of the valet station. "You okay?" She moved toward the tall woman.

Park gave her an okay sign and looked back to Anthony. "You?"

"A clean in and out," the large man replied, his left hand pressed into his right shoulder. "Pride bruised."

Cordelia looked around for Sebastian. She sighed when she saw him stand up on the other side of the car. She sighed again when she saw Ujah helping Andre up with Thomas's help. She was surprised to see him with a pistol.

Park put a hand on her shoulder. "We'd all be in worse shape without you."

Seamus came to help Anthony up and said, "We need to leave." Police sirens grew louder.

A crowd started to gather. Sebastian shook his head clear. "Andre, you good to stay with me and deal with the authorities? There're security cameras all over. We can't get out of here clean."

The graceful Slovenian nodded. "Of course."

The absent valet pulled up with their Infiniti QX80, confusion on his face. Park pulled him out. "Thomas, let's get Oni into the car." She opened the back door as Thomas and Seamus eased Anthony to his feet. She looked at Sebastian. "Where're we going?"

Sebastian shot Cordelia, closely flanked by the bleeding Ujah, a look. "The apartment. We'll meet you." He spoke into his comm. "Jarske?"

A disembodied voice broke into their comm links. "Yeah, boss."

"Get Crosse and Morely to the apartment. Leave Barth at the hotel to secure the rooms in case someone tries there. We need the med kit." He holstered his weapon; his irritation at not firing a single shot pushed out toward Cordelia.

She rolled her eyes. "Of course," she muttered.

His acute hearing drew his eyes to catch her look. "What?"

She shook her head. "Not a thing."

Park waved at Cordelia and Ujah. "Let's blow this pop stand."

Cordelia felt Sebastian's quizzical eyes on the back of her head as they pulled away.

Crosse opened the door for them. "Status?" he demanded of Park, who was first through the door.

"Anthony has a through and through, right shoulder. Ujah's left arm is creased. Rest of us are fine."

Haager charged them. "What the hell happened?"

Park gave him a look that froze him. She and Crosse moved to allow Seamus and Thomas to muscle Anthony into the flat. Cordelia and Ujah brought up the rear. She pushed the protesting Ujah onto the stool next to Anthony. "We need to look at your arm."

"Who attacked you?" Haager asked. Seamus snorted and Park's sneer spoke volumes. General contempt for Haager pulsed strongly from the entire group; Cordelia imagined she could see it.

"Sebastian's on his way. They cleared it with the authorities," Jarske reported, ignoring Haager's question.

"Wonder how much that cost," Thomas mused, helping Anthony sit on a stool at the bar. "Going to have to stitch you up, mate."

Anthony nodded. "Help me get this jacket off. Shame to ruin such fancy duds." He looked appreciatively at the blood stain on the deep purple silk.

"Eh, aside from the hole, the blood's barely noticeable," Park sniped, winking at Cordelia.

Cordelia's smile froze. She stiffened when she noticed the approaching presence.

Mai Li sauntered into the room. "Trouble?" Her gaze traveled over the newcomers.

Suspicion fueling her disdain, Cordelia pushed into Mai's brain trying to see if the woman knew anything about the ambush. Mai wasn't surprised they had been attacked, but Cordelia couldn't find any specific link. "You don't seem surprised."

The slight woman shrugged. "This is a high-stakes auction. Not a shock if someone's trying to narrow the competition."

"She's right," Haager said, sitting on the sofa. "It could be Wong or any of the other buyers."

Thomas took the medical kit from Crosse. "Did you hear something?" He looked around at the others. He helped Anthony unbutton his shirt.

Haager frowned.

Cordelia nudged Ujah. "You too, buster."

Ujah looked chagrined. "I told you, it's only a crease."

"Either way, your arm needs to be cleaned and dressed," Park said, moving into the kitchen. She opened the fridge and peered at the selection. "Anyone need a drink?" She pulled a beer and popped the top.

Anthony nodded, but Thomas interceded. "Nope, water only." He took a syringe and a vial from the case. "I'm going to anesthetize your shoulder and give you a tip of morphine. No booze."

The patient sighed.

Ujah spoke up, peeling off his shirt. "At most, I'll only need the lidocaine." He looked at Park. "I'd like one, please."

"Seamus, take a look at Ujah's arm." Thomas squinted at the hole in Anthony's shoulder. "This needs to be cleaned up. The bleeding has slowed, but you need stitches." Thomas rummaged through the medical case, setting aside a blister pack with a suture kit. "Mine won't be as neat as Ian's."

"As long as it heals." Anthony gritted his teeth as Thomas worked to clean both sides of his wound.

Seamus peered at Ujah's arm. "I think a few butterfly strips'll do the trick." He retrieved a box of steri-strips. "Cord, I'll need you to hand them to me while I hold this gash closed."

Cordelia stepped closer and opened the box. "Sure thing."

"I would be remiss if I didn't mention, auction aside, my uncle does have enemies." Ujah grunted as Seamus applied the white adhesive strips with force. "I thought you were going to numb it."

"Pansy." Seamus snorted.

Cordelia held back her snicker and handed the tall ginger another bandage.

The front door slammed open. Sebastian strode into the room, his anger blazing in front of him.

Cordelia winced at the force of it.

"Everyone okay?" He glared around the room.

Andre glided into the flat behind him and shut the door.

Thomas looked up from the last suture in Anthony's entrance wound. "None the worse for wear. I'll be done with Tony's stitches in a minute and I think Seamus is about finished with Ujah's arm. Considering the firepower, we're in pretty good shape." He indicated to Anthony to turn around.

"The police are going to pull surveillance tapes from the surrounding buildings, but I didn't get the feeling they would be helpful." Andre moved to sit opposite Haager in the living room.

"Any problem with us leaving the scene?" Thomas asked, anesthetizing the other side of Anthony's shoulder.

Sebastian shook his head. "Is there another beer?"

Park popped a new bottle open and handed it to him. "What did it cost? Andre, anything?"

Andre shook his head. "Thank you. Not as pricey as you might think in Hong Kong."

"They're not hurting for resources here," Haager sneered. "Did they have any idea who did the shooting?"

"No, and it's unlikely they'll find out," Andre answered with a cool glance.

Cordelia admired his manners. Haager's voice set her teeth to grinding. She looked at Sebastian. "Do we still move forward?" She willed his eyes to move from glaring at Haager to her.

He turned, his relief she wasn't injured ebbing around her like a caress. "Yes."

Haager stood. "Yes? We don't know who shot at you. Our cover could be blown. Walking into the auction now is a guaranteed mess." His voice, shrill and sharp, drew irritated looks.

Park walked out of the kitchen, veered wide around Mai Li, and plopped down next to Andre. "Six of one, half dozen of the other." She took a sip of beer.

"What the hell does that mean?" Haager swung around to face Park.

"The who doesn't matter." Sebastian's tone matched the general feeling of the room.

Mai Li smirked at Haager. "They have to go regardless."

Andre stood, a serene smile on his face. "Well then, I'll order lunch. Showers all around because we have dinner plans."

The Fringe Club glimmered in concert with the glint and shine of the women exiting expensive cars at the doors. Rock stars, celebrities, and criminals flooded the multinational crowd. The air crackled with excitement to mingle at the invitation of Madame Mdivani, the glamorous and constant companion of the leader of the Triad. Notes of a string quartet drifted down to the street from the rooftop patio. Local paparazzi blitzed the dazzling crowd with flashes.

"Oh my," Cordelia gasped, hesitating for a moment.

Andre placed his hand at her elbow. "Steady now. The General and Madame greet guests in the foyer. Sebastian and the others are right behind us."

She gripped Anthony's arm and felt him wince. "Sorry, are you sure we needed to come?"

"Yeah, we need to be seen. Even if the press didn't publish our names, the street drums would have spread the word." He smoothed a hand down the front of his jacket. "Better to show we're fine and on our feet."

Park flanked Anthony on the left. "Brave faces, people. We're next."

Adam Morely, fidgeting in his tuxedo, flanked Andre on the right. "Last time I cut cards with Trevor."

"He cheats," Anthony remarked. "Here we go."

General Wong stood under six feet but exuded confidence and composure. Cordelia read nothing of the violent monster from Mai Li's memory. He reminded her of Gerald Cole, all quiet mastery. The tiny woman next to him sparkled with mischievous grace. Her gown dazzled a stained glass masterpiece against her alabaster skin. Black eyes gleamed with intelligence under long, fanning lashes. Her mind buzzed with excitement in a familiar but unclear language. Cordelia felt a shift in Andre. She resisted the urge to look at him, a question in her eyes.

Madame Mdivani grasped Cordelia's hand in both of hers. "Welcome, welcome." She bobbed her head to Anthony. "So lovely, both of you."

Taken aback by her host's exuberance, Cordelia couldn't help but smile. "Thank you, Madame."

Anthony offered a brief bow to the General. "General Wong, I appreciate the invitation."

The older man dipped his silver-maned head. "Mr. Oni, I'm glad to finally meet you." He gave a pointed look at Cordelia.

"My apologies, this is Celia Wright. Ms. Wright, this is General Wong and his companion, Madame Mdivani." He gestured to Andre. "This is my majordomo, Andre Juricic."

The General offered Anthony a look of pleasure. "A majordomo. How wonderfully elegant." The Dragon offered a gracious bow of the head to Andre.

"Juricic?" Madame Mdivani's eyes brightened. "Madžarski in Slovenski?" *Hungarian or Slovenian?*

Cordelia caught a familiarity between Andre and the Hungarian. Something passed between them.

Andre's serene smile didn't waver. "Az sem slovenski, Madame."

Madame Mdivani clapped her hands together. "How wonderful! You'll dance with me, young man. I miss speaking my native languages."

"Of course, Madame," the slender man said.

Cordelia felt Sebastian's presence behind her. She willed her face to remain impassive.

General Wong's smile beamed. He stepped past Cordelia. "Sebastian, Thomas. Old friends, welcome."

Sebastian bowed slightly. "General, it's a pleasure to be invited."

Cordelia picked up his amusement. *This is a chess game.*

He gestured to the redheaded Irishman. "I don't believe you've met Seamus MacColgan."

Seamus offered his own bow. "General Wong."

The sterling-headed general turned to Anthony. "It's my understanding you know Mr. Oni?"

"Yes, for a long time." Sebastian offered Anthony his hand. "Nwora."

"Sebastian," Anthony replied, his stony mien in place.

Madame Mdivani swept her arm toward the ballroom. "I've placed you at the same table." She gave Andre a sharp look. "Ne pozabite, my young man, you owe me a dance."

Andre nodded. "I won't forget, Madame. Shall we go in, sir?" he asked Anthony.

"After you." Anthony held out his elbow for Cordelia.

She took it, ignoring the heat from Sebastian's eyes on the back of her head.

Park sidled up on her right side and muttered wryly. "Ought to be some party."

Cordelia snorted.

CHAPTER FIFTEEN

Sebastian watched Andre gracefully lead Madame Mdivani to the sounds of the orchestra. He scanned the room from his seat next to Anthony. Thomas and Seamus stood near the bar chatting with their operative Wai Ling and a couple of other low-level Triad members. "Figures Seamus would find the bar."

Morely gave a light laugh. "And the low lives. He's consistent."

The Englishman's eyes moved to Cordelia, who outshined a pair of women the Madame introduced to her. He frowned imagining her awareness of his gaze. Glancing at Anthony he asked, "How's the shoulder?"

"Stiff. Thomas wanted to give me a shot of Dilaudid, but I took some ibuprofen instead. Not the worst I've had." He took a sip of wine. "One of Wong's cronies is staring at us."

Sebastian casually swept his eyes across the room. "Líu Qīngyún. He's second-tier management. Líu's outspoken in his argument Wong has outlived his role as Dragon. He's a loudmouth." Sebastian focused on Cordelia making her way back to the table.

"Think he'd act?" Anthony stood to pull out Cordelia's chair.

"Who's a loudmouth?" she asked, placing her wine on the table. Sebastian noticed a lock of hair drifting along her throat. She met his eyes and reached up to adjust it.

He sighed. "Slim guy to our left, leaning against the bar in the shiny suit."

She leaned her elbow on the table and pretended to study her ring.

Sebastian recognized it as the one he bought for her in Italy. He imagined her mind press on him. It felt as though she'd whispered in his ear. *Not now.*

"Hm. He's ambitious, bitter, and self-righteous. I wish I knew Chinese. That's the best I can do." Cordelia straightened up and took a sip from her glass. "I get the feeling he'd shank Wong the first chance he could, but I don't think he'd do it openly or without prompting."

"A straw man," Anthony remarked. "Who's pulling the strings?"

Sebastian saw an idea bloom on Cordelia's face. "We can talk about it later."

A hand fell on his shoulder; he looked up to see General Wong. Seeing his attempt to stand, Wong waved him back down. "No need, my friend." The Triad leader sat next to Sebastian. "You're enjoying the party?" He looked at the ballroom awash in color and sequins.

"Yessir. Madame is a marvelous dancer." Even seated, Sebastian looked down at the man.

"Ah yes. She loves a gala and such a debonair partner." Wong acknowledged Anthony. "You don't dance, Mr. Oni?"

"Why yes, I was about to take Celia for a turn." The Bostonian rose and held out his hand. "C?"

Sebastian knew she kept her eyes from glancing his way. She stood and took Anthony's hand. "Of course." She nodded her head to the two powerful men and accompanied Anthony to the dance floor.

General Wong patted Sebastian's arm. "You're a formidable man, Sebas." He surprised Sebastian with the use of the nickname. "It's not healthy to covet what a friend possesses."

The head of Global Sureties leaned back into his seat. "I'm obvious, Fo Lung?"

The older man chuckled at the casual title. "Your eyes rarely leave her. I empathize, my boy. I found myself entranced in such a way by Eleonora, but good business and a good friendship demand more." He sighed. Sebastian believed his sincere regret. "You may never find its like again."

Changing tacks, Sebastian picked up his scotch. "Is coveting Liú's sin?"

The Dragon tinkled the ice in his own glass. "Impatience and ignorance. Are you sure about your plan? The Nigerian's been targeted."

The long pause hung between the two forceful men. "As long as I have your word, one way or another we'll both remain standing on the other side."

Mischief alight in his eyes, the General raised his glass to Sebastian. "To old debts."

"And new ones," he said, his voice determined. Sebastian clinked glasses and drank. He set his glass on the table and stood. "If you'll excuse me."

Wong shook his head. "Of the three ways we learn wisdom, experience is the bitterest, my friend."

"We've both had our share of bittersweet, Confucius or no." Sebastian tipped his head and strode to the dance floor.

****

"You're a good dancer," Cordelia complimented.

Anthony smiled. "My grandmother demanded dance lessons." He kept an eye on the crowd.

Cordelia felt a familiar presence. "Well, she's a smart cookie. A good dancer is hard to resist."

"He's a regular twinkle toes." Seamus broke in on the comm link.

With a snort, she took a glance at the bar where the sizable Irishman leaned against the bar. "Don't see you out here."

"He's afraid of the River Dance jokes," Anthony rejoined with a smirk.

Seamus raised his glass toward the dance floor.

Cordelia saw Andre walk Madame Mdivani back to General Wong at their table and locked eyes with Sebastian coming toward her and Anthony. She held back her sigh.

Sebastian tapped Anthony on the shoulder. "May I?"

Her dance partner stiffened so briefly, she might've imagined it. "Of course." He offered a slight bow toward her and headed back to the table.

Sebastian slipped his hand to her hip and held out his other hand. "Shall we?"

Her mind hummed at his touch. "Certainly." She placed her hand in his and they began to move as the orchestra began the next measure.

"He's a good man." The amused respect in his voice matched his thoughts.

"Cole." She warned, knowing Anthony could hear them over the comm. *Don't stir the pot.* She pushed at him.

Winking, he moved her to the strains of a Delibes waltz with ease. *Relax.* "We're all professionals here."

"Really?" She raised her eyebrow.

His eyes narrowed, but she knew he mocked. "Ouch."

"You'll live." She allowed her eyes to travel the room, confident in her partner's ability. "Poor Morely, he's so uncomfortable."

Without looking, Sebastian chuckled. "He'd rather be on watch in the pouring rain than sitting here in a tux. Next time, he won't gamble with Trevor."

The waltz shifted to Brahms. He shifted steps without hesitation. "Anthony's grandmother forced him into dance lessons. What's your excuse?"

Another chuckle escaped him. "Boarding school. Proper British education includes Latin and the waltz."

She laughed. "Well rounded. Who'd you practice with?"

He paused. "Alfie Hoskins." Humor wrinkled the corner of his eyes. A snort broke in over the comm from Thomas. "All-boys school. He was quite graceful." Sebastian defended.

Tucking her chin, her chortle caused her to stumble a bit.

"You're no Alfie." He skillfully righted her.

"Be glad of it," she jabbed wickedly.

He locked eyes with her. The intensity of his look matched the energy pulsing from him. "Careful, we might be having a moment."

Sighing, she swallowed. "Just dance."

His snicker vanished into a smashing reverberation. Screams, glass, and smoke flew from every direction. She slammed onto her back. Fire alarms screeched in time with emergency strobe lights. Ears ringing, dazed and coughing, Cordelia couldn't breathe. A weight pressed heavy upon her chest, immobilizing her. Sebastian had shielded her with his body and flattened her to the floor.

"Cord, you okay?" He pushed off of her, coughing against the smoke billowing through the debris.

She nodded and tried to lean on her elbows. Pieces of ceiling tiles hung at crazy angles. A table sheltered their legs from a cracked support beam. Shattered glass glittered on the floor. People gained their feet slowly as realization spread through the living. Crying and moaning traveled along the hot currents as bodies lay still here and there. She didn't look too closely. "The others?"

He shook his head and gained his knees. "Can't see." He peered through the murk. "The water main's been shut off. No fire sprinklers." He nodded at a small blaze to his right. "We've got to move before this place lights up."

Cordelia flexed her feet. "Legs work." She squinted through the soot. "I've lost my shoes. Andre's going to have a fit."

"He'll deal." He stood up carefully. Reaching out, he offered her his hand. "Try to stand."

A figure emerged from the wreckage. Sebastian leaped to a defensive stance in front of her.

She placed her hand on his leg and coughed. "It's okay."

Out of the smoke, the figured took the shape of Wai Ling, one of the men Seamus had been chatting with at the bar. He had tied his kerchief around his nose and mouth. "Hey, boss, good to see you standing."

Cordelia felt her companion relax. "You too. What's up?"

"Two devices. One on the roof, one in here. Comms are out. The fires are localized, but without sprinklers, they're going to spread. I was in the stairwell sneaking a smoke." Wai Ling's eyes crinkled in humor. "Rumor has it they're gonna kill me."

Sebastian snorted. "Not today."

Wai Ling glanced at her. "Got to get out of here. I saw some *say pok* guys creeping up here with semi-autos. Someone wants to be sure the target is dead." He slipped back into the debris and haze.

"What now?" Cordelia asked, unable to get a read on Sebastian's racing thoughts.

Their wiry Chinese ally reappeared with a pair of men's loafers. "Put these on." He handed them to her.

She shook off her grimace. *No time to be squeamish.*

Sebastian helped her stand and steadied her while she slipped on the shoes. "Everyone will rabbit. Once we're all in the clear, Jarske will roll call." He nodded at Wai Ling. "Let's go."

"Mau was with me in the stairwell. He's gone around the other side to see who he can round up." Wai Ling started his way back through the disarray and wreckage, keeping his body low. "This way."

Cordelia took Sebastian's hand. They wound their way crunching over the debris, following Wai Ling's shadowed figure. Sirens wailed in the distance echoing the sobs and moans of the injured. A press of bodies gathered, flowing in the same general direction. Cordelia kept her focus on their guide's back. She didn't dare let the surrounding pain and alarm into her thoughts. Her worry over the others in their group threatened to spill over.

"They're okay," Sebastian said, over his shoulder. He tightened his grip on her hand. "Let's get through this crowd then we'll regroup."

She nodded, keeping her mouth and nose covered with her other elbow.

Wai Ling reached the door to the stairs and noticed they had stopped. He waved them to hurry. More people hobbled and pushed their way into the stairwell.

"Okay." Cordelia tamped down her worry. "Let's go."

****

They burst out of the building among the herd of survivors. The street filled with emergency vehicles. Firefighters worked on containing the flames while EMTs moved among the crowd assessing injuries. Police held a perimeter and tried to move traffic. The chaos inside spilled out into the streets.

Wai Ling pulled them to the left, winding his way through the maze of police cars and traffic at a standstill. "Next block over," he encouraged.

They kept moving, finally breaking out of the tumult. A taxi parked on the opposite corner flashed its lights as Wai Ling turned the corner. "Here." He herded them to the car. Leaning down, he gestured at the driver. "This is Choi. He'll take you where you want to go. Just give him the address."

Choi waved a hand with a huge grin.

Sebastian put a hand on Wai Ling's shoulder. "Thank you."

The lean Cantonese man beamed. "It's never boring when you're in town. Be safe. I'll contact you tomorrow." He bowed to Cordelia. "You're a trooper," he said and loped off, disappearing in the noise and bustle of the city.

"Put this on." Sebastian opened the door and slipped off his jacket.

The coat draped over her shoulders, he watched her slide in gingerly. *I don't blame her.* Adrenaline rush over, he began to feel bomb bruised.

He joined her in the backseat. Leaning forward, he told Choi, "The bus station at Old Peak Road, near Dynasty Court Tower."

The young man nodded and handed Sebastian a phone. "Burner. We'll be there in no time."

Sebastian glanced at Cordelia as the car pulled into the swarm of traffic. She leaned back, eyes closed. He couldn't tell if he felt her exhaustion as he had her thoughts earlier or if he registered it in response to his own. He dialed an eleven-digit number.

"Crosse." Trevor's voice clipped with tension.

"It's Cole." Sebastian's worry amped up in response to Trevor's tone. "What's your status?"

"Jarske and I moved to higher ground as you suggested. Just as we set up surveillance, four armed bodies breached the hotel. Nothing much for them to do there; Barth followed them as far as the Central District. We lost the comm link after the blast at the Fringe Club. Jarske thinks a low-level EMP pulse fried our comms."

"Can he get them back?" The city lights dwindled as they left the noise of the Central District behind them.

He heard disgruntlement in Trevor's answer. "No, we'll need new tech."

Sebastian kept a sigh in check. "Anyone else check in?"

"No. You heading to ground?" Trevor sounded tired.

"Yes, Cordelia's with me. Wai Ling managed to help us out of the building. We'll settle in and I'll check with you every two hours." He suspected something else weighed on the man.

"One last thing." Irritation filled Trevor's voice. "Mai Li has disappeared."

"There's nothing for it." Sebastian couldn't worry about her. He rubbed his eyes. "Anything from Haager?"

"Nothing, but I don't think we're lucky enough for that to hold," he snorted.

Sebastian silently agreed. "Get hold of Alonzo. He'll arrange a new location for us."

"Yessir and boss, glad to hear your voice," Trevor said.

Sebastian cleared his throat. "You too, Crosse."

CHAPTER SIXTEEN

Choi pulled the taxi over near the bus station. "Here you go."

Sebastian gave him a pat on the shoulder. "Get yourself underground. There's no telling who's a target."

He opened the door and stepped out into the neighborhood. The street remained quiet and dark in the early morning. He offered a hand to Cordelia, who almost stumbled getting out of the cab.

"Thanks. I'm beat." She turned and offered Choi a pleasant smile. "And thank you for the ride."

The young driver blushed. "No problem."

Leaning against the driver side door, Sebastian looked serious. "Choi, I mean it. Be safe."

"No worries." The young man beamed and pulled into the darkened street.

After the cab had disappeared around a curve, Sebastian surveyed the street. He placed his hand against Cordelia's lower back. "Let's move."

They hurried across the street toward a towering building. Even in the dark, its surface shimmered with glass and steel. Some windows glowed with light, but most remained shadowed. He led her to the lobby doors, pausing only long enough to fix his thumb against a biometric scanner near the door.

She chuckled. "Great for when you're escaping from a bombed building and forget to grab your keys."

Sebastian shrugged. "A safe house wouldn't be any use if you couldn't gain access in an emergency." He made a show of patting his pockets as he yanked the door open at the audible click releasing the lock. "Honey, did you grab the keys?" Sweeping his arm, he said, "After you."

He thought he could feel more than just the amusement on her face as he followed her, being sure to firmly pull the door shut behind them.

The lobby lights, dimmed for the night, glowed soft and warm off of the honey-colored marble. They made their way to the reception desk where a night concierge tried to appear alert at this early morning intrusion.

Sebastian smiled, glad to recognize the man. It eliminated some of the complications he anticipated. "Néih hóu, Lam Yuán." He bowed warmly.

The older man smiled and stood. He returned the bow. "Ngoh hoh hoh. Very good, boss." He pointed to the small television behind the counter. "I watched the hubbub at the club." His eyes twinkled. "I thought it might have something to do with you."

"I don't wreck the town every time I visit." Sebastian chuckled.

"No, but the word is, how you say? On the street?" The jovial man verified his slang.

"Yes." Sebastian nodded.

Leaning in with a conspiratorial gleam, the Cantonese man lowered his voice. "Whispers of Líu's coup against the Fo Lung float on the wind."

Sebastian shot a glance at Cordelia, who shrugged and shook her head. He felt her surprise along with his own. "Are you sure? Where'd you hear this?"

"Murmurs. Rumors. The ba gua about Líu is he's backed by a Gwai Lo." His salt and peppered head bobbed. "Some people have said it's you, but I know you have zun zhong. You wouldn't interfere with the Fo Lung."

Pursing his lips, Sebastian added the information to his own suspicions. "My thanks for your loyalty, Yuán. Can I get the key card for the apartment?"

He pulled his wallet out and took out several Hong Kong Dollars. "Would you arrange for some food to be delivered?"

Yuán took the money with a bow. "Of course." He entered a code in a safe in the wall behind him. Pulling out a tray of key cards, he found the one he wanted. Handing it to Sebastian, he bowed again. "My wife is a good cook. I'll have my nephew run something up to the apartment. His name is Lok."

"Again, my thanks." Sebastian took the card.

"Elevator three." Yuán pointed to the doors to the left. He pressed a button and the elevator opened.

Sebastian bowed to the concierge as the elevator doors shut.

****

The elevator doors opened on the twenty-sixth floor. Cordelia stepped out after Sebastian and followed him down the hall. She spotted a garbage chute and slipped the loafers off of her feet. She pulled the door down, then dropped them into the trough. They clattered and clanked down.

Sebastian didn't say anything. He moved to the next door on the right. Slipping the card through a magnetic swiper, he waited for a green light to press his thumb to another biometric scanner. A loud snap announced the lock release. He held the door open for her.

She stepped from the carpet of the hallway to the cool, smooth blonde walnut floors in the darkened apartment. Heavy blinds masked the bank of windows that faced the door. She moved aside to let Sebastian past her.

He walked to a light panel on the left wall. Sliding three switches part way on the panel, he gradually lit the apartment to a warm glow. "Shower's through here." He motioned her to follow down a hallway to the right. He flipped on lights as he went. "Master is in here."

Cordelia entered an airy room with another wall of covered windows. The bathroom waited on the other side of an enormous bed. She shrugged off his jacket and tossed it on the bed. "I'm taking the hottest shower I can stand."

"I need to call Trevor. I thought I'd get some water on for tea. A drink?" he asked.

"Damn straight." She stepped into the bathroom and winced at her reflection in the mirror. Soot smudged her face. Her hair flopped in a tangled mess. Turning to get a look at her back, she started to feel the sting of the scratches she saw. She called out the door. "Maybe a first-aid kit?"

Sebastian's voice came back to her from across the apartment. "Yeah, under the sink. You want I should take a closer look?" His voice came closer as he brought her an old fashioned glass sloshing with three fingers of scotch. He held out the glass.

"After the shower, I think." Cordelia took a sip, reveling in the smoky heat sliding down her throat.

He nodded, sipping his own scotch. Sebastian opened a drawer in the nightstand and pulled out a different cell phone. He moved into the hall as he dialed. "Trevor."

Cordelia returned to the bathroom. She reached back to get hold of the zipper. Her body grumbled in a few places. *That's going to be a huge bruise under my shoulder blade.* "Great." She managed a fingertip pinch on the zipper but couldn't get it to budge. Cordelia heard Sebastian speaking with Trevor. Carrying her glass, she walked into the living room.

Sebastian looked up. "Okay. I'll call again in two hours. Have Alonzo call my father. I'm sure he's watching the news. Also, give him this number, I need him to get some information for me." He ended the call. "You okay?"

"No. I can't get out of this dress. Any word on the others?"

He shook his head. "Not yet."

Holding back a sigh, she turned her back to him and asked, "Can you muscle the zipper?"

She picked up his alarm at the sight of her back. Looking over her shoulder, she said, "Looks worse than it feels."

He snorted. "I'll check back with you tomorrow." Squinting, he looked closer at the zipper. "It's broken. Looks like your skid across the floor crushed it."

"Shit. How're we getting it open?" She craned her neck to see the damage.

"You're not going to like it. More to the point, Andre's not going to like it." He smiled.

Cordelia whirled on him. "Oh no, I lost the shoes. You're not taking scissors to this silk." She tugged on the aubergine fabric trying to smooth out the creases and wrinkles.

"Would you like out of the dress?" he asked, eyebrow raised.

His amusement tumbled over her. She puffed her irritation. "Yes."

"Okay." He motioned her toward the master bedroom. "You know, it's filthy."

She stomped down the hall. "Yes, I'm aware. Thanks for the news flash."

He chuckled. "You're welcome."

"What're we doing?" She walked into the bedroom.

He went past her into the bathroom and returned with a large first-aid kit. "We're going to cut you out of it."

"You're loving this, aren't you?" She plopped down on the bed.

"I'm not loving it. I've imagined getting you out of your clothes, but this isn't how I pictured it." He fished through the box. "I think after being shot and bombed worrying about the shoes and the dress is—"

She read his reluctance to finish his sentence.

She swallowed. "Andre devoted his energy and imagination to this wardrobe and we don't know.—"

Sebastian put his hand up to stop her, calm radiating outward. "Cord, worry paralyzes. When we know something certain, then we deal." He brandished the scissors. "Now, priorities. Getting you a shower."

"Okay, but I can't watch." She covered her eyes with her hands.

He snugged the scissors against the zipper. "I'll keep close to the seam. Andre might be able to save the dress." He leaned back and made a show of looking her over. "It's a nice dress."

She laughed as his attraction washed over her. "It is a nice dress." The triage scissors parted the fabric, exposing her back. Anger flared from him. "Really, Sebastian, it'll look better after a shower."

"I think we'll be working on some glass shards later."

Cordelia swished her scotch glass at him. "I'll need another and some food first." On cue, her stomach rumbled. Clasping her dress to her, she stood to get in the shower. "For now, I'm not coming out until you tell me food is here."

"Shout if you'd like any help in there." He waggled his eyebrows.

Rolling her eyes, she shut the door. "You shouldn't ever do that again."

She heard him shout through the door. "Leave me some hot water!"

****

Sebastian chuckled. He heard Cordelia start the water as he returned to the kitchen. Rummaging through the pantry, he found the teapot. He rinsed it and filled it with filtered water, then paused to sip his scotch. The Royal Lochnagar twelve-year tantalized his mouth with hints of coffee and brown sugar. *Not bad.* He lit the fire under the pot.

"Now to find some tea." He started opening cabinet doors. The new phone rumbled on the counter. "This is Cole." He found a tin of Lin Cang Green. "Aha!"

"Aha?" His father's voice twinkled with humor. "You've had an epiphany?"

"No, Dad, I've found tea." He cupped the phone between his ear and shoulder to look for mugs.

"Glad to hear you're alive. Either of you hurt? Ian's asking."

Sebastian could hear his brother whispering in the background. "We're fine. Some bumps and bruises. It's a good thing Cordelia's bones have grown denser. Between me and the debris falling on her, she's come out fine. As it is, we may be pulling some glass shards from her back."

Ian grabbed the phone from Gerald. Sebastian chuckled listening to the two scuffle. "Sebastian? Do you have a first-aid kit?"

"Of course he has a first-aid kit. It's a safe house," Gerald said in the background.

"Dad," Ian scolded then returned to talking to Sebastian. "Have her soak in hot water and then use the antiseptic to clean the area. Use tweezers if any glass is visible, but you may have to get to a clinic. I don't know if she'll heal as fast as you."

"Ian," Sebastian said, keeping his voice neutral. "This isn't our first day out. I am experienced at in-field triage. We'll deal. Cordelia'll be fine."

"I know you're an old hand at this, but Cordelia isn't." His brother fretted.

He sighed. "Cordelia is strong, stronger now than ever, and she's capable. You have nothing to worry about. Who's the fusspot now? I need to talk to Dad."

"Hmph." Ian snorted but handed the phone back to Sir Gerald.

"What's up, son?" the elder Cole asked.

"Yuán mentioned a Gwai Lo. I need to know who it is. I thought you could reach out to some of your MI-6 contacts and see if there's any word on operations with the Triad."

"Hmmm, a ghost person. Wouldn't be the first time Westerners tried to control a foreign cartel. I'll see what I can find out." His father's voice held a hint of distaste. He asked, "What are you thinking?"

Sebastian poured the hot water over the tea filter into the pot. "I mentioned Bishop to Haager and he didn't deny his hand in this. If Bishop's running an op to replace the Dragon of the Triad, I'd like to know. I need to know the players. The auction is in two days."

Gerald thought in silence for a moment. "I'll get to it on this end. Mind you keep your wits about you and bring that young woman back in one piece."

"Yessir." Sebastian smiled at his father's perfunctory click ending the call.

CHAPTER SEVENTEEN

Cordelia stepped out of the shower and eased her aching arms into a plush, white robe from a hook on the wall. Draping the fabric low over her shoulders, she peered into the mirror craning her neck to take stock of the damage. "Not too bad." She flexed her back and it with the burn. "Doesn't feel like there's any glass."

Murmuring and a different thought pattern from the living room drew her attention back to her growling stomach. She hoped the food arrived. Wrapping the robe snuggly, she wandered out into the main space of the apartment.

Sebastian heard her approach and nodded. "Cordelia, this is Yuán's nephew, Lok. He's brought dinner." He gestured to several brown bags waiting on the dining room table.

The jet-headed teenager bobbed and grinned. "My English not so good, but glad to help." He backed toward the door. "My aunt is good cook. Lots to eat."

"Thanks, Lok," Cordelia offered warmly.

The young man blushed and scooted out of the apartment lightning quick.

She turned to Sebastian. He announced, "Tea is ready. Mind if I shower? You can dig through those bags."

"Go, go. Isn't there a second shower?" She flushed with a twinge of guilt.

"No, only one bedroom. I won't take long. I'm starving too." He topped off his glass of scotch and brushed past her. "I'll take a look at your back. How does it feel?"

"Better, I don't think there's any glass. Take your shower, I'll get the food out and set."

The sound of water accompanied her rummage through the bags. Several stacking food baskets tempted with warm aromas. She set them out on the table peeking but keeping them closed. Better to keep the heat in and the food warm. A cup of tea poured, Cordelia went into the kitchen to find dishes and flatware.

By the time Sebastian returned in a robe matching the one she wore, Cordelia had set the table. "Primarily vegetable dishes, which suits me. A basket of steamed rice and some dumplings." She gestured to the table.

"Smells great." He held out a chair for her.

Cordelia chuckled. "Thank you, sir." She started spooning food onto their plates. "Some of this smells spicy."

"Can you handle it?" He grinned as she rolled her eyes. "Wine?" He went into the kitchen.

"You bet." She enjoyed the relaxed humor he radiated. His thoughts sometimes darkened with images of Thomas and the others, but he pushed those shadows down with firm resolve. It calmed her own pangs of worry.

Sebastian returned with a chilled bottle of Pinot Gris. "This'll balance the heat." He poured and sat down to a heaping plate.

"I could only find chopsticks," she apologized.

He spun his set nunchuck style. "I think I can manage." Taking a swath of noodles from his plate, he slurped them.

Cordelia worked more delicately. "Very attractive."

"I'm a regular Prince Charming." Sebastian winked and then his thoughts clouded. "Or rather, I'm more the polite Beast, eh?"

"Careful, Cole, we're close to having a moment," she admonished.

He nabbed a couple of dumplings. "A moment, huh? What exactly does an actual moment entail?"

She snorted into a bite of tomato. "Wow, you're really out of practice aren't you? If I have to explain what makes the moment." She wrinkled her nose. "The moment's over." She shook her head and sipped her wine. "I do have a question."

"Okay." He poured more wine into his glass.

"What's your deal with Wong? I got the impression he's a pretty bad guy." Cordelia slurped some noodles.

Sebastian took a sip of wine. "Back when we were Marines, Wong worked as a double agent for the CIA. He worked his way up the military chain of command and realized he was expendable." He paused to nibble a dumpling. "Someone sold him out. He was placed in a work camp in Fujian province. We were sent in to bring him and a few others out. He was in bad shape."

"This is an honor thing, isn't it?" Cordelia rolled her eyes reading his principles front and center in his mind.

"Wong was an asset. I discovered later Mai Li was the informant who exposed him. They tortured him and kept him in a hole. We pulled him out." Sebastian shrugged. "He can be brutal and he's definitely a criminal, but he feels he owes me," he said, wrapping some noodles around his chopsticks. "We set him up."

"You mean the American government?" Cordelia read it in his mind but asked anyway.

"Remember that day in the piazza? You said politics is wrapped in propaganda and I was free to follow my own code of honor working for myself. You were right. Nwora is a criminal. Wong is a criminal. Criminals I trust more than the CIA agent working to set up a straw man leader for the Triad." He drank his wine.

They ate in silence for a few minutes.

She read his reluctant question. "What?"

"What do you mean what?" He squinted suspiciously. "You're in my head again."

"I hate to tell you this." She leaned in. "Your head is spilling over."

"Spilling over? I'm not spilling over." He glared. "Your psychic mumbo jumbo has grown stronger."

"It has, but this is more about us." She stuffed a dumpling in her mouth.

Sebastian scanned her face. She felt his thoughts spin around her comment. She watched him line the last several days up. The understanding of her need to keep the prophecy silent rushed into his mind. The feeling of her irritation led him to follow Mai Li at the Norfolk house. Tumblers of a lock clicking and clacking into place to reveal something nagging at him since their reunion.

A sigh escaped her and he leaped at the answer. "You're not just reading me, I'm reading you?"

"Will you promise not to spiral into the abyss of 'Woe is me, I'm a monster who's dragged you into my world of anathema'?" she mocked.

His brows furrowed and indignation bloomed in his head. "Anathema? Are you even using that correctly? And I don't sound like that."

She threw her head back and let out a bell of a laugh. "As in curse, heresy, abomination? I think I know what anathema means. Have you listened to yourself? That's exactly how you sound."

Tightening his robe and then sipping more wine, he looked at her. "Well, bugger all, I'm a pompous ass."

Cordelia's eyes crinkled. "The first step to recovery is admitting it." She raised her hands in celebration.

"Okay, give. Why am I able to hear you more clearly?"

She nodded to him to fill her wine glass. After a sip, she started. "The first time I met you and Thomas, I thought I felt something nonverbal between you two. I chalked it up to military training and familiarity. You know how some couples can finish each other's sentences?"

He snorted. "We're like an old married couple?"

Cordelia laughed. "Oh yeah, but that's not what I'm talking about. It felt as though if I tilted my head the right way I might be able to hear it. It's tangible. I experienced the same feeling with Lorena and Seamus. And then there's Elsa."

"Elsa?" Sebastian wrinkled his brow.

"I know you haven't spent much time with her, but she and I easily communicate."

Shrugging, he popped the last dumpling into his mouth. "I kind of went Walk About."

"She makes you uncomfortable." She tapped her head.

"Phhhttt." He drank his wine.

Eyes rolling, Cordelia moved the conversation forward. "In the lab, when I—" She swallowed. "Elsa knew you were coming. She sensed you in the same manner I perceived the connection between you and the others."

"You didn't tell me." He grew thoughtful.

"You didn't give me much chance." She raised her eyebrow.

He cleared his throat. "How does that explain the connection between us?"

"Seamus guessed. Elsa and I were talking. Seamus picked up the vibe. Don't you see? There's a lot of anecdotal evidence of nonverbal communication among animals. Elephants use subsonic frequencies in rare cases to communicate long distances. We could even discuss twins and their ability to sense each other's emotions. Ian's theory is along those lines. You and I?" She shrugged. "Has anything between us ever felt mild?"

"Ian's theory? No one thought to mention this to me?" His look grew stony.

"For heaven's sake, Sebastian, give us a break. You disappeared. And since we found you, we've been flying all over the place. You can't be in control of everything." She felt her eyes might pop out of her head from all of the rolling. "You take on too much responsibility for all of us. You are not singularly culpable for the misfortunes of the world."

"If Vivienne Carlson hadn't—"

"If you hadn't become a Marine. If the U.S. had invaded Afghanistan when it should have rather than Iraq. If I hadn't taken the job with Matthews. Don't you see, it's an endless sinkhole of what ifs?"

He started to speak, but she ran right over him. "What if you weren't the man you are? What if Haager had been changed? What if Andre hadn't helped you find me?"

"Okay, okay, you've made your point," Sebastian said. "You're not human because of all of this." His guilt washed over her.

"Hell for breakfast! You don't listen." She stood to pace. "Let's get one thing straight: what Vivienne Carlson did to me wasn't your fault." She put a finger up to shush his argument. "That's life, Sebastian. We make choices and do the best we can. In my mind, that's the very definition of humanity. I can't say I would've chosen the way Seamus did, but it was out of my control. Why do you think there are so many myths and legends, even comic books, about heroes? Because people long to be extraordinary, Sebastian. Growing up with this ability sucked. I didn't have friends because I knew who lied and who cheated. I didn't learn to pretend ignorance until later and by then being alone became my norm." She whirled on him. "And then you appeared. Looming, humming with energy, and something else, maybe purpose. I don't know, but you intrigued me. I could've shut you down in Rome. I decided to see you again and I don't regret it for a minute. I was that kid who ran everywhere in slow motion making the sh sh sh sh noise pretending to be the Bionic Woman."

His eyebrow rose. "We can rebuild her?"

She scoffed. "Seriously? That's the Six Million Dollar Man. Get your shows straight."

Leaning back in the chair, he ran a hand through his hair. "I'm more of a John Wayne guy."

Striding over to him, she placed her hands on either side of his head. "As though I couldn't tell." She touched her forehead to his. "Even he had a sense of humor. You need to lighten up." She felt his hands settle at her waist.

"Does that make you Elsa Martinelli?" he asked with humor.

She balked. "I've always considered myself the spunky Maureen O'Hara type. Now, I'm the stronger, faster version." She sighed. "What was your plan coming to Vancouver?"

Sebastian moved her away to meet her eyes. His thoughts swirled as he stood. "I don't know." He shook his head confused. He lowered his lips to hers as he wrapped his arms around her.

Cordelia gasped in pain and he sprang back.

"Shite, your back. Are you okay? I still need to take a look at it." He stepped away from her as he would a hot flame.

She took a deep breath. "I'm good, just sore." She laid a hand on his arm. "Let's take a look at it, and then we need to check in with Trevor."

"So much for another moment," he said, sliding his hands to her wrists.

"Seriously, Cole?" She burst out with a laugh and shook her head. Taking his hand, she led him back to the bedroom. "First-aid kit." She pointed toward the kit resting on the counter in the bathroom and plopped down on the edge of the bed. "Call Trevor. We both need to try to sleep."

****

The twilight of dawn pierced the gaps in the curtains only a few hours later. Sebastian resisted opening his eyes to the encroaching sunrise. Cordelia, warm and relaxed, nestled against him. He thought about the previous night's discussion. As a test, he pulled his awareness to the instinct settled deep in his gut. Listening to the sounds of the apartment, he breathed in the scents of the room. Tingling with perception, he channeled the feeling into a thread, visible behind his closed eyes. He let the tendril of thought drift toward Cordelia.

He could've imagined the quiet thrum of her dozing mind, if not for the rousing tremble of thought he perceived as she stretched. Reaching wide, her mind hummed in the comfort of the bed. He sensed her reluctance to open her eyes to the day ahead of them. Her mind turned to the thought he sent. The curious sensation of her mind pulling at his startled him. She wove a strand of awareness with his and the two tangled, connected.

Parallel to her cognition, her hand came to press inside the gap of the robe onto his bare chest igniting heat where skin touched skin. A bloom of purple spread across his eyelids accompanied by a burst of flame deep in his belly. His thought or hers, he couldn't tell. Her fingers trailed down the center of his ribcage scorching a path as she parted his robe. His erection reared at her delicate touch.

A groan escaped him. He opened his eyes as Cordelia slipped a leg over to straddle his hips. He slid his hands into the opening of her robe exposing the gentle curves of her body. Feasting on the sight of her bare, olive flesh, he met her eyes as he cupped her breasts. A gasp of pleasure escaped her as he brushed his thumbs across her nipples. Gaze locked with his, she lowered her lips to press against his mouth. He slid his hands around her ribs pressing her closer only to have her rear back with a grimace.

"Shite, I'm sorry," he mumbled, the agony of restrained energy thickening his words. He felt humor and exhilaration radiate through her violet arousal.

She settled his hands on her hip bones and then moved a finger to his lips. "This is a moment, Cole."

His chuckle shifted to sigh when she cosseted his rigid member between the velveted folds of her body. Her hands pressed into his shoulders while she slid along the length of his erection. A surge of lust rushed to his head. He tightened his grip on her waist.

Raising her body up, Cordelia reached behind to brush the skin between his balls and ass. His testicles tightened and he groaned. He forced his body to remain still while she placed the tip of his cock at her ingress. With agonizing leisure, she guided him into her depths. He held her fixed for a moment reveling in her heat. He watched her head tilt back, delight flushing her skin and issuing out to smother his mind. *I'm drowning.*

He lightened his grip and she responded to the invitation to move, slowly rocking her hips. Sebastian held his breath struggling to keep his roaring excitement in check. Losing himself in her increasing rhythm, he fought to keep his eyes on her face. Seeing Cordelia close her eyes, relinquishing control to the demands of pleasure, he sank into the waves of intensity crashing over them.

Succumbing to the thunder of orgasm, Cordelia cried out and ground against him. His answering thrust released his own climax, sending ripples of desire and gooseflesh over his body. She crumpled with ecstasy across him, resting her head on his shoulder. Afraid to shatter the quiet reverie, he stroked her hair in silence. He felt her relaxed amusement.

"I'll go ahead and say it. Holy shit." Her casual chuckle surprised him.

He laughed, easy and restful, pressed under the weight of her body. She attempted to shift her weight, but he stilled her with the press of his hands. "Don't move."

"Pretending the world isn't waiting can only go so far," Cordelia pointed out, her thoughts pleasant.

Unencumbered, Sebastian grunted. "I know. Let me lie here for a minute longer."

"Someone else might've considered the intrusion rude in the morning," she said, her tone teased.

He opened his eyes to see the smile in her voice mirrored on her face. "I was testing the theory."

Rolling off of him, she stretched her arms overhead and said, "One helluva test. Too much to ask if there's coffee in this joint?"

"Pretty sure." He chuckled. The phone chirped from the bedside table. Groaning, he reached for it.

She moved to the edge of the bed. "Told you, the world wouldn't wait."

He swatted her mocking tone away with one hand and answered the phone with the other. "Cole."

Trevor's voice broke into his mood. "I've heard from Thomas. He and Seamus are singed but good. They ended up underground for the night. Alonzo arranged new digs and organized delivery of the luggage from the hotel. I'll text you the new address."

Sebastian remained silent for a minute. "No word on Park, Andre, Anthony, and Morely? Any word on Wong?"

"Nothing so far. Líu is standing up as Triad leader until the rubble can be cleared. Emergency crews are still pulling people out of the club," Trevor informed him.

"Wong was the target," Sebastian stated.

"Not enough information yet. Could've been fortunate collateral damage," Trevor said.

Swinging his legs over the edge of the bed, Sebastian stared into the pale light growing in the room. "Text me the address. We'll meet you."

"All right." Trevor ended the call.

Sebastian turned to Cordelia. "Time to get moving."

She tugged the robe close. "Any clothes we can wear? We'll draw some attention roaming the streets in these."

He tamped his good spirits down as reality crowded in on his thoughts. "We should talk."

Cordelia put her hand up and he felt her mind press toward him as well. "Look, let's keep it simple for now. Don't say anything, don't promise anything. Truth is, neither one of us knows exactly what this is." She looked over her shoulder as she walked into the bathroom. "It's a moment. Right now, that's good enough."

He listened to the shower start, surprised by her ability to compartmentalize. The women in his past typically demanded some proof of connection from him. He didn't pick up any resentment or anger in her mind.

Her voice rang out from the bathroom. "Be glad and get over it."

CHAPTER EIGHTEEN

Given their disheveled state, Cordelia noticed few people paying attention to them. They weren't the only Westerners on the bus, but they were by far the shabbiest. The address Trevor sent had them en route to a building in the Aberdeen neighborhood. Getting off at different stops and transferring to three different buses turned the twenty-minute trip into a ninety-minute trek. She didn't doubt the necessity for caution after being shot and bombed.

A little punchy from lack of sleep, she dozed off a couple of times, finally jerking awake when Sebastian nudged her.

"Our stop." He pulled the signal cord.

The area didn't look promising. Overgrown with lush greenery, the bus stop felt abandoned. The other side of Tin Wan Praya Road stood blocked off by concrete construction barriers. Cranes and the partially complete steel skeletons of skyscrapers loomed, isolated and quiet for the weekend. Waiting for the bus to vanish around the curve, Sebastian took her hand. He checked the GPS on his phone and led her east toward a storage yard filled with shipping containers.

"You're sure we're in the right place?" she asked, feeling exposed and awkward in the industrial area.

He stopped at a gate in a chain-link fence barring the way to a building made entirely of shipping containers. It blended into the landscape of units littered around. Sebastian entered a security pin and scanned his thumbprint.

"I need to upgrade my security. A life without keys would be a luxury. Can I get my car retrofitted to thumb scanner?" she joked.

He shot her a look. "I'm sure we can arrange something."

The gate swung open to a storage yard backed up against a verdant, wooded hill. Empty containers were piled in stacks along the road. Gravel paved the yard to the main structure, which was made up of stacked shipping containers three stories tall, resembling a child's off-kilter pile of building blocks. Windows opened outward from the corners and reflected the stacks of rectangular containers. Mismatched in color, faded green rose above the trees and sandwiched a silver, graffiti-splotched container with a dark russet capsule.

Seamus exploded out the door. He rushed Cordelia, embracing her bearlike and spinning around. "Goddamn, it's good to see your face."

Laughing and gasping, she winced a bit but hugged him fiercely. "You pie-faced Irishman, put me down."

"You're hurt." He stepped back to examine her.

Thomas followed close behind and clasped his old friend's shoulders with both hands. "You sod, you're good?"

Sebastian gripped Thomas's shoulders. "I'm good. Cord could use a little more care. Anyone else?"

On cue, Anthony stepped out of the building. "Park's upstairs getting some sleep. A couple of broken ribs, some superficial burns and bruises, but otherwise fine. Barth is on scene monitoring the progress of the rescue."

Before he continued, Cordelia's sharp intake of breath drew the group's attention. She covered her mouth with her hand. She shook her head unable to speak thinking of the young man squirming in his tuxedo.

"Anthony?" Sebastian asked.

The big man's grim face said it before the words hit. "Adam is dead."

Everyone remained silent a moment to grasp the loss of their young compatriot.

Sebastian wiped his hand across his face and swore. "Shite." He looked determined. "Let's get inside. I've a call to make and we need to adjust our plan."

Seamus slung an arm over Cordelia's shoulder. "Come on, love, some food and some coffee will fix you up."

Shifting her gaze from man to man, she felt their dauntless calm in the face of wreckage. "Yeah, food and coffee." She longed for Lorena's sardonic humor. "Wait, what about Andre?"

Thomas said it as his thoughts, echoing the other two, hit her. "Don't know yet."

Cordelia pressed the heels of her hands into her closed eyes.

Seamus's meaty hand patted her shoulder as he propelled her forward. "No body means there's a chance." His hopeful lilt belied the grim resignation in his head.

Stiffening her spine, she let out a breath. "Well, at least I don't have to tell him what happened to the dress."

An amused grunt escaped Sebastian. "That's the spirit."

She turned to meet his eyes and felt him direct a blast of dogged tenacity toward her. They shared a grim smile.

Seamus shivered and winked. "Whew, I don't have the hang of this, but even I'm getting the blowback. I think I need to hear what happened to the dress."

Cordelia jammed an elbow into his ribs with a stern thought. *Shut it.*

"Ouch, you know you're stronger than you used to be. Watch it," he said, his lilting brogue filled with humor.

Anthony cleared his throat and opened the wide front door. "Emergency crews are still digging people out. General Wong and Madame Mdivani haven't been found yet either. It's a mess over there."

"It'll take time to get things sorted," Thomas chimed in.

Sebastian approached the slapdash edifice. "We don't have time."

Once inside, all remnants of the ungainly structure disappeared. Still industrial in atmosphere, the inside surprised with a clean, modern style. The main area expanded with an open floor plan extending out the back of the framework. Hidden from the front, the space opened up to the triple width of containers. An outdoor deck spread beyond the huge sliding glass doors reaching into the camouflage of the dense greenery.

"Where does Alonzo find these places?" Cordelia mused out loud.

Thomas chuckled. "The man's a wizard."

"Of course I am. This place belonged to a French financier. The entire block is zoned for off the grid construction. Bold and innovative idea, really. Sadly, the man has a gambling addiction. Global Sureties is now a prime investor in the project that will include commercial and residential properties." The rich, Italian baritone of the man in question rang from the kitchen in the southeast corner of the main floor. He stepped into view, wavy jet hair tinseled with silver, eyes sparkling with vibrant energy. "Ciao, bella."

In quick strides, he crossed the living room to hug her. "Anche in tali circostanze, sei raggiante." *Even under such circumstances, you are radiant.*

He reminded her so much of her father; immersed in his comforting grasp, her eyes welled. Breathing back tears, she murmured into his ear. "Sembra buffo, ma sono così felice che tu sia qui" *It seems silly, but I'm glad you're here.*

"No, non e' buffo. Piccoli ricordi di casa possono portarci attraverso le ore più buie." *Not silly at all. Little reminders of home can bear us through the darkest hours.* Alonzo straightened. Releasing Cordelia, he moved to clasp Sebastian's hand. "Ciao, signore. Good to see you're alive."

Taking the Italian's hand in both of his, Sebastian showed a rare warmth. "Good to be alive. My father sent you."

Clapping his hands, Alonzo's face brightened. "Oh si, I have news and with Andre assente, I thought I'd be more effective here. I have fresh clothes." Giving the rag tag pair a once over, he commented, "Which you sorely need, but first food and drink." He waved them to the kitchen.

"What's Jarske have?" Sebastian asked.

Trevor answered, grabbing a croissant from a pile on the counter. "He's tapped into the police chatter to see if anyone else has been identified and he's talking to Barth. The word is the auction's still on for tomorrow, so we're guessing it's Liú's deal. Wong is MIA, no body yet."

Gladly taking a mug of coffee from Alonzo, Sebastian asked, "What did my father find out?"

The dapper Italian offered Cordelia a mug. "Bishop is unsanctioned. Word from MI-6, unconfirmed, of course, is he's working rogue. CIA refuses to comment. Doesn't look good for them if they can't take care of this in-house. As soon as they find out where he's hiding a cleanup crew will be all over him."

Cordelia tore a piece of croissant to pop into her mouth and chose a slice of cantaloupe. "Does Haager know?"

"Depends," Thomas answered, taking another roll. "I suppose we need to verify."

Seamus topped off his mug. "The guy's a wanker, but if he's under the impression this is official ops we can't take him down with Bishop."

Even Cordelia, withdrawn from the minds in the room, could see the wheels turning in Sebastian's mind.

"Have Jarske tap our new source. Get whatever intel from him we can and set him up with a backdoor. On this end, let's see if we can tap some of Wong's people. We need the blueprints of the auction location. We'll plan this as though Haager's ignorant of Bishop's status; it's not a far reach. We'll keep some options open if our information changes. I don't like the idea of burning an agent if he's on the up and up, but I'm happy to knee-cap Haager if he's involved."

Loath to bring it up, Cordelia asked, "What about Mai Li?"

"We assume she's turned over everything she knows to either Bishop or Liú," Thomas said, mouth full of croissant.

Trevor offered a grim smile. "Good thing she doesn't have the whole picture."

"Don't count on that," Sebastian said. "She's smart enough to guess we weren't keeping her in the loop. We'll confirm, but my guess is Bishop is behind Liú's grab for power. Better a Dragon you can control than one you can't. Wong's demise is in Mai Li's best interest. She's involved either way. I'd bet she has been from the beginning."

"We'll have to deal with her one way or another," Thomas pointed out, munching on his croissant.

Sebastian took a sip of coffee. "It's already in the works."

Cordelia didn't need to read his mind to know what he thought. Her grave smile corresponded with the rest of the looks in the room. Sebastian moved to stand next to her and placed his hand gingerly on the small of her back. He held his mug out to Alonzo, who moved to top everyone's mug.

Seamus, not missing a beat, waggled his eyebrows at Cordelia.

She read mischief in his mind and shot a stern thought at him. *I know where you sleep.*

The ginger-headed titan choked his sip of coffee and dribbled down the front of his shirt.

Anthony shoved him. "Jesus, Mac, can't take you anywhere."

A low chuckle drew every eye in the room. Cordelia sensed Sebastian's awareness of her exchange with Seamus, but even she turned to look at him.

An eyebrow raised, Sebastian's usual reserve dropped and he almost smiled.

Without pause Thomas, gaping at his longtime friend, remarked, "Now I'd like to hear what happened to the dress."

****

Travis monitored his screens, fingers flying on the keyboard. *This is all rudimentary stuff.* He sniggered thinking about the recruitment agent's assurance he'd be working on complex stuff.

Bishop strode in. "Travis, anything yet?"

"Nope. Wong's presumed dead. Rescue is still digging out the rubble. No chit chat on the comm networks. I'm guessing your other guy is either dead or licking his wounds. They're cut off from Wong's contacts."

Mai Li scoffed.

"Liú has told the Triad it's under investigation led by Sebastian." Bishop smiled. "I doubt he'll get much help, but keep a line on the communication channels."

Travis gave a slight nod and kept his skepticism focused on the screen. *Douchebag.*

"When I kick the bastard's cold, lifeless body is the day I'll believe Wong is dead," Mai Li shot at Bishop. "Liú is a dolt."

"Of course he is. You think I set this up to waste my time. I need a malleable Dragon, not someone who's going to fight me every step." Bishop placed his hand on Travis's shoulder. "Travis is tapped into the police database. Once they find Wong, we'll know. In the meantime, Liú is running the show and the auction is still on. We've limited Cole's play with Wong out of the picture and we know his Nigerian is a fake."

Mai Li snorted again. "Don't underestimate Sebastian. He'll figure out you tried to tie him to the theft at the lab if he doesn't know already."

"I'm not underestimating him. I just know him." Bishop looked at Mai Li. "He's the kind of man who'll never change. It's unfortunate he didn't die in the bombing. With Wong missing and presumed dead, his resources are limited." Bishop ticked a list off. "We have the research files. We have the clone and his Nigerian is a fake. Sebastian has to know we won't let him anywhere near the building. Even after the auction, we'll be able to farm out the data and Liú will be running the Triad permanently."

Mai Li gave him a measured look. "You're getting ahead of yourself. We have to let his fake Nigerian into the auction. The other players saw Wong vet him at the party. If you shut the Nigerian out of the auction, it will raise suspicions. Right now, the bombing is a power play against the Triad. Someone looks closely enough and they'll discover Liú is being backed by the CIA. Your bidders may scramble and Liú's credibility as a successor dies."

"Goddamn it." Bishop smacked his hand on the table. "This is getting messy."

"You're the one trying to frame Sebastian. You can't let it get personal," Mai Li said.

Bishop frowned. "This from the woman trying to kill General Wong? Need I remind you this was your idea?"

"I didn't tell you to involve Sebastian," Mai Li shot back.

"Enough! I needed someone to take the fall for the inside intel at the lab. Get Haager and the crew. We need to figure out a way to contain Sebastian and his Nigerian without losing control of the auction," Bishop said.

Travis, running three screens, caught a popup in his encrypted feed. A few keystrokes later, he opened another window and started writing a new script.

****

"Time to wake her up," Liú told the physician. "We need to move her to the warehouse for tomorrow's auction. Facilities are in place. Once there, you'll keep her conscious, but biddable."

The graying doctor nodded and bowed. "Ngóh mìhngbaahk la, Seen-sahn." *I understand, sir.*

"You'll address me as Lung," Liú commanded, puffing his chest.

Blanching, the older man bowed more deeply. "Yes, Lung jiéxià."

Lying still behind closed eyes, the little girl listened to the exchange. Wake her up, she thought. It was easier to fool these doctors than it had been in the lab. Dr. Carol suspected, but could never prove anything. *Dr. Carol is dead.* Without attaching judgment to the thought, Nadja ruminated on the next forty-eight hours. They were moving her to a different building. She didn't know exactly what an auction was, but she knew it involved her.

Somewhere between the new location and the auction, she might be able to find a chance to get loose. Sighing out a breath, she returned her attention to the imaginary blocks in her head. She created a warm, braided rug and spread the wooden shapes out in front of her. One after another, she laid the foundation for a fortress similar to the one she'd built the last morning in the lab.

The equipment in the room maintained the rhythmic beep tracking her heart rate.

CHAPTER NINETEEN

Jardine's Crescent bustled with locals haggling over the street market goods. Food vendors hawked and hooted expounding on the quality of their product. Old women draped their silken scarves over their shoulders and arms to highlight the superiority of their goods. Shoes, clothing, purses, and myriad other items shocked in vivid colors and displays along the narrow alleys. Several scrubby children darted through the crowd selling trinkets and gum.

Thomas scanned the crowd. "It doesn't matter where we end up. These markets are all the same."

"Just goes to show, people are more similar than they'd like to think," Sebastian remarked, hands tucked into his pockets. He caught the eye of a purple-haired teenager leaning on one of the doorways leading up to one of the crowded apartment buildings lining the market's sidewalks.

The young man rested his fingers on a skateboard propped against his thigh. Giant earphones cradled his neck while the music spilled out thinly.

Thomas chuckled as he handed a girl no older than seven or eight a folded American bill. "Listen to you, sounding almost warm about mankind. Dare I speculate the source of this magnanimity?"

"No." Sebastian didn't spare him a glance despite his friend's cheerful tone.

The two men stumbled apart as the skater blew through them.

"Bollocks, there's got to be an easier way to do this." Thomas regained his balance and straightened his shirt.

Sebastian shot him a look. "Has anything the last year been easy? For that matter, I feel we've been slogging through the mud since Afghanistan."

"Look, mate, even if we solved all of our problems are you going to retire to a place in the country and take up gardening?" Thomas chortled at the flat look on Sebastian's face. "Didn't think so."

Despite the smug amusement coming from his best friend, Sebastian remained impassive. "It'd be nice to go a stretch of time without being kidnapped, cloned, shot at, or bombed."

His mop-headed companion tsked. "Now you're just whining." Thomas stopped at a booth displaying silk tunics. He ran his hand over one shimmering peach and gold. "Rachna would love this."

The tiny, ebony-haired woman working the booth approached him in the blink of an eye to haggle in broken English.

Sebastian frowned. "We don't have time for this."

Ignoring his friend, Thomas took a couple of Hong Kong bills from his pocket.

The petite woman shook her head and rattled off a higher price.

"There's always time, Sebastian, your problem is you don't realize it." He shook his head and offered the woman the two bills.

Reluctantly she snatched them out of his hand and grumbled as she folded the tunic into a bag.

The tall, raven-haired Sebastian growled. "Your problem is you don't realize how little time we have. We're against the wall. I'm worried how we're going to win this one."

"You'd think with all of your John Wayne movies you'd remember one important thing, old chap. We're the good guys and the good guys always win." Thomas jauntily strode away.

Sebastian sighed and caught up with his friend. "Except we're not really the good guys."

Thomas nudged a sharp elbow into his compatriot's ribs. "You're the only one of us who believes that statement."

"You've all gone round the fuckin' bend." He ran his hand through the jet tangle of his hair.

****

Cordelia reclined on a cushioned chaise looking out at the lush rainforest climbing up the hill from the building. She needed a quiet minute away from Seamus's ribbing. His innuendo and entendre had already incited her to throw a dishtowel at his head. Anthony had punched him and even genial Alonzo excused himself to his room to take a break.

Park came out with two cups of tea. She offered one to Cordelia. "If my ribs weren't cracked, I'd have clocked him with a pan." She sat in the other chaise with a slight wince.

Cord blew on her tea. "Normally, I'd enjoy the jokes at Sebastian's expense, but Seamus doesn't know when to quit."

"I'll admit he's driving me a bit crazy, but I'm enjoying it too. 'Bout time the boss got laid." She lifted her cup in salute. "No offense."

"None taken." Cordelia found a little laugh. "It's like an Italian family around here, everybody knows everybody's business. I've got a thick skin." She ran a hand through her hair, still damp from a shower. "Seamus is laying it on to keep me from worrying about Andre, so he means well."

"The road to hell," the lanky blonde said. "He'll rein it in when Sebastian gets back. Thing is, C," Park said, joining the others in shortening her name, "focus on finishing the job. There'll be time enough later to lick our wounds. Surely Slovenia proved that."

"Yes, it did." She drank the last of her tea. "I think I'd prefer something stronger."

"I think we have something stronger." Park stood up. "Come on, there's food too."

Cordelia followed her into the house. She scanned the building without picking up Seamus's distinct presence.

Alonzo returned to the kitchen speaking Italian-flavored Cantonese into a headset linked to his phone. He waved the two women to the table where he placed a bottle of red wine to breathe. A cornucopia of baguettes, cheeses, olives, and fruit stretched along the polished grain of the table. Park grabbed a couple of wine glasses from the bar and held them out.

Cordelia obliged with two large pours. She whispered, "Where does he find baguettes in Hong Kong?"

Park sat down positioning Cordelia's glass next to her. "Huge French Nationalist population. Leave it to Alonzo to find the French patisserie. Even odds he's stashed some la religieuse and pain au chocolat away for tomorrow."

"I love la religieuse au café. The year I graduated high school, I visited France with my French teacher. I think I ate one every day of the trip." Cordelia sighed.

"How long was the trip?" Park asked.

Cordelia laughed. "Twenty days."

Park tore off a chunk of baguette. "I ate a baguette every day for breakfast my senior trip."

"How many days?" Cordelia asked and took a drink of her wine.

"Fourteen," Park answered around a bite of bread. She raised her glass. "Here's to reveling in foreign travel while your ass gets bigger."

Laughing again, Cordelia raised her glass.

The Italian mastermind ended his call. "What are we toasting?"

"Exotic travel to foreign lands and the food we love," Cordelia answered.

He took a glass from the table and leaned toward Park, who still had the bottle. "I must confess I loathe poutine."

Park snorted. "You and me both, Lonzo."

"I do love maple syrup though." He brightened with a smile at Cordelia.

"Who doesn't?" Cordelia asked.

The older gentleman nodded guiltily at Park. "And I can't help it, but I love a good hot dog."

"Now you're talking." Park smiled. "Chicago's my town. Drag it through the garden."

"I like mine with spicy mustard, chopped onions, and sauerkraut." Cordelia raised her glass.

Both women looked at Alonzo, who blushed with contrition. "Mustard and … ketchup."

Park burst out with a groan. "Sacrilege!"

All three laughed into their wine. Cordelia stopped with a thought. "Where's Seamus?"

Alonzo grew serious. "I sent him to pick up the weapons supplies." He popped an olive into his mouth. He raised his glass to Cordelia. "Of course, I applaud your influence on Sebastian. The kiss is to love as lightning is to thunder. Doubtless, the man needs you, but even I thought about killing that overgrown Hibernian." He pulled a handkerchief from the pocket of his straw-colored Ferragamo shirt to wipe his forehead.

The women, seeing his distress at his loss of composure, did the only thing possible. They let loose with howls of amusement.

Alonzo joined them.

The trio still guffawed when Sebastian and Thomas entered the house.

Thomas scanned the group and turned to his friend. "We're working and we miss a party."

Cordelia waved a hand over the table. "Actually, we just started." She wiped the tears from her eyes.

Sebastian poured a glass and sat next to Cordelia. "We missed something else." She warmed feeling his hand press into her lower back.

Alonzo shook his head, a merry expression on his face. "Non è importante. It's nothing."

Cordelia felt Sebastian's confused amusement as he looked sternly at the flaxen-haired titaness across the table. "Park?"

"Don't look at me, boss. Just pals sharing a joke." She paused a second and then asked, "Though what's a Hibernian?"

Not missing a beat, Thomas answered with a twinkle in his eye. "It's Ancient Greek for arsehole."

Cordelia and Alonzo collapsed into a fresh round of hysterics.

"Seamus has been his usual, charming self I see," Sebastian said dryly.

****

Alonzo set one of the upstairs rooms up as a work space. A long, narrow table stretched across the room covered in paper. The fishing expedition in the market proved fruitful. Sending out handwritten, coded inquiries using the beggars and urchins of the street resulted in notes arriving from all over

Hong Kong. Sebastian poured over missives and maps working out the logistics in his head.

Sebastian and Thomas stood on either side of the table. Several of the urchins from the Jardine returned notes in response to the money given them.

"Bishop'll be monitoring the phone chit chat and internet traffic. I doubt he would think to monitor the jungle drums," Thomas said, prioritizing piles of paper. "Good thing he's such a snob."

"He's never had much respect for the natives. He's only interested in controlling them," Sebastian said, remembering the man's reluctance to deal with the locals. "Even if he intercepts something, it won't matter."

Cordelia appeared and leaned in the doorway. "Can I ask why?"

Absorbed in his thoughts, Sebastian didn't notice her presence. Looking at her now, he picked up the pressure of her thoughts the way he detected her fragrance. Both drifted as though carried on a breeze. He recognized the smile on her face. *This is damn irritating.*

Really? I find it amusing. Her eyes glinted with humor.

Out of the corner of his eye, Sebastian saw Thomas studying the space between them. He frowned. "Seamus is right, it's there. I can almost—"

"This is ridiculous," Sebastian snapped. Cordelia's thoughts melted away. He could still sense her, but she wasn't in his head. "I didn't know you could do that," he said.

Cordelia shrugged. "The messages are coded and Bishop doesn't have the cipher?"

Sebastian studied Cordelia the way he studied puzzles.

Thomas answered, "Exactly. We're using the fish market wholesales."

"Don't those change every day?" she asked.

"That's why we're using them," Sebastian said. "Depending on the day, the cipher changes."

Trevor slipped past Cordelia. "Here are two more." He handed the slips of paper to Sebastian.

The first note came from Lam Yuán. He glanced at Cordelia. "This one's from Yuán. His nephew Lok has been tapped to staff the auction."

"That makes five," Thomas said. He ticked off names. "Leung, Man, Wai Ling, Choi, and now Lok." He pulled the blueprint of the building to the center of the table. "Think two sentries for each door and loading dock." He tapped the schematic where doors were indicated. "Sixteen to eighteen men."

Trevor leaned over the table. "At least two guards on each side of the helipad and two men each for the road access between buildings."

Sebastian pulled out the satellite map and drew his finger along the road. "Bidders are entering from Sai Tso Wan Road to the parking lot. They'll drop off at the main doors and drivers will exit to the west past the oil depot to a holding lot on the east side of Sai Tso Wan."

"Keeping the parking lot empty prevents any covered approach to the front of the building," Thomas said.

"Jarske said they're pulling more juice into the southwest corner." Trevor pointed to the floor plan. "I'd guess they're keeping the girl in the flex space between the warehouse and the office. It offers a buffer from the outer perimeter."

Sebastian looked at the space Trevor indicated and said, "We can put at least two guards in the room with the clone." He glanced up to see Park step into the room.

She leaned against the wall across from Cordelia. Scanning the floor plans, she said, "Two guards on the hallway because they have a visual line on both the outer doors and the hallway. Figure two inside and maybe two on that south-facing door."

"Where will Bishop and Haager be?" Thomas asked.

Sebastian said, "They won't participate in the auction. For this to sell as Triad business, Líu has to appear in control."

"My guess is holed up in this four-story building." Trevor pointed to the map. "I'd also have a team in this building to the north. There's a docking door here." He gestured to the northwest corner of the auction building. "Simple enough to slip across the access road and into the building."

"They've also left the parking lot clear," Park reminded them. "It would be a quick sprint from this flex space building across the lot to the main doors."

Sebastian looked around the room and asked, "Ideas?"

"What are they allowing in the building?" Trevor asked.

Thomas picked up the invitation. "Two escorts, no weapons. There's a metal detector and a patdown."

"That means Anthony, Cordelia, Ujah, and me on the inside," Trevor said. "If we can get one of our contacts on the door, we might be able to get a couple of weapons through."

Sebastian looked at Cordelia, noticing a thought behind the surface of the wall she put up. "Cordelia?"

She hesitated. "You've been running all of these notes—will they suspect you have inside people?"

Sebastian caught her frown as he pushed a thought into a deep corner of his brain. "With General Wong dead, Líu will have cleared the upper ranks of any of Wong's officers. I'm guessing Bishop believes our resources within the Triad are limited."

"And so they are," Thomas said dryly.

"I'll have Jarske running frequency scans in the area. Bishop's bound to have web cams on the south and west sides," Trevor said.

Park moved to the table. "We disable the cameras and move in from the southwest and northwest." She pointed to the building to the north. "Seal any exits in this north building preventing Bishop's people rear access. Clear the west side for egress."

Sebastian thought a minute. "We have our inside people plant weapons for Anthony's group."

"Wait, what happened to being the highest bidder or tracking the girl after the auction?" Cordelia asked.

"Bishop isn't going to let us out of there alive," Trevor said.

Sebastian caught a brief flash of resignation in her mind and then she buried it. She pointed to the northeast corner of the auction building. "Then you should draw Bishop's eye to the north with a distraction. Make him think we're coming from between these two buildings."

Bounding footsteps up the stairs drew everyone's eyes to the door of the room. Seamus popped his head in. "Did someone say distraction? I think I have just the thing."

"What about Bishop?" Cordelia asked. "Who gets him?"

Sebastian stared at the building where they suspected Bishop would be. "I'm going to call in a favor."

CHAPTER TWENTY

With a plan in motion, the house quieted down for the night. Thomas and Alonzo made arrangements with Wai Ling regarding weapons via the fish market notes. The purple-haired skateboarder from the market turned out to be Wai Ling's son. *Lucky break.* The boy impressed Sebastian with his cheeky nerve. Several of the other street kids had come and gone.

Park and Barth sat on the patio after dinner. Sebastian thought he heard them debating the merits of scotch compared to bourbon. *Scotch. No question.* Yuán's wife had arranged for an enormous meal. Sebastian felt full and relaxed. He gave Anthony a nod as he walked through the living room. The Bostonian sat across from Ujah studying a chessboard.

Speaking of scotch. He snatched two glasses and a bottle of Bunnahabhain twenty-five-year from the bar. Taking a close look at the bottle, he chuckled. *Alonzo's gone raving mad buying three-hundred-dollar scotch.* He shook his head. Following his thoughts upstairs, he knocked on Cordelia's door.

"Come in," she called, her thoughts still tucked away from him.

He looked past the door to see her sitting out on the tiny patio, the sliding doors open to the humid night air. Sebastian moved to sit in the chair next to her. "The auction starts at seven."

"You and the others will be setting up. We'll be here waiting around twiddling our thumbs," she said. "At least you're taking Seamus with you." She nodded at the bottle. "You going to pour that?"

173

He felt her mischievous poke in his head. He placed the glasses on the small glass-topped table between them, popped the cork, and poured the amber-hued liquor. "You know, very few women I've met enjoy scotch." Sebastian swirled his glass inhaling the toffee and ginger wafting up.

"Don't start thinking I'm perfect," she said. "I happen to enjoy scotch." Cordelia took a sip. He watched her savor it. "I know you think you have to destroy the girl."

"Cord, if I could be normal I would. Thomas, Seamus, and now you. This clone," he ran a hand through his hair, "is—"

"You," she finished. "This little girl is a part of you."

"I don't want more of us out there." He frowned into his glass.

Cordelia looked at him. "Listen, I'll take mutant freak over dead any day."

He snorted. "There wasn't any choice. Not for any of us."

"Seamus chose, but I suppose he doesn't count because he's … Seamus," she said and chuckled into her glass.

"You all treat this as a lark. Anthony's the only one who seems to grasp the wrongness of it all." He felt her argument before she voiced it aloud.

"Oh no you don't, you don't get to force us into the monster box because you haven't come to terms with who you are. This girl may be a part of you, but she's *not* you. Destroying her won't change anything. In fact, I'm beginning to see my divination more clearly. You destroy her, you give up your humanity." She shook her head and held out her glass for more scotch.

"Don't you see? We're a threat to humanity," he asserted and filled her glass halfway.

Her laugh sounded forced. "News flash Sebastian, you have no control here. Are you going to tell Thomas and Rachna not to have their baby? Are you able to stop the changes in me? Are you willing to eliminate us all in the name of—I can't even guess what? We're back to you and your bloody need to control things. The tighter you grasp, the more slips through your fingers." She glared at him.

Her rancor surprised him. He cleared his throat. "No, I would never do anything to hurt any of you, especially Thomas and Rachna. Don't you see? I don't know how this is all going to play out!" He knew she felt his desperation.

Cordelia's face softened. "None of us do and that's okay." She took a deep drink of her scotch.

Following the line of her throat as she swallowed, he opened up his physical senses to feel the heat rise in her belly.

"That's so weird," she said, looking at him.

Returning her gaze, he tilted his head. "What is?"

"This whole in your head in my head thing." She took another sip. "I get the heightened responses. I swear I am able to see better in the dark, but you hearing my pulse, noticing the change in my body temperature — I can feel it in your thoughts and it's a little freaky."

"Stay out of my head," he said, teasing her a little. "I know you can. Tell me how you shut me out."

Cordelia shrugged. "A couple of weeks after I went home, the fog from the coma cleared." He smiled, attentive to the trail of her thoughts. "The only way to explain it is to compare watching television with a wire antenna versus high definition. Not only am I hearing people's thoughts clearly, I can turn off the volume." He saw her eyes narrow and felt the scrutiny in her mind. "You held something back from me today." Her tone accused.

He tossed back the last of his drink and poured another. Holding out the bottle to Cordelia, he smiled at her nod. Topping off her glass, he pinned her with his eyes. "I guess we're even."

She laughed. "Now you know why I kept to myself. It's a relief to be able to shut people out. Even you."

"Ouch." He raised an eyebrow at her. "If there were a way to keep you out of it tomorrow, I would." He looked out into the shadowed greenery of the hills. He could hear the murmur of Park and Barth talking from the patio around the corner of the structure.

"There you go again trying to control everything." She stood up to lean on the railing. "You don't get to tell Ian that I can handle myself and then question sending me into the auction." She turned to face him and said, "You aren't second-guessing sending Anthony or Trevor."

He wrestled with his thoughts. "You asked me what I planned on saying to you when I came to Vancouver." He paused to take a drink. "I'm back in the world. Not only because of you, but you're a part of it. So yes, I'm worried about sending you into what is absolutely a trap." He felt her impulse to speak and he put a hand up. "You can fight. You can shoot. You're stronger than some of those men and you have an advantage because you'll be able to see a threat coming. With more experience, you'll be the equal of any of us. All of those things are true and I'm worried about putting you in danger." He sensed her threading thoughts with his own.

She moved forward and touched his face. "I think you're a lucky bastard." Her voice and mind bubbled with humor. "You've met a woman to whom you needn't explain anything."

He kissed her, tasting the scotch on her lips. Pulling back, he gave her a small smile. "Good thing too because I've been told I'm terrible with people."

"Oh." She settled into his lap. "I think you're improving."

He raised his glass to hers. "We need to get some sleep."

"I agree." She reached behind her for the bottle. "After another drink." She poured a bit more into his glass and then three fingers into her own. "Now," she said, enjoying his chuckle as he picked her thought out of the air. "Your room or mine?"

****

Cordelia braided her hair, then wrapped and tucked it into a knot with pins. Park had suggested it. "Don't give 'em anything to grab. You'll need to keep moving once the shit trips."

She took a deep breath and tamped down her nerves. *You've been in a fight before and you're in much better shape now.* She pulled on a pair of black low-heeled boots and zipped them up over the slim-fitting olive green pants. A knock on the door interrupted her thoughts.

"Cordelia?" Alonzo poked his head around the door. "Are you ready?"

"Yes, come in." She stood up adjusting the tuck of her white blouse. She spread out her arms. "Do I look like the concubine of a Nigerian criminal lord?"

The Italian clapped his hands. "Lovely, but we need some finishing touches. Don't want to look too ready for a fight." He crossed to the dresser and opened her valise. Rummaging for a moment, he brought out a pair of diamond earrings and a serpentine platinum chain with a diamond pendant. Alonzo handed her the studs.

"These have to be at least three karats. I can't wear these." Cordelia gaped.

He shushed her with a wave of his hand. "Four Karats and how else would a Nigerian crime lord adorn his girlfriend? Let me help you with the chain. Turn please," he commanded.

Cordelia turned around. "Alonzo." She couldn't think of a thing to say when the sparkling round pendant settled perfectly in the opening of her blouse.

"Beautiful things for a beautiful woman." He chuckled. "No rings. You may have to hit someone." He looked her over head to toe. "We're ready to go. The car is in front and the others are setting up."

She followed him out of the room and down the stairs. Anthony looked handsome and grim. He wore the Spanish leather holster and the SIG Sauer P226X over a dark eggplant cotton shirt. His shirt remained untucked over a pair of dark wash jeans and he had cuffed the sleeves showing lavender lining.

She whistled. "Wow, you look terrific." Cordelia kept out of his thoughts. Sebastian had slipped back to his room early in the morning hoping no one would notice. She accidentally read Anthony's thoughts. He had noticed.

"Back at you." Anthony's smile didn't quite make it to his eyes.

Trevor and Ujah wore black shirts and jeans. Both wore holsters and carried pistols.

Park stood near Alonzo. "I know you carry a Bursa, C," she said, "but since they're not allowing weapons these are for show."

"Our weapons should be waiting for us inside," Trevor said, holstering his pistol. "Good thing too, I prefer my H & K USP."

Ujah grinned. "Not as good as the SIG Sauer P220 .45 cal for stopping power."

"Boys, boys, you can compare sizes later," Park said, rolling her eyes. "We gotta get this circus on the road."

In the driveway, Barth stood leaning on the roof of a large black Mercedes. "You girls done primping?" His wicked grin made Cordelia smile. His thoughts hopped with excitement.

"Yeah, yeah, shut up and drive." Anthony opened the rear passenger door for Cordelia. "After you."

Ujah took the front passenger seat and Trevor went around the other side. Cordelia found herself between Trevor and Anthony.

Park leaned down and Anthony lowered his window. "See you on the other side."

The engine purred to life and Barth pulled out of the compound.

"Cordelia." She jumped at the sound of her name. Anthony looked at her. "You ready for this?"

"Yeah." She took a deep breath. "We go in. There'll be an explosion. Guards move toward the chaos. We make our way toward the room where the girl is being held. Sebastian and the others eliminate the guards on the south side where we'll exit and meet Barth on the road running along the waterfront."

"Right," Trevor said. "Our contacts will have our weapons and they'll let our two teams into the building."

She didn't try to keep the sarcasm out of her voice. "What could possibly go wrong in a room full of Triad gangsters, underworld criminals, explosives, and the CIA?"

Barth snorted from the driver's seat. "That's the spirit."

CHAPTER TWENTY-ONE

The sun sank low over Ma Wan Channel as they approached the turnoff from Sai Tso Wan Road. Cordelia's anxiety ratcheted up when she saw how many cars queued to drop off for the auction. "Did you expect this many people?" she asked Anthony, taking a quick peek into his mind.

"It's not unusual," he said. His bland tone matched the lack of excessive concern in his thoughts. *He's all about the job right now.* "Many of these people aren't bidding. They're here to see the spectacle."

Trevor said, "It's not just the clone being auctioned off. I'd bet she's the big ticket item but at events like this there are arms dealers, smugglers, and black market types. We'll have to wait for the girl to be offered. There could also be consignment items available."

Anthony added, "There will be a walk-through for bidders to preview the items up for sale."

Cordelia shook her head. "You mean they run these like art auctions?"

"Exactly," Anthony said. "There will be food and a bar. With a ban on weapons, this is typically an event where these people can mingle without worry about violence or double-cross."

"Except this is a huge double-cross," Cordelia said.

"I hope we're the only ones who know that," Trevor said. "Otherwise it's going south sooner than we think."

"If Bishop wants Líu to be seen as the new Dragon everything about this auction is on the up and up." Anthony paused. "For criminals."

Barth added, "He's drawn a big crowd for a smokescreen. There are five cars in front of us and who knows how many behind." He nodded his head at the headlights twinkling on in the growing dark trailing them.

They approached the main door to the building. Several guests milled on the stairs waiting their turn to step through the metal detectors. Cordelia couldn't believe the scope of dress in the crowd. Some looked ready for a night at the Met, and others could be attending the Grammys. "This is more like a Cirque du Soleil show than an auction," she said. "Is it stupid to feel bad for the people caught in the crossfire? First the bombing and now this, it seems … gratuitous."

"You're right," Anthony said. "It's a production. Bishop is looking to burn us with this crowd. Word will spread and we'll lose credibility." He waved a hand at the queue. "Like it or not in our line of work, relationships with the criminal element can help."

Trevor nodded. "Not to mention these types are big on payback."

"Good news is," Barth said from the front as he pulled the car up to the doors, "Sebastian has a good reputation and Bishop is a tool. Here we are." He stopped and put the car in park. "If it makes you feel better, a lot of these people will disappear quickly once the commotion starts." He hopped out of the car.

Trevor bent down to look at her. "Wait until I come round."

"You can do this," Anthony said. His urge to put a hand over hers leaked through her screen.

Cordelia straightened her spine. "I know." She let her filter drop so she could get a sense of the crowd.

Barth opened the passenger door. Trevor stood sentinel on the right as Anthony stepped out. Ujah moved to the left. Anthony held a hand out to assist her and she took it. Murmurs rolled through the crowd. She sensed the excitement at the appearance of the Nigerian. Several minds projected curiosity at their arrival. The multinational group meant an easier read. Cordelia felt emboldened by the familiarity of languages. Their presence in the city, as well as the shooting, had been a topic of gossip for many.

The crowd moved steadily up the stairs and through the wide double doors. Cordelia could see four guards, two on each side guiding people through the metal detectors. Four more men stood divided on either side patting down those guests who set off the alarms. Several guns appeared from jackets and holsters to be tagged for pickup after the auction.

Anthony offered his arm. "Folks are staring at you."

"They're staring at us," she said, looping her arm through his. "We've been the talk of the town."

She sensed his unspoken question. *You can read this crowd?*

"A lot of English speakers and several native Germans and Italians," she whispered up at him pretending to smooth out his collar.

Anthony slipped his hand to the small of her back and he leaned closer. "You'll be able to sense Sebastian and the others." His breath brushed her ear.

Nodding, she said, "Nwora, about Sebastian." She caught a momentary glimpse of his feelings.

He snapped back into his role as the Nigerian, pushing back the desire she'd seen. "The job, C." He straightened and gestured her up the stairs. "Focus on the auction."

Trevor and Ujah veered to the right where Cordelia saw Lok working patdowns. Stepping through the panels of the metal detectors their group triggered the beeping. Lok's face remained blank as he approached them.

Sensing a shift in the crowd, Cordelia placed her free hand on Anthony's shoulder. "Nwora," she said.

Líu Qīngyún approached them with a welcoming smile. "Mr. Oni, I'm so glad to see you survived the incident at the Fringe Club." He offered a genial bow.

Anthony returned a bow matching the depth of the Triad lord's. "Líu Xiānshēng, I don't know if you met my companion, Celia Wright." He gestured to Cordelia.

Taking a cue from Anthony, she addressed the man with the generic honorific. "Líu Xiānshēng, it's a pleasure." She read the man's ambition loud and clear. *Dragon.* He reveled in this interaction with the man he believed to be the Nigerian.

The guests continued to proceed through the other side of security but Cordelia noticed the onlookers slowing their pace to observe the exchange.

Líu Qīngyún bowed a little deeper to Cordelia, enjoying the audience. "The pleasure is mine," he said. He waved a hand at Lok, who waited to frisk Trevor and Ujah. "You understand our precautions?" He asked with respect.

"Of course." Anthony nodded to the men. They relinquished their guns to Lok.

Anthony unholstered his own weapon, but Líu took it before Lok could. He turned the pistol over in his hands. "ASIG Sauer P226X-Six Scandic. I've heard you carry one. It's a gorgeous piece of weaponry." He ran his fingers over the burnished wood. "What kind of wood is this?"

"It's birch," Anthony said.

The acting crime lord handed the gun back to Anthony with ceremony.

Playing to the crowd. Cordelia heard a whisper move through the people around them.

"I'm happy to check it," Anthony said.

Líu shook his head. "Please, please, keep your gun. Let me offer this measure of respect." He bowed a little deeper. "Enjoy the rest of your evening."

Holstering the gun, Anthony returned the bow. "We will. My thanks, Líu Xiānshēng."

The interim Triad leader beamed as he moved away greeting the occasional guest. Cordelia kept her gaze down as they moved past Lok.

"What was that about?" Anthony asked out of the corner of his mouth.

Cordelia felt on display as people nodded and tried to catch her eye. She said, "He wanted the room to see him chatting with you. The gun was meant to garner your support."

"Politics," he said, his thoughts tinged with irritation.

"Exactly," she agreed. "You're a big fish, Nwora." She smiled up at him.

His lips pursed, Anthony scanned the crowd. "The sooner we're out of here, the happier I'll be."

Trevor fell back to Anthony's side. "At least you have your gun."

The building opened into a wide space broken by a ring of raised tables with stools. A long table bordered the only wall to the left serving as a bar. To the right, interspersed along the end of the building, stood parcels and stacks of crates. Several groups of people wandered among the goods lifting lids and reading labels.

A man in waiter's garb approached Ujah and whispered to him. Ujah turned. "A table has been set aside for us, sir."

Anthony gestured for them to follow the man. Cordelia recognized him to be Choi, the taxi driver.

The table stood near the end of the bar at the corner where a hallway began. Cordelia glanced down the corridor. It extended almost fifty yards until it opened up into a bigger space. She recalled the floor plan they studied. The wall directly behind their table bordered the room where they thought the girl was being held.

Anthony slid a stool out for her. She perched on it and pushed her mind beyond the wall into the space behind it. *Two guards bored and wishing they were out here.* Cordelia straightened, drawing a look from Anthony as he sat next to her. "You okay?"

Not willing to break contact, she waved a hand at him. *A thrum.* Cordelia reached with more force. She felt the little girl focused on something to the exclusion of noticing Cordelia's presence. *Her heartbeat. She's controlling her pulse.* Leaning into Anthony, Cordelia said, "They've tried to sedate her, but it didn't work. She's pretending to be unconscious."

"Did she notice you?" he asked.

Choi, the waiter, delivered a bottle of champagne with an ice bucket. He gave Cordelia a little wink as he nodded to another waiter to set up a tall bucket stand. "With compliments from Líu Xiānshēng." He smiled placing two glasses at their table.

Ujah, standing with his back to the wall, watched the crowd. Cordelia felt Trevor counting Líu's men.

"I'll pour," Choi said to his helper and shooed him off. He draped a towel over the cork and with skill released it. "Sir?" he asked.

Anthony nodded. "Sure." He lowered his voice. "Weapons?"

"Of course, sir," Choi said loudly. He poured the sparkling wine into Cordelia's glass. "I'll deliver your meal shortly." Returning the bottle to the ice, Choi melted into the crowd.

Cordelia returned her attention to the little girl on the other side of the corrugated tin wall. She focused the thinnest thread of energy toward the child. *I'm going to help you.*

The woman felt her thought jerk the young girl's attention. *Focus on the heartbeat, little one.* Cordelia didn't think it would be good for anyone to notice the child's farce. *Think about your pulse, but listen too.*

Anthony touched her hand, yanking her back to the table. "Everything okay?"

"Yes, why?" she said. She strained to keep a light presence in the girl's mind while she looked at Anthony.

"You're looking—"

"Creepy," Trevor said from Anthony's shoulder. "You're staring into space."

"Look." She glared. "You try touching the mind of another person in another room while trying to keep some attention on the room around you." Cordelia grabbed the wine flute and took a swallow. "This is new to me and it's hard."

Anthony took a sip from his glass. "Okay, just try to keep her calm, but you have to listen for the others. We'll need lead time on the diversion."

An explosion rocked the opposite side of the warehouse, followed by another at the front doors. Cordelia toppled off the stool and landed on her hands and knees. Ujah knelt next to her. He pulled the table, which had fallen over, in front of them as a shield. Shouts from the crowd echoed in the metal building. A third explosion shot pieces of sheet metal into the room just to their right. Cordelia saw Anthony face down on the concrete floor. "Ujah." She gestured toward Anthony. She couldn't see Trevor anywhere.

Her companion coughed in the smoke but nodded. "Stay here and keep low."

The sharp pops of semi-automatic guns punched through the noise and panic of the crowd. Cordelia reached wide with her mind to pick up faint traces of Sebastian and the others. She felt Sebastian push a single thought at her. *We're coming.*

Ujah scooted backwards toward her pulling Anthony a few inches at a time. Peeking over the table, she saw a distinct split in the crowd. *Barth was right.* She saw many people duck and make for the exits without too much concern except for speed. Others frightened and confused in the smoke and amid gunfire milled around in circles. They had gone unnoticed so far. She moved next to Ujah and took up one of Anthony's arms. Between the two of them, they moved the big man past the bombed east wall and into the corridor.

Glancing over her shoulder, Cordelia didn't see the two guards posted there earlier. *Must've moved to a different position.* "We've got to get into this room." She pointed at the wall on their left. "The little girl is there." She reached out, relieved to find the young mind remarkably calm for the noise and destruction. *We're coming. Hide.* Not sure her advice was sound, Cordelia focused on inching Anthony down the hall. The smoke covered their position low on the floor but set both of them coughing.

Ujah stood when they finally arrived at the door. "Stay here." He tested the door, which proved to be unlocked. Sliding the panel an inch, she saw him peer into the room. Ujah glanced at her and signaled two fingers. *Two guards.*

"Can you take them?" Cordelia mouthed.

Ujah's face bloomed into a cocky grin. He shoved the door open and disappeared into the room. She heard a crash and a shout. With a quick glance at the unconscious Anthony, she jumped up ready to launch through the door. Ujah's head popped out. "Let's get him in."

They slid the injured man through the doorway and slid the door in place as four armed guards ran past them into the main warehouse. As she closed the door Cordelia saw a slide bar and pushed it into place. She turned to face the room. Two men lay unconscious in a heap in the corner. A hospital bed lay empty, tubes from an IV dangled free, but no patient could be seen.

Ujah looked at her. "They only have tasers. I didn't see the girl."

Cordelia scanned the space with her mind and walked to a large metal cabinet opposite the bed. She glanced at Ujah with a nod and pulled the door open. Tucked deep into the bottom shelf, the little girl hid. Legs tucked up against her ribs with arms looped around, she looked out with eyes of the deepest jade. *Sebastian's eyes.* Cordelia held her breath and dropped to a crouch. "I'm Cordelia," she said aloud. With her mind, she added, *We came to help you.*

Without a sound, the child slid her legs out and crept from the cabinet. Standing, she just met Cordelia's eyes. Curly waves of ebony hair tumbled below her ears. Face solemn and still silent, she reached for Cordelia's hand.

Cordelia felt the tumult of the child's thoughts but could only pick a single emotion from her mind. *Resignation.* "Oh boy," she said.

Ujah looked confused. "C?"

Cordelia stood up with the little girl's hand clutching her own. "We've got to get out of here. That explosion wasn't ours." She pushed out with her mind. "Sebastian and the others are outside, but we're on our own until we can get out of the building."

Another explosion punctuated her words and sent the IV and monitors to the ground.

Anthony groaned. "We can get out to the west to the channel."

Ujah knelt to look at the injured Bostonian. "We need to clean him up."

Looking at the open doors of the cabinet, Cordelia shot a thought at the child. *I have to let go for a minute.*

Those enigmatic pools of green watched her without expression. The girl dropped her hand but moved a bit closer to Cordelia's side.

Pulling out several boxes, she found what she needed. "Here." She tossed them to Ujah. "Compression bandages." She grabbed a pair of blunted scissors and kneeled next to Anthony. Ujah opened the boxes while Cordelia sliced the fabric of Anthony's shirt. Peeling the cotton back, she gasped. "Fuck."

Anthony grunted. "That bad, eh?"

Ujah looked around the room. Reaching across the floor, he scanned the label on the IV bag. "This is saline. We can use this." He took the scissors from Cordelia and snipped the top of the bag. Pouring the fluid over Anthony's back elicited a loud swear from their patient. The liquid flowed to the floor with a wave of blood and soot. Anthony had taken the brunt of the closest explosion. His back gaped open with shreds of flesh and glints of shrapnel. Ujah met Cordelia's eyes over the wounds. "Is there any anesthetic or medication?"

She stood, her tiny shadow close at her side, and poured through the cabinet. "Secobarbital?" she asked, picking up a vile.

"Perfect." Ujah waved her over. "There should be some syringes if they were using that to dose the child."

"Yes." Cordelia found one and brought it with the drug over to the young Nigerian.

"Anthony," Ujah said while he drew a dose of the sedative. "This is going to numb you a bit and probably knock you out."

"You have to leave me," Anthony said with a grimace of pain.

"Absolutely not," Cordelia said.

"The others will be here soon," he argued. "They can get me out."

Cordelia looked at Ujah, who pressed the bandages against the wounds. The younger man shook his head. *He might bleed out.* Nodding at his thought, she looked around the room again. "There's a back board." She moved to grab it from the corner. "We'll take you out on this."

"Smallest dose, Ujah," the big man said, head resting on his arm. "I can hold on to the end, but you can't dope me."

Ujah injected a small amount of the medication into their patient. He motioned to Cordelia. "I'll lift him, you slide the board." More gunfire cracked closer to their position. "One. Two. Three."

He lifted and Cordelia pushed the board under Anthony. She grabbed the hand hold with her right hand and held out her other to the girl. She remembered the girl's name. "Nadja, right?"

Nadja nodded, taking hold of Cordelia's hand.

Ujah grabbed an emergency kit in a black canvas bag. He stuffed the secobarbital and an extra syringe along with extra pressure bandages into the bag. Looping the bag across his chest, he picked up the left-hand hold. "Let's go." He opened the door to the hallway leading to the south. Shouts and more gunfire boomed out from where they came. They dragged Anthony through the door into the smoke.

CHAPTER TWENTY-TWO

Sebastian leaped onto the dock surprising the first guard standing near the water. Whirling around, he thrust the man between the other guard and himself. In the darkness, the second guard fired. Dropping the dead guard, Sebastian heard Thomas launch onto the dock behind him. With blinding speed, he drew his weapon and shot the remaining guard.

Another explosion rocked the waterfront. "Goddamn it," Thomas said. They moved toward the south side of the building.

Over the comm link, Seamus reported, "Boss, it's a fuckin' mess over here. The north building is on fire. Won't matter if we secure it, doesn't look like anyone is getting out of there. We're going into the main warehouse through a hole in the wall."

"Copy," Sebastian answered. He looked to Thomas, who nodded. He said, "There's no way Anthony and the others received their weapons. They should be moving our direction but keep an eye out. Our guys should have bright green armbands so keep an eye open."

"Roger," the Irishman said. "Here we go."

Gunfire drifted across the freight yard. Moving silently toward the front of the building, Sebastian saw crowds of people running across the parking lot. Several of the waiting cars had managed to pull in to pick up passengers.

Thomas examined the door. "I can snip this lock. We can lift the door and roll under." He pulled a small pair of bolt cutters from one of his pockets.

"Do it," Sebastian said, covering his partner.

Thomas cut the bolt and rolled the door up a few inches. Smoke wafted out over the ground. "Can't see much."

"Then they won't see us." Sebastian gestured with his head. Keeping their entry covered, he waited until Thomas heaved up over the ledge. After a quick second glance, he strapped his gun over his shoulder and threw his leg up over the concrete. He rolled into the building and Thomas let the door drop.

Regaining his feet, Sebastian stood next to Thomas trying to get his bearings in the debris and smoke. "You know, bombs are getting old on this job," he said.

Thomas shook his head. "We're in loading. I don't see any guards up ahead and to the left is where Anthony and the others were headed."

Sebastian closed his eyes but couldn't feel Cordelia anywhere. At the first explosion, he had pushed a thought at her without knowing if she could hear it. "Seamus," he said into the comm link.

"We're in." The Irishman coughed. "I've found Leung and Lok. Wai Ling and Mau are already out. Looks like the Triad guards are spooking. What do you want us to do?"

Sebastian thought a moment. "This wasn't Bishop and he's not going to stick around to find out who it was. Hook up with the others and swing around to the office building. Our friends might need help if Bishop has disappeared."

"Copy that," Seamus said.

"We're going to sweep the building and see if we can find the others," Sebastian said.

Thomas moved to take point sliding along the west wall toward the main warehouse. A couple of Triad guards burst out of the smoke, took one look at the Westerners, and ran toward the gaping hole at the front of the building. "If it keeps up like this, we'll have it made," Thomas said with a toss of his head.

They'd covered several yards when they approached the room where they thought the clone was held. Thomas still on point sent a questioning look at Sebastian. He gave Thomas a nod and moved up as his friend turned down the hall to check the door. His quick wave brought Sebastian to join him. They went into the empty room.

One guard lay dead. The room had been tossed over. Blood and what looked like water pooled on the floor. "Shit, Thomas," Sebastian said, kneeling down for a closer look. "One of them is injured." The pit of his stomach clenched thinking about Cordelia.

His friend placed a hand on his shoulder. "We don't know who it was." Thomas looked at the door to the northeast. "We do know they're not here." He walked over and unlatched the sliding panel. "Let's keep moving."

Sebastian stood to follow, sensing something in the smoke. "Thomas!" Too late, he saw his partner realize someone stood on the other side of the door. A gunshot rang out. Thomas took a hit to his left shoulder and stumbled back.

The door flew wide open and Líu blocked the way with two men on either side of him. "I should have known you would be working against me," the lean man said, his eyes narrowed.

Sebastian glanced out the corner of his eye to his injured friend. "Thomas?"

The answering growl triggered his own rage. "Yeah." Thomas's voice grew thick and heavy.

Letting the familiar scourge flame up through his body, he felt a mirroring heat from Thomas. Red haze filmed his eyes as guns dropped from their opponents' hands. Líu and his men turned, shouting in terror as the two enormous figures rose up. Burnished gold fur and tapered claws reached out to cut two of the men down.

Leaping across the space, the jet black titan landed in front of Líu and the other two guards. Throwing his head back, Sebastian opened his yawning jaws. The reverberant bellow roared through the entire building.

The two guards collapsed in terror while a puddle of urine spread around Líu's expensive shoes. The would-be Dragon stood trembling, unable to move.

Out of the smoke, the silver-haired figure of General Wong emerged. "Líu Xiānshēng." The General bowed shallowly. "It seems you've made quite a mess and possibly cost my dear friend," he said gesturing to the looming hulk of Sebastian, "someone important to him." He continued, his tone chastising. "Not to mention, the cleanup after all of this and dealing with the rumors of monsters." The General clucked his tongue. "Then there's the matter of involving the CIA in our business. What will the Triad elders think?"

Four burly men appeared from the smoke. Sebastian saw one of the men spare the tiniest glance at the tawny-maned figure of Thomas imposed behind Líu. A growl escaped him, causing the big men to take hold of Líu with haste.

A phone rang from the General's pocket. "Hóu." He listened for a moment and said, "Jóutáu m`hgòi." He turned to Sebastian without fear.

Gotta respect the man.

"Bishop has been taken by your friends. However, the matter of our mutual acquaintance remains unfinished. I trust you to deal with it according to our agreement." The General bowed deeply. He offered a second low bow to Thomas and then turned on his heel. "We'll deal with Líu," he said, walking away. His men with Líu in tow moved past Sebastian without a word.

Seamus came bounding through the gaping hole in the building carrying a duffle bag. "Thought I heard you call." He tossed the bag to the floor. "Think it's time to find Cordelia and the others. Don't need too many more folks claiming to see monsters in this haze."

****

Spurred by continuing sounds of gunfire, Cordelia and Ujah kept moving. The bulk of Anthony's weight fell to Ujah. Cordelia carried the litter with her right hand and held the little girl's hand in her left. It made for slow going. Cordelia glanced at Anthony and smothered her nauseating worry. *Can't think about it.*

"I think the bleeding has slowed," Ujah said.

"He's already lost too much." She tried to remember the layout of the building. A corridor crossed their path. She motioned Ujah to stop. "The loading docks are to the west. I think we're heading south."

Anthony roused. "Yeah, take the right corridor and get out to the docks." He coughed, slipping down on the back board.

Cordelia needed a minute. "Okay," she said, looking at their silent ward. "I need to help Anthony. I'm going to let go for a sec."

Nadja nodded with the same withdrawn disinterest she'd shown since they'd found her.

"Let's put him down. We need to figure out a way to keep him from falling off." She racked her brain to think of a way.

"I can hold on," Anthony said weakly.

Ujah kept his face blank, but Cordelia read his doubt their patient would survive. She shook his thoughts out of her head. "Bullshit. You're fading fast."

Her gaze fell on the strap over Ujah's shoulder. "Yes! Ujah." She gestured at the bag they'd taken from the medical room. "The strap, does it come off?"

The young Nigerian slipped the bag over his head and unbuckled a band from around his boot. "It will." With a slight twist, he freed a compact knife. The handle of the knife was disguised as the buckle.

"How'd you get it through security?" Cordelia asked.

With a wily grin, Ujah sliced the straps. "Ceramic. Doesn't trip the metal detectors. Not great in a fight, too brittle, but handy if you need it."

"I'll kiss you later." She grinned at his blush. "We'll need two lengths." She turned to Anthony. "This is gonna suck."

"More than it already does?" He winced.

"Good point."

Ujah handed her a cut length of the strap. "Okay, loop it with a knot leaving length on the ends to tie to the corners." She showed him. "Like this."

"Ahh! Yes, this'll work." He mirrored her work.

She looked at Anthony, forehead resting on his arm. "When you're ready, loop the strap around your wrist. You can hang on to the loop rather than the end of the litter. It should be easier and if you slip or pass out, the strap'll keep you from falling off."

The tired man nodded, slipping his large hands into the loops. "Let's get moving."

Signaling to Ujah, she reached out for the passive Nadja with one hand and lifted the end of the litter with the other. "Right turn."

Working together, they moved Anthony around the corner and proceeded toward a set of heavy double doors.

"Imagine meeting you here."

Cordelia and Ujah turned together at the sound of Haager's voice.

She curled her lip at the thoughts in his head. "You're a dick."

"Oh." He aimed a taser with one hand while the other covered his heart. "I'm hurt. Have the girl walk over here."

The little girl's hand clutched tighter to Cordelia, the first sign of spirit she'd displayed. "Come get her." Steel edged Cordelia's voice.

He moved his gaze over their motley group with scorn. "Anthony's dead. The boy is green and you? Seriously? This isn't the way to play this."

A glance at Ujah and they each put their corner of the litter down. She moved Nadja behind her. "Sebastian called it from the beginning."

Mild curiosity stirred in Haager's brain. "Called it?"

"Worthless."

Ujah snorted.

Haager fired the taser at the young man. Reading his intention, Cordelia launched across the hallway at the same moment. She heard Ujah drop to the floor but didn't slow her charge. Leading with her right elbow, she clubbed her target across the jaw. Haager lost his grip on the taser and stumbled forward. Without breaking her momentum, Cordelia drove her left elbow into his kidney. He grunted and doubled over, but twisted with both hands to shove her. Stumbling back over Anthony's outstretched legs, she lost her footing. She heard the big man grunt in pain as her weight came down directly on his wounded back.

As Haager straightened, she rolled off. Anthony grabbed her wrist before she could gain her feet. She paused on her hands and knees, meeting his pain-glazed eyes with grim agreement.

The traitor coughed and tried to catch his breath. "Underestimated you, but who's worthless now?"

Without a word, Cordelia whirled to her back and fired Anthony's P226X pistol. A shot to his leg and one to his shoulder brought the former Black Wolf to his knees. She slowly rose, maintaining her aim.

"Damn." Another cough came with blood.

"That was for us," Cordelia said, coolly. From the corner of her eye, she saw Ujah struggle to recover his feet. Pausing a moment, she allowed ice calm to envelop her. "This is for Lorena." Eyes open, she squeezed the trigger. Without a second glance, she handed the gun to Ujah. "Let's get out of here."

Anthony coughed. "Well?"

Reading his weakened thoughts, she said, "Three inches above the seven."

Her injured friend tried to laugh.

"Any ideas?" Ujah asked.

With more confidence than she felt, she said, "Let's continue out. We can't stay here. Anthony needs help."

Ujah nodded. He slid the gun into his waistband and bent to put his hand on the litter. "On three?"

"On three." Cordelia bent to lift Anthony. "One. Two. Three." She opened her free hand to the three-year-old. "Ready?"

Solemn and quiet, the little sprite placed her hand into Cordelia's without hesitation.

Wish I could read her more clearly. She nodded at Ujah and he pushed open the door.

They stepped into a circle of armed men. One of the men spoke harshly in Chinese. It didn't take much for them to understand. One of the men disarmed Ujah.

She couldn't pick up much besides brusque irritation. "This man needs a doctor," she said, hoping one of them spoke English.

Four of the men shoved Ujah and Cordelia aside to pick up Anthony without much care.

"Can you tell what they're going to do to us?" Ujah asked.

She snorted, pulling the little girl closer to her side. "Thinking in Chinese. Angry. I can tell they're angry."

Two men moved to either side of her and Ujah, muscling them to follow along with the group. Moving quickly, their captors hustled them out to the docks. A helicopter sat on the landing pad, rotors spinning in low idle.

Cordelia stopped. "Shit."

Her guard shoved her forward with a push of his rifle.

"Keep hold of the girl." Ujah gestured to the child. "And hope we're the only ones who know who she is."

She watched them load Anthony. "No choice, is there?"

"No."

Looking down at Nadja, Cordelia reached out and lifted the small girl to her hip. "No matter what happens, try to keep close, okay?"

The little girl nodded solemnly.

CHAPTER TWENTY-THREE

The helicopter landed on the helipad of a sleek yacht moored in the harbor. Cordelia tried to make out the name, but between the darkness of the night and the speed of their approach she failed. The ride could only have taken fifteen minutes, but her constant glances at Anthony stretched the time out. He'd lost consciousness on the pier as the men loaded him into the helicopter. He hadn't roused. Cordelia couldn't tell if he still breathed.

Nadja's head lolled against her shoulder. The little girl nodded off, pacified by the throb of the rotors. Cordelia didn't have to imagine the amount of stress the child experienced. Ujah's thoughts remained calm. He continued to scan the men holding them looking for an opportunity. What he thought they could do in a helicopter, even he didn't know.

The armed men hustled them out onto the deck. Cordelia carried Nadja. She tried to follow as they carried Anthony to a lower deck. Two of the men stepped into her path. They led Cordelia and Ujah through the ship to the second salon deck. Shoved through a large sliding glass door into the salon, Cordelia almost lost her grip on Nadja. The little girl roused and indicated she wanted to be put down.

Ujah moved to flank the youngster, giving Cordelia a grim look. "I fear we're sitting near the fire rubbed in oil."

She didn't exactly understand the saying but nodded at the gist of his thought. *Frying pan, fire.*

"I'm sorry about the brusque treatment. They didn't like being pulled from the fight to rescue you. Welcome aboard the *Berehynia*." Madame Mdivani's bright, intelligent eyes beamed. Graceful and lovely, she gestured they sit on the plush, yellow sofa. "Please, your man is being attended to by my physician. Please."

Without much choice, Cordelia nodded to Ujah. They moved as a unit to collapse on the couch.

Cordelia spoke. "Not to be ungracious, but … we thought you were dead."

The glamorous woman pressed a button. "Of course, of course, that was the plan. Sebastian and the General thought it best to keep it, how do you say, close to the vest?" She stood to direct the two porters who entered with trays. "Please, put them right there."

Nadja perked up at the sight of the sliced fruit and petit fours.

Madame Mdivani smiled at the girl's interest. "Eat, eat."

"Go ahead." Cordelia knew the eccentric woman posed no threat. Her thoughts jumbled in three different languages, but she effused warmth and charm.

"Let me pour you some cognac." She stood, her heavy gold bracelets clinking.

"Our friend?" Cordelia asked, taking a crystal snifter.

"Oh yes, I'll take you to him soon. Give the doctor time." Madame Mdivani smoothed her silk brocade cheongsam.

Cordelia stood; impatience filled her. "What's going on?"

The elegant woman stepped around a gleaming, full-size replica of an ivory tusk. "You, my dear Alice, have stepped through the looking glass." She gave a throaty laugh. "And I suppose that makes me the March Hare."

Taking a sip of the cognac, Cordelia let the heat and butter warm her throat. "Just to clarify, General Wong is alive?"

Their hostess's laugh chimed. "Yes, my dear Dragon is alive. We were sorry to have people believe our demise, but you understand, this is a dangerous game, and you've plopped right into the middle. Even if I hadn't promised Sebastian your safety in the event of any trouble, I'd be answering to another dear to me." She moved to stroke Nadja's head. "And you've found the prize." The little girl shied. "Every reason to be nervous, malo draga."

"I'm sorry to be ungracious, but what is your stake in all of this?" Cordelia asked, feeling Nadja press closer into her ribs.

Swirling her goblet, Madame Mdivani gazed into the caramel liquid.

Cordelia felt a subtle shift of energy. She looked sharply at the petite Hungarian.

"Ah yes," the Madame said and lifted her perceptive and bright eyes to meet Cordelia's, "I've my own little gift." She clicked her tongue. "Not as formidable as yours, but insightful never the less." She sipped her cognac. "Please understand, I love the General and remain loyal to him, but I also understand who and what he is." She looked evenly at Cordelia to be sure she grasped the nuances. "I also know who Sebastian is."

The younger woman forced her body to remain still. Unable to keep the tremor from her voice, she asked, "And?"

Madame brushed aside the concern with a swish of her hand. "Everyone is the blacksmith of his own fortune. I don't believe it's serendipity that Sebastian is a good man."

Ujah spoke thoughtfully. "My uncle says he is an Orisha."

Cordelia questioned him with a look, but Madame Mdivani answered first. "A conduit of the divine spirit." She meditated into her snifter. "Hmmm." She nodded. "Yes, yes, I believe he is, but egy fecske nem csinál nyarat. *One swallow does not make a summer.* Poor Sebastian is confused about his true nature." The sharp Hungarian woman pierced Cordelia with her eyes. "You will help him, yes?"

Raising her hands in mock defense, Cordelia shook her head. "I agree Sebastian is a good man. He's definitely suffering a martyr complex and I'm willing to knock him upside the head, but divine conduit? Predestiny? I'm not sure I buy it."

Madame Mdivani placed her hand on Cordelia's knee, sending a shockwave through her. The hair on her arms tingled in recognition. The Madame's intensity filled her voice. "You are a powerful augury. Do you doubt your own knowledge?"

Cordelia looked from Ujah to Madame Mdivani. She glanced at Nadja, who nibbled on a petit four. The little girl keenly felt the energy in the room as she struggled to understand the adult language. "No, I don't. Call it fate, call it magnetic fields. Sebastian and the others generate something."

"And the girl plays her own role." The elegant woman passed a bejeweled hand over Nadja's hair. "A role she cannot fulfill if the General possesses her."

"This is insane." Cordelia took a large swig of the cognac.

Ujah let out a brief laugh. "She did call you Alice."

Madame Mdivani raised her glass. "'The time has come,' the Walrus said, 'To talk of many things: of shoes and ships and sealing wax, of cabbages and kings!'"

Cordelia laughed into her glass feeling the comfort of the alcohol.

A porter entered the salon to whisper into Madame Mdivani's ear. "Oh, dear." She turned to Cordelia and Ujah. "Your friend's lost a lot of blood. My physician stabilized him, but his injuries are serious. He needs a transfusion and a hospital."

"I'm O-negative. I can give him blood." Cordelia stepped forward. She shoved her misgivings down.

Ujah touched her arm. "You're sure?" His worry about the situation radiated off of him.

"I'm sure." She nodded and put down the glass. "Fortuitous. Dober pocitek je pol dela. *Well begun is half done.* Let's head down to the infirmary and I'll have my captain move this barge." Madame Mdivani swept a bejeweled hand toward the door.

Cordelia hesitated.

"No worries, Szépségem. I've contacted Miszter Sebastian. He'll join us on the island," the petite woman assured her.

Ujah moved to Cordelia's side. "I'll go with you."

Madame Mdivani motioned to Nadja as well. "I think it's best if we all stick together. I'm not foolish enough to think my love hasn't eyes and ears among my crew."

Nadja moved close to Cordelia and slipped her tiny hand into Cordelia's warm one. Her thoughts began to settle into a calmer state and the woman thought she could pick a few out of the maelstrom.

You're safe. Cordelia looked down at the little girl. *We're going to help Anthony. Remember him?*

The sprite's luminous eyes locked with hers and she nodded.

Looking up to Madame Mdivani, Cordelia gestured. "Okay."

Their host's eyes twinkled as understanding bloomed. She gave Cordelia a mischievous look and clapped her hands. "Things are never boring when Sebastian visits. Come, come. Let's get your man settled and then," she placed an affectionate hand on Cordelia's arm, "you and I will have another drink, yes?"

Cordelia felt every corner of the yacht brimmed with opulence. Moving down to the lower decks, two factions in the crew became clear. The dour-faced, beefy men belonged to security and the cheerful, nodding smilers ran the ship. *I can imagine who appointed whom.* Cordelia hefted Nadja to her hip to keep the group moving. Despite the size of the ship, the infirmary didn't take long to reach.

The little troupe walked in and the doctor looked up from attending Anthony. "Oh good, can one of you give blood?"

Cordelia nodded. "I'm O-negative." She noticed Nadja's grip grow tight. The little girl's thoughts moved from calm undulating waves to frantic whirls. *It's going to be okay.* She hugged the child with reassurance. "I need Ujah to hold you," she said out loud, moving toward the young Nigerian.

Ujah nodded with a kind look and reached for Nadja.

The little girl showed more agitation than she had the entire night. She clung to Cordelia with a powerful grip for a small girl. She shut her eyes tight and shook her head continually. Cordelia looked aghast to Madame Mdivani.

"Poor thing, she's upset about the infirmary," the eccentric Hungarian said.

Cordelia felt stupid. "Of course, she's only known clinics and laboratories." She put Nadja down and crouched to the girl's eye level. "Honey, I need to help Anthony. No one is going to hurt you here."

Madame Mdivani placed her hand on Nadja's head. Cordelia felt a hum of energy travel through the woman to the child. "Malo draga, Itt leszek, és nem lesz nekem," she murmured in Hungarian. Cordelia understood the sentiment. Madame Mdivani promised to keep Nadja safe.

The doctor hurried Cordelia to a bed near Anthony. "He's sedated. I've been managing his pain through his IV, but he needs blood. We'll do more for him at the onshore clinic. I have a surgeon meeting us at the island." He brought over a saline IV. "I'm going to start you a saline drip to keep you hydrated while we transfer the blood to your friend."

The calm that had settled over Nadja started to fade. She began tapping her hand nervously against her leg. "Maybe it's better if I take her back to the salon?" Madame Mdivani said with a worried look for the girl.

Ujah stepped forward. "I'll stay with Cordelia."

"I don't know," Cordelia said, still feeling trepidation about the night's events.

One of Madame's smiling crew members entered and whispered something in her ear. She clapped her hands with delight. "Yes, yes, bring him in." She turned to give Cordelia a hawkish look. "I hope this quells all of your concerns."

Andre stepped into the clinic. He patted Ujah, looking shocked, on the shoulder and placed a kiss on Madame's cheek. "Nagynéni, my lovely aunt. I'm full of thanks for scooping up my friends." The two clasped hands; warmth and affection flowed between them.

"That's what I picked up the night of the party!" Cordelia all but shouted. The doctor shushed her. "Please don't jerk around."

"I hoped you hadn't," Andre said, moving to squeeze her hand. "The General doesn't know. My aunt likes to keep some things to herself. I'm sorry I worried you."

Madame Mdivani took Nadja's hand in her bejeweled one. "Now, Andre and I will attend to our little angyal and, Ujah, you will bring Cordelia back to the salon when the good doctor is finished, yes?" Without waiting for an answer, she coaxed the child out of the room.

Nadja looked back at Cordelia. *It's okay. I promise.* She nodded at the girl. Face still impassive, Nadja allowed the Madame to lead her out. *Those eyes.* Cordelia shook her head.

Andre shook his head smiling. "You know, she's a temptress. I remember being small and thinking she was a sorceress to make my wishes come true."

He looked at Anthony. "She owns a little island where she started a school and a clinic. We're headed there to get Anthony to the surgeon."

The doctor nodded. "His injuries are superficial, but they're extensive. We'll remove the shrapnel and suture the lacerations. It will be slow going but he'll recover."

Cordelia started to feel fuzzy. She looked at the doctor. "Did you medicate me?"

"A very small dose of valium to alleviate the discomfort of the IVs." He flashed an LED light into her eyes. "You also look exhausted. It might be magnifying the medication effects. I wager Madame tempted you with some fine cognac as well." He smiled and patted her hand.

She puffed out her breath. "Andre, did Sebastian know you were alive along with Wong and the Madame?"

The slender, doe-eyed man tilted his head. "Yes, I'm sorry, Cordelia. We thought it would offer us an advantage when it became clear Mai Li was working with Bishop. Sebastian worried he wouldn't be able to keep it from you."

She thought about Sebastian pulling his mind tight around something the day before. "We both know how to keep some secrets," she said. *Good thing or bad thing?*

As though he could read her mind, Andre said, "Nagynéni says plain dealing and honesty are the keys to a happy life but a little artifice is the key to joy." He shrugged. "No one needs to know everything. I'll make sure she doesn't spoil the child too much." He patted Cordelia's hand and turned to follow his aunt.

"Andre," she called.

He stopped at the door. "Yes?"

"I'm really glad you're alive," Cordelia said, eyes brimming.

The graceful young man tipped his head with a warm smile. "Me too, drágám barátja, me too." He disappeared into the passageway.

"Ujah," Cordelia said, "I think I'm going to close my eyes a minute."

He moved a stool to her side and perched on it. "I'm not going anywhere."

"Good, because I'm not sure I can handle any more surprises today," she said. She placed a hand on his and rested her head back. Her eye lids drifted down and she blissfully let things go quiet.

CHAPTER TWENTY-FOUR

Sebastian pulled a black t-shirt over his head. With General Wong's men moving cleanup through the building, the place settled down quickly.

"The CIA guys are waiting for us over at the parking lot east of the office building." Seamus handed Thomas a holster. "Bishop's making all kinds of noise."

"I'll bet," Sebastian said, buckling his own new holster. "Jarske put together the packet?"

Seamus checked the chamber of an H & K USP. He released the clip and pushed it back into place. Handing the gun to Sebastian he said, "Yeah, and that new guy, what's his name?"

"Travis," Sebastian said, placing the gun in his holster.

"Yeah, Travis. That kid's hilarious. He's gonna be loads of fun to have around."

Thomas adjusted his holster and gun. "Great, just what we need, someone to encourage you."

The tall ginger grinned ear to ear. "Oh, it gets entirely too serious around here. You love me." He blew a kiss at the shaggy-headed Englishman.

"All right," Sebastian said. "Let's go deal with Bishop. We need to get Cordelia and the others and then there's one last thing to deliver."

Seamus heaved the duffle over his shoulder. "Deadly, can I wrap her up with a bow?"

Thomas patted him on the shoulder. "With curly cues and sparkles if you like."

"Come on," Sebastian said, taking long strides toward the parking lot. "Bishop's waiting."

It didn't take long to cross the main parking lot to meet a group of suits in front of the office building.

"Do my eyes deceive?" Thomas said, making a show of peering into the dark.

Sebastian raised an eyebrow. They both saw easily across the distance. "No deception. I wonder why they pulled him out of retirement."

"Huh, Jack Pepper. Bishop must've wound him up," Thomas said.

Seamus whistled. "Three-Fingered Jack Pepper? I thought he was a myth."

Shaking his head, Thomas made a face. "No one calls him that to his face and don't you either."

"Bishop forced him into retirement," Sebastian said.

"Did I say wound up? The tosser's lucky he's not dead," Thomas said.

"That doesn't look like retirement to me," Seamus said, pointing to the man with a silver ponytail ordering men around. "He looks like a man on a mission."

"To bury Bishop," Sebastian said.

"Looks like he brought his own shovel," Seamus said, with a smirk.

The man in question strode toward them. "Cole, damn glad to see you, son." The older man shook Sebastian's hand with a powerful grip. "Word is I have you to thank for putting this show together."

Sebastian put a hand up. "We had some help."

Jack Pepper stroked his beard. "I gathered. No one moves in this town without the Dragon knowing. I'm surprised Bishop had the cojones to try."

He turned back toward the group of men and stopped. "Scratch that, I'm not surprised. He's in the car."

Seamus leaned close to Thomas. "He really only has three fingers."

The glee in his voice caused Sebastian to nudge him with an elbow. "You're such a git."

"May have lost the pointer on a job in Honduras but my hearing works just fine," Pepper said over his shoulder.

"Yessir," Seamus said, shrugging his shoulders at Sebastian with a grin.

Sebastian shot a low snarl at Seamus.

Pepper approached a black sedan and pounded the roof. "Open her up," he commanded. The back window rolled down.

Bishop sat in the backseat, hands zip-tied in his lap. He glared at Sebastian and Pepper.

"So we've got misappropriation of funds, illegal medical experiments, international human trafficking, possible treason, and weapons trafficking. Anything you'd like to add?" Pepper asked.

Sebastian looked at Bishop. "Not a thing."

"I owe you one on this thing, Cole," Pepper said, offering a hand. "Only thing I regret is Hawthorne ain't here to see it."

Shaking Pepper's hand, the jet-haired Englishman pushed down the familiar sorrow he felt whenever Hawthorne came up. Sebastian said, "I thought you retired."

The older man waved a hand in dismissal. "Semiretired. They need old coots like me to catch piss ants like Bishop." He winked. "Speaking of relics, you tell that codger of a Dragon he owes me one. Oh, and your old man owes me a fishing trip." He nodded at the driver and opened the passenger door. "He'll know what I mean." Getting into the car, he stopped and pinned Seamus with his bright blue eyes. "I prefer Colonel Pepper; no one calls me

Three-Finger Jack." He flicked a casual salute toward them with his three-fingered hand. The window rolled up and the car pulled away.

Thomas let loose the chuckle he had been holding back while Seamus hooted with amused triumph.

Sebastian watched the government types disperse. "Come on," he said. "We need to clear out. The local authorities will be coming in now that Jack and his crew are pulling out."

"Where are we headed?" Seamus asked.

"Town Island," Thomas said. "That is if we can find Barth with the car."

"He headed back to the car with Wai Ling," Seamus said, pulling out a cell phone. "I told him I'd call when we were ready."

Sebastian asked, "What happened to your comm link?"

A sheepish look on his face, Seamus said, "After you shifted and toasted your links, I left mine with Barth." He looked at the two men. "What? It hurts my ear."

****

Madame Mdivani insisted it would be best for Cordelia and Nadja to remain on the *Berehynia*. The fewer people who knew they had the girl the better. Cordelia couldn't argue with her logic, but she worried about Anthony. They had arrived at the island in the wee hours of the morning. After giving Anthony what blood she could, the doctor allowed Ujah to escort her back to the salon.

"I've arranged for a stateroom so you can rest," Madame Mdivani said. "Anthony's being moved to the island clinic where my surgeon can repair his injuries." She motioned to Ujah. "You, young man, will go with him. Sebastian is on his way to the island."

The exhausted Nigerian started to protest, but the Madame shushed him. "Go, go, Andre will stay on board with us." Her eyes crinkled with humor. "So suspicious for such a young man," she said.

Cordelia, leaning back on the sofa with Nadja tucked against her side, waved at Ujah. "Go, Sebastian will need a briefing. We'll get cleaned up."

"Also, there's no guarantee the General won't show up," Madame Mdivani clucked. "He's not fond of boats so you're better off here."

Ujah offered a stiff bow and turned to follow one of the crew members to the deck.

"If you'd like some fresh air, we can certainly sit on the bridge sun deck and have coffee." She smiled. "Nothing like taking coffee in the sea air."

"I think a shower and a nap would be grand," Cordelia said. "Could I get my clothes cleaned?" She looked down at her now dingy blouse covered in soot and Anthony's blood.

"Oh, my love, Andre arranged for some new clothes for both you and the kislány." The elegant woman clicked her tongue. "Imagine, letting that little angel schlep around in a hospital gown." She shook her head with a frown. "Miska." She gestured to an older steward standing patiently near the door. "Miska will show you to your room. There is a generous bath as well as some robes. I think your clothing should be delivered by now." She patted Cordelia's arm. "Take your time, rest. I know I need some after the last few days of excitement." The lively gleam in her eyes contradicted her statement, but Cordelia definitely needed some sleep.

She stood up, causing Nadja to blink her eyes open. *Poor thing falls asleep at any quiet moment.* Cordelia lifted the tiny thing to her hip. "Miska, lead on."

Without a word, the diminutive man bowed and hurried from the room. Cordelia felt rushed to keep up with him.

"I'll send Andre for you in a few hours," Madame Mdivani called after her. "I'll need at least that much time to freshen up myself," she said, waving her hands dramatically.

Characters. My world has filled with eccentrics. Cordelia shook her head with a smile.

A voice from the doorway made her turn. "Variety keeps things diverting, kedvesem!" The Madame blew her a kiss and disappeared down another passageway.

Miska led them to a stateroom. He opened the door and with another silent bow vanished down the passageway. "Alice through the looking glass indeed," Cordelia said.

The room beckoned with soft golden lights. A king-sized bed draped in honeyed satin took center stage on the creamy alabaster carpet. Cordelia placed the drowsy girl on the bed and turned to look into a cavernous bathroom. An immense tub sat framed by a stained glass wall of peacock feathers. *I could drown in that tub.* Three large marine windows revealed the shadowed outline of an island catching the first glimmer of the rising sun. She walked over to draw the heavy curtains closed.

The low glow of lights set off the warm burnished glow of the gilded colors. She smiled at the clothes spread out on the plush white sofa. Andre had left a couple of sets of new clothes. A pair of soft, black cargo pants with a white tank to go under a camel, loosely fitted blouse. She chuckled at the new bra and panties. *He has a great mind for details.* Seeing an almost identical outfit in Nadja's size mirroring her own, she paused. *You are delightfully calculating, my friend. Let's hope we don't all burn because of it.*

"Okay, little duck," she said turning to the sleepy child. "We need a hot shower. Can you shower on your own or would you like help?"

Cordelia felt the little girl's mind twirling around the foreign idea of choice. She watched the tiny face puzzling out the new experience. "Jeez, you look like Sebastian just now." She reached out her hand. "How about we head into this glorious bathroom and decide?"

The little girl slid off of the bed and took Cordelia's hand.

"We'll get cleaned up and catch a quick nap before the insanity begins again," she said, rolling her eyes. "As if that's possible."

Two luscious robes, one adult size and one child size, hung on hooks beside the shower door. The smooth marble floor spread out with creamy polish swirled with layers of caramel. Cordelia sat down on the dressing table stool to unzip her boots. "I'll need both of my hands," she said to the silent sprite.

She saw the reluctance in Nadja's eyes as the girl let go. "I'm not going anywhere, well, maybe the shower." She pointed to the frosted glass door in the corner of the large room. Cordelia gazed at the bathtub with appreciation. "Though I could soak in the tub for days," she said.

The little girl stood quietly while Cordelia peeled off her boots. Standing up to stretch, Cordelia looked at the slippers on Nadja's feet. "Your turn." She crouched to the girl's eye level and gestured for her foot.

Nadja placed a small hand on Cordelia's shoulder and lifted one foot at a time.

"Good job," the woman said. "Now out of our filthy clothes and into the shower." She looked at Nadja and sighed. "Can you shower on your own?"

Nadja tilted her head and Cordelia finally felt her mind clear. *Not the same as with Elsa or Sebastian. More like images.* She felt the distinct idea of the little girl in the shower on her own.

"Okay," she said, moving to turn the shower on. "You first; hand me out your clothes when you get in." Steam began to spill out of the stall. "You know how to fix it if the water is too hot?"

Nadja offered the smallest of nods and stepped into the cavernous shower.

Hallelujah! Cordelia waited for Nadja to hand out the hospital gown and tossed them into the bin she found under the sink. She unfurled a plush, folded towel and draped it over the counter next to the shower door. She opened a drawer to investigate the contents and found a brush. "Yes!" Cordelia pulled the pins out of her already loose braids and unwound her hair. "Nadja," she called, "you okay in there?"

A little hand waved behind the glass.

Cordelia felt the girl's pleasure with the hot water and huge shower. "Okay, I have a towel ready when you're done." She worked the braids undone with her fingers and started working the brush through her hair. The water in the shower shut off. She held out the towel. "Come on out," she said.

Nadja opened the door releasing another cloud of steam and stepped into the folds of the towel. Cordelia rubbed vigorously and then tucked the towel around the tiny form. She grabbed the petite robe and helped the girl slip her arms through. Grabbing a smaller towel, Cordelia rubbed the child's hair. "I think I saw a comb in the drawer." She took out the big toothed comb and sat on the stool.

Nadja belted the robe and stepped out of the damp towel. She looked at it lumped on the floor.

"I'll get that," Cordelia said, "but you're right, it isn't good to leave it." She motioned her to move closer. "Let me comb your hair before it dries tangled."

Nadja stood between Cordelia's knees and let her run the comb through her hair. The child's hair stopped just below her ears. "Probably for easy maintenance." Cordelia thought aloud. She finished quickly and the girl turned around.

The tiny fingers reached out to graze the end of Cordelia's locks, which rested well below her shoulders. Cordelia smiled. "Yours will grow." She tucked a piece behind Nadja's ear. "Can you get dressed? Andre left your clothes on the couch."

Nadja's luminous eyes turned to the stateroom and she gave another minute nod.

"Whew," Cordelia said with a light tone. "You're going to have to tone that down."

The little girl looked at her without expression, her mind blank.

Cordelia smoothed Nadja's head. "Sorry, it's a joke." She stood up. "Come on." She held out a hand and led the girl to her clothes. "Okay, my turn to shower. You get dressed." She moved to return to the bathroom, but the girl didn't let go. "I'm just going to be a minute," she said, "or two. I'm grimy."

The child released her hand and watched Cordelia walk to the bathroom.

Cordelia peeled out of her soiled clothing and placed it without ceremony into the bin atop Nadja's things. She felt the diamond pendant against her chest with relief and glanced into the mirror to see both of her earrings. *So glad I didn't lose them.* Stepping into the shower, she twisted the knobs to adjust for scalding water. She washed her hair with economy and scrubbed without leisure.

She toweled off and wrapped her head with a smaller towel, tucking the ends tight behind her head. Cordelia returned to the room to find Nadja dressed and tucked into a ball on the bed asleep. She took a velvety throw off of a chair and covered the little girl. Finding a dimming switch, she lowered the lights in the room. Cordelia grabbed her clothes and went into the bathroom to dress. After running the comb through her own damp curls, she hung the damp towels on the rack and slid onto the bed with care.

Her lids closed heavy with exhaustion. Sleep took her without delay.

CHAPTER TWENTY-FIVE

Sebastian stood in the doorway of the Town Island Hospital room fuming. Anthony lay on his side still unconscious after his surgery.

The doctor explained his condition. "We're keeping him lightly sedated for the time being. The injuries to his back were extensive but, fortunately, superficial. The sedation will prevent him from moving around too much the next few days." The doctor continued, "It was lucky the woman on board the Madame's ship was type O-negative. Without the transfusion, he may have experienced fatal blood loss."

"When will we be able to move him?" Thomas asked.

"Maybe four days, but I'd prefer to keep him a full week," he said.

Sebastian ignored the man's nervous glances, aware his anger bloomed out of him in a heated aura. "I'll have my brother contact you and arrange his transport for the end of the week," he said. He spun around and took long strides down the hallway.

Thomas moved to catch up. "The wounds are superficial. He's going to be okay."

"What woman on board the *Berehynia* do we know could've given him blood?" Sebastian asked, his sigh exploding from him.

"Look," Thomas said. "Ian may be able to sort this out when we get Anthony home. Isn't it more important she saved him?"

Sebastian burst out of the clinic doors to see Seamus coming up the paved walk. He turned to his friend. "There never seems to be an end to this." He gestured to himself.

"How is he then?" Seamus asked.

Sebastian sighed.

Thomas said, "He's going to be fine. Better than fine." Sebastian ignored the blatant look of exasperation Thomas shot him.

Feeling the electricity crackle between the three of them, Sebastian slapped his forehead. "Everything keeps growing more and more complicated."

Seamus grinned. "Haven't you figured it out yet? Complicated's your only man."

****

A light knock at the door opened Cordelia's eyes to the low light. Disoriented for a moment, she scanned the room to catch the muted purr of Nadja's sleeping brain. *What time is it?* Outside of the door, Cordelia recognized Andre's serene thought pattern. Nadja lay facing her on the bed at arm's length touching Cordelia's hand with just her fingertips. She eased up as carefully as she could. Cordelia slid off the bed and crept across the plush carpet.

She eased the door open and whispered, "Come in, she's still sleeping."

Andre slid into the room with a cup of coffee. He handed it to Cordelia. "Breakfast is going to be served on the sun deck. Sebastian and the others are on the island."

She sipped the latte with a hum of pleasure. "Oy, I'll need more of this." She gestured to her new clothes. "Thanks for this and are you out of your mind?" she asked, nodding to the tiny figure curled up on the bed with toes peeking out from the throw.

Her lithe friend shrugged his shoulders. "Since we started this search, he's called her the clone. Never her, never the little girl. The clone." Andre stared at the child. "She's equally the miracle he is, but he's steering himself to destroy her."

Cordelia sighed. "I've noticed. He thinks he's buried it where I can't see it." She took another sip of coffee and focused on the glimmer of sunshine slicing through the narrow gap in the curtains. "She's him and she's not. I catch hints of him in the way she studies me or when she's thinking, but she's a person, an individual."

"She has a soul," Andre said, his thoughts shining with joy.

"That's not going to move him," she pointed out, frowning.

Andre patted her arm. "But, seeing her in connection with you will make it so much harder for him to impersonalize her. Don't you think?"

"I need pancakes. That's what I think. A big stack of pancakes swimming in butter," Cordelia said as she wrapped her fingers around her mug. "And more coffee."

The sun shone brightly on the calm waters of the South China Sea. Cordelia enjoyed the contrast between the cooler sea breeze and the heat of the midday. She had slept longer than she'd originally thought though it didn't keep the exhaustion from hanging at the edge of her thoughts. Patiently waiting for her pancakes, Cordelia smiled to see Nadja eating.

The little girl sat next to her nibbling on a bowl of strawberries while Madame Mdivani scanned the Hong Kong Standard for news of the auction and following arrests. "Oh, Zyu Chuntao was arrested." She threw her head back to laugh with glee. "She's a nadrágért. A harpy, you would say." She nodded to Cordelia and returned to reading the article.

Andre chuckled. "Nagynéni, surely you know some old proverb about enjoying the suffering of others."

Madame Mdivani sniffed. "Aki másnak vermet ás, maga esik bele. She dug her hole."

"That's not exactly what I meant." He smiled with affection.

Cordelia looked at them for translation.

"Whoever digs a hole for someone else will fall into it themselves," the Madame said with a cunning little smile. "Madam Zyu has long desired my absence in Hong Kong. Serves her right."

"Instant Karma?" Cordelia offered, enjoying the morning.

Madame Mdivani opened a hand to Cordelia. "Exactly!" She noticed Nadja's bowl empty of berries. "Oh Édes, you've devoured all of your strawberries. Can Auntie get you more?"

Cordelia watched with interest as Nadja turned those jade eyes on the Madame. Her impassive features belied her busy mind. The hair on Cordelia's arms stood on end as she felt the snap of energy between the lively Hungarian and the child.

"Some pancakes? Yes, we have pancakes on the way." Madame Mdivani smiled. She turned to Miska, who hovered in silence. "Miska, do check on the pancakes kérem?"

The steward bowed and disappeared into the salon doors.

Nadja hopped out of her chair to stand close to Cordelia. She placed a small hand on hers. Cordelia sat up straight at the familiar echo coming from the little girl. She pushed out with her own gift to catch the thrum of three recognizable minds.

Cordelia felt Madame Mdivani's keen stare. "When there's time, my sweet, you and I will discuss this growing power of yours." She clapped her hands with appreciation. "I can't wait to see what you become!"

"Let's see if I survive Sebastian," Cordelia said. She looked at Nadja. "It's going to be okay. He's scary at first, but he'll come around." *I hope.*

Madame Mdivani's eyes sparkled. "He must be on his way?"

The sound of a motorboat floated over the water from the island side. Andre stood. "Why don't I go meet them and we'll all have breakfast together?"

"You tell that young man I'll have no disreputable behavior at my table." His aunt wagged a finger. "I'll have Miska and Armin throw him overboard." She moved her tiny form to the chair Nadja vacated and patted the girl's arm. "Trust me, little one, no one crosses Auntie."

Cordelia blew out a breath. "I know I wouldn't. Look what happened to Madam Zyu."

Madame Mdivani laughed with confidence.

The child leaned close to Cordelia and divided her measured gaze between the two women. Framed by Cordelia and Madame Mdivani, Nadja focused on the walkway where Andre disappeared.

Cordelia's heart fluttered with nerves. She forced her free hand into her lap when she noticed it tapping her anxiety on the glass table.

Madame Mdivani's composed voice broke through her worry. "He'll make a mess of it. Most men do, but we won't hold it against him, will we?"

Cordelia jumped in her skin at the words, almost an exact echo of the words Lorena spoke to her. She let out her breath with a deep sigh and forced the tension in her body to melt. "You're absolutely right, Madame. It's going to be a heaping shambles."

"Of course I am." The buoyant woman's voice chimed with laughter. "Now, remember we love him despite his weaknesses and it won't do to blow him off the ship with your gift."

Suddenly aware of the boiling strength of her mind, Cordelia realized she had been readying a similar push to the one she'd given Haager in Virginia. *Only much more forceful.* "I'll do my level best, Madame." She took a few more deep breaths and felt Nadja's fingers nervously drumming the back of her hand. Cordelia placed a free hand over the girl's. *Be brave.* "We'll both be brave," she said wryly.

The sound of Sebastian's voice answered by Andre's cool tones traveled to the sun deck before the owners. Cordelia took her hand from under Nadja's and curled her arm around the girl's waist. She thinned her shield allowing the touch she'd sensed from Sebastian with a firm thought of her own. *Behave yourself.* She sensed his pleasure of her connection and surprise at her stern order. Cordelia felt him frowning. *I mean it, Cole.*

Andre appeared leading the trio of large men onto the deck. Cordelia caught Sebastian's jet eyes with unyielding flint. His relief to see her unharmed whirled toward her mixed with aggravation and gloom.

"Jayzuz! She's the bleedin' image of you," Seamus shouted to Sebastian, slapping his hands on his thighs. He straightened with a look from Madame Mdivani. "Pardon, ma'am." He blushed under her stern gaze.

Madame Mdivani stood to her full five feet. Though she barely came to Sebastian's chest, Cordelia swore the woman felt bigger. "Sebastian." She inclined her head slightly. "Welcome aboard the *Berehynia*. We were just going to enjoy breakfast, will you join us?" The Hungarian's tone said she would brook no disruption from the big man.

Cordelia felt his eyes on her and saw him stiffen at the sight of her arm around Nadja. His thoughts revealed he hadn't missed the similarity of their clothing. He raised an eyebrow. "We're happy to join you for breakfast." His mind hummed. *We will talk about this.*

She can hear us. Cordelia cautioned.

He sighed. "Gentlemen?" He motioned Thomas and Seamus to the table. Taking Madame Mdivani's hand, he offered her a bow. "You win, Madame. I'd prefer pancakes over being tossed in the South China Sea."

Cordelia whipped her shield into place glaring at Sebastian, whose eyes twinkled with satisfaction.

Seamus pulled a chair close to Cordelia's side opposite where Nadja stood. "Howya, Dove," he said to the girl, leaning forward. "Don't mind him." He shook his head at Sebastian. "He's touched." The redheaded giant tapped a finger to his temple with a grin. "Did I hear we're having pancakes?"

Nadja met Seamus's sparkling emerald eyes with her own and Cordelia thought she saw the tiniest flutter of her lips. *Of course.*

Seamus shot Cordelia a wicked grin. "It's my charming guile." He waggled his bushy eyebrows.

Cordelia rolled her eyes. "Nadja, this is Seamus."

Thomas pushed past his dark-humored friend to squat down in front of the little girl. "You have to watch Seamus. He's a bit dodgy." He balanced on the balls of his feet and offered her a hand. "I'm Thomas." His bright grin and golden hair matched his sunny thoughts. He winked at Cordelia waiting with his hand out.

Nadja moved her gaze back and forth between Seamus's mischievous beaming and Thomas's chummy smile. Cordelia noticed a shift in her energy as Nadja placed her tiny hand in Thomas's outstretched one.

"Ha ha!" Thomas exclaimed, startling Nadja. "Oops." He covered her hand with his own. "Just so excited to meet you." He looked at Sebastian with an expectant smile.

Sebastian exhaled with irritation. *Mutiny.* He shot at Cordelia with a mulish look. *Mutiny and rebellion.*

Madame Mdivani patted the tall man's arm with understanding. "A little rebellion is good from time to time. Keeps things from stagnating." Ignoring his stunned look, she opened her hands with satisfaction. "Pancakes!"

Miska led three crew members bearing two huge platters stacked with pancakes.

Without warning, Seamus reached across Cordelia to swing Nadja into his lap. He rubbed his hands together framing the sprite. "Oh boy, I love pancakes. Are you ready, little mot?"

Cordelia shot daggers at Seamus and watched Nadja warily. *The barmy eejit.*

The little girl met Cordelia's gaze with no signs of alarm. Instead she turned her eyes earnestly to the platter of pancakes.

"Take the seat next to Cordelia, Sebastian," Madame Mdivani commanded. "Thomas." She gestured to the seat near her. "Please sit by me."

Thomas stood with a smile at Cordelia and moved to hold a chair out for the Madame. "My pleasure, Madame Mdivani."

The bejeweled Hungarian waved at Andre. "Sit, sit, my dear." She took in the table of men with indulgence. "Handsome men keep me young." She beamed. Winking at Cordelia, she said, "Disaster averted."

"For now," Cordelia said with a glance at Sebastian, whose thoughts were tinged with exasperated humor but occasionally dipped into a shadowed corner of his mind.

CHAPTER TWENTY-SIX

Madame Mdivani hugged Cordelia with strength belied by her size. "Keep me informed about where you are so I can come visit soon. Promise to visit me." She drew back to look at the taller woman. "We'll take Nadja on the Danube in the spring." She smiled at the little girl clutching Cordelia's hand.

Cordelia nodded. "Of course, maybe my grandmother will join us." She smiled. "I think you two would get along."

The tiny Hungarian clapped her hands, delight shining on her face. "We'll have such fun!" She turned her dark eyes on Sebastian with force. "You don't dare upset my travel plans, *te makacs ember*."

Bowing with respect, Sebastian still towered over the Madame. "Absolutely not, Madame Mdivani. If Cordelia is in England, I offer an open invitation to stay at our estate." His voice earnest, Cordelia still read conflict in his thoughts.

"Good, good." Madame Mdivani beamed. "Now, I need a moment with my nephew before you whisk him off." She motioned Andre closer. The elegant woman placed a hand on Nadja's shoulder. "*Jó dolog az én kis angyal.*" *Things will work out fine, my angel.*

Cordelia offered a bow to the eccentric woman and led Nadja down the gangplank behind Sebastian. She felt relief to see Barth loading equipment and bags into the back of an SUV. The large Mercedes they rode in to the auction sat behind the SUV.

Seamus leaned against it with a roguish grin watching the three of them step onto the pier. "Thomas is on the phone. Alonzo found our missing bird."

She felt the grim satisfaction flowing between the two men. *Mai Li.*

Sebastian turned to her. "You want in on this?"

"Oh yeah," Cordelia said, letting her own dark sense of justice merge with the energy weaving around them. She glanced at Nadja, who shifted her weight from foot to tiny foot. The child's mind began to flitter with anxiety at the shared energy of the adults.

Seamus crouched down and placed two heavy hands on Nadja's tiny shoulders. "You and I are going to meet Alonzo. He's a cheerful Italian who has a booming laugh and loves pastries."

Cordelia felt the image Seamus built in his mind. *He picked up how she thinks. Gotta hand it to him.*

Nadja turned her sober green eyes to Cordelia. Feeling her worry, the woman dropped to eye level. "You go with Seamus. I promise the rest of us will meet you soon."

The little girl placed her fingers on Cordelia's face with the barest touch and then turned into Seamus's open arms. The hulking Irishman lifted the tiny pixie. "Good girl." He carried her to the SUV and opened the door to the backseat.

Barth moved to help him. "Double-check the seatbelt is tight." He hovered behind Seamus. "The seat might be a bit big for her. She's pretty small."

"A car seat?" Cordelia asked, blinking in shock.

Barth nodded with a serious look. "Alonzo said we were traveling with a kid. Kids need car seats."

Cordelia ignored Sebastian's frown and irritation. She strode to Barth and kissed him on the cheek. "You're marvelous."

The swarthy man flushed under his neat black chin-curtain beard. "Yeah, well … thanks." He moved to the driver's side quickly.

Sebastian's eyebrow rose. "You freaked him out."

"Gee, couldn't tell," Cordelia said.

Thomas shut the back of the SUV and turned to Seamus. "We'll meet you at the Aberdeen house when we're done. Park and Alonzo are arranging for our flight out in the morning."

Cordelia shook her head. "Shit, I just realized Ujah is missing. Where is he?"

"He's staying with Anthony at the clinic," Sebastian said. "I had Andre send him out before we left. I didn't want him to travel alone."

She put her hand on his arm. "Did I do the right thing?"

His thoughts and his face echoed her turmoil. "I don't know." He nodded his head toward the SUV. "Send her off," he said.

Cordelia walked to stand next to Seamus. She looked at Nadja engulfed in the big car seat. "This won't take long."

Seamus winked at Nadja. "I'll make sure Barth doesn't drive like a maniac."

Cordelia heard Barth cough loudly from the driver's seat. "Only one maniac in this vehicle and it ain't me."

The towering redhead shut the door. "She'll be fine."

"I know," Cordelia said. "She's just so—"

"Don't worry," Seamus said. "She's with me."

"That's supposed to be comforting?" she asked, giving him a dubious look.

He pressed his hand over his heart. "Ouch." He pushed her in the shoulder. "Go take care of business." He linked his fingers and cracked his knuckles. "Would it be wrong to ask you to take a picture of her face?"

Cordelia laughed and looked to the sky. "Just a little."

Barth gave a short honk of the horn.

"Oy, rein it in, ye gombeen! I'm coming." Seamus climbed into the front seat. "See ya soon."

She raised her hand as he shut the door.

Thomas stood one foot in the open door of the Mercedes. "We ready?"

Cordelia felt Sebastian's gritty resolve. He held a hand out to her. "Let's go."

Taking his hand, she noticed a familiar face at the wheel. "Choi?"

The bright-faced man waved.

Cordelia slid into the seat behind Thomas. "We good with this plan?"

The typically cheerful Englishman looked solemn, his thoughts calm. "I'm good with it."

She nodded ruefully. *White hats, eh?*

Sebastian slid into the car. "I told you we weren't the good guys." He'd picked up her thought.

"This isn't good or bad, it's recompense," Thomas said, flint in his voice.

"You ready, boss?" Choi asked from the front seat.

"Yep," Sebastian said, folding a hand around Cordelia's.

Choi pulled away from the waterfront and into Hong Kong traffic.

"You have the address?" Sebastian asked.

"Yep." Choi smiled into the rearview mirror. "Mr. Jarske texted me. Twenty or thirty minutes in traffic."

Thomas leaned forward. "Who's on surveillance?"

"Wan and Lok have eyes on the street. Jarske and the new guy are covering the building," Choi said.

"New guy?" Cordelia asked.

"It never fails he picks up the strays." Thomas laughed at his friend.

Sebastian ignored the jab and stared out the window. "Travis. We took on one of Haager's tech people."

"Is that wise?" she asked, feeling his agitation.

He shrugged. "He helped us out. We'll see how it goes."

Cordelia had another thought. "You haven't mentioned Trevor." She thought about the dry-humored man who had disappeared in the explosions at the warehouse.

Sebastian shook his head.

"Oh," she said deflated.

"Mai Li planned to double-cross Bishop," Thomas said, his thoughts weary. "Her team blew the warehouse up before we had a chance."

"She disappeared as soon as she realized we were on the scene," Sebastian added.

"Recompense," Cordelia said, feeling more resolved about their destination.

"Yes," Sebastian said.

****

"She is exiting the building." Travis's voice came over the comm link. "Jarske says she's hired a car."

Sebastian leaned against the building across the street from their target. "Okay," he said. "Is our friend in place?"

"Roger," Travis said.

Sebastian felt Cordelia's amusement. He could see her and Thomas sitting outside at the Classified Cafe a stone's throw away from his position.

"Jarske says she's gonna come out of the door next to the coffee shop," Travis said.

A steel gray BMW 535i pulled up to the curb. Tinted windows prevented any view of the interior of the car.

Sebastian motioned to Thomas, who stood up and offered Cordelia an arm. "Shall we?"

"Yessir." Cordelia joined him.

The tall Englishman kept an eye on the doorway across the street. *Glad to have this done.*

"Glad to have this business sorted," Thomas said moving to stand next to his friend.

Sebastian shot him a look just as Cordelia laughed. "Blast it, this is going to grow dull," he said with a grumble.

Thomas looked back at him in askance. "What're you on about?"

"He doesn't even know he's doing it," Cordelia said. "You're noticing it more because of me." Her cheeky smile irked him.

Sebastian put his hand up when he noticed movement across the street. "Here we go." He held back his anger when Gao Mai Li stepped onto the street. She glanced up and down the block before walking to the BMW. She carried a light overnight bag. Sebastian watched Wai Ling hop out of the driver's side to place the bag in the trunk.

The carefree man who had guided them out of the fire and smoke and the Fringe Club glanced across the street. Sebastian gave him a slight nod.

He felt Cordelia's edginess as her eyes followed Wai Ling opening the back passenger door for the ex-MSS operative. Sliding his arm around her waist, he spoke low. "She thinks she's free and clear."

Gao Mai Li disappeared into the smoky sheen of the vehicle.

Wai Ling shut the door firmly and gave Sebastian a sporty salute. He returned to the driver's seat. As the sleek European Tourismo pulled into traffic, the tinted window facing them descended. General Wong bowed his head to the trio with a contented smile. He raised his hand and the window floated up, swallowing Gao Mai Li and the man she had betrayed.

Travis came over the comms. "Package delivered. The General sends his regards. Over and out."

Cordelia let a nervous chuckle go and she turned her comm off. "For goodness sake, someone needs to teach that boy voice procedure. Even I know *over* requires a response and *out* means don't reply." She threw her hands in the air. "He's been watching too many movies. Why isn't Jarske on the line?"

Thomas gave a little wink. He turned off his comm so Jarske wouldn't pick it up. "The new guy loves the spy jargon and Jarske is morbidly shy. It's a win-win."

Sebastian nodded as Choi pulled up in the black Mercedes. "I'll have Jarske talk to him." He raised an eyebrow at Cordelia. "No need to squash the kid's enthusiasm right off the bat." He opened the door for her. "You're going to introduce that kid to my father, aren't you?" He felt her amusement and relief.

"Oh yeah." She nudged Thomas with her elbow. "He said kid this time." She beamed.

His best friend chuckled. "Round one to Cordelia." He winked at Sebastian.

"Mutiny and rebellion," he growled, getting in the car. "I'm not promising anything." His statement did little to diminish the giddy confidence blooming from the woman next to him.

"Have I ever asked for promises?" she asked, a hint of impish wit in her voice.

Thomas harrumphed and choked into his hand.

"Can it, Shaw. Nothing's to stop me from knocking you arse over elbow." He glared at the blonde mophead. "And get a haircut."

"Violence is last refuge of the defeated," Thomas managed to choke out. "Face it, my dour friend, once Gerald and the boys get hold of that little girl, they'll put paid to any arguments you have."

Sebastian let out a weary sigh. "You've all gone round the fucking bend."

Cordelia patted him on the cheek with an overly sweet smile, her thoughts as wicked as her words. "Who do you think is driving the train?"

Thomas threw his head back whooping with laughter.

CHAPTER TWENTY-SEVEN

The Cole Estate

The caravan of vehicles pulled through the large black iron gates. Sebastian braced himself for the inevitable brouhaha. He hadn't avoided Cordelia the last two days but the little girl clung to her side, making it impossible to have any conversation. Each time he'd floated a thought at Cordelia, she shushed him with a reminder the child could hear them. He sighed. It unnerved him to see his formerly emerald eyes staring into his now jet ones. He turned the one thing Cordelia had managed to say through clenched teeth over in his mind. "She's not you."

Thomas drove with restrained anticipation. Sebastian knew he looked forward to seeing Rachna as well as fancied what Gerald and Ian would say about the girl. *Nadja.* He didn't have to scan Cordelia's thoughts to hear her voice in his head.

"You ready for this?" his friend asked, nodding to the small crowd gathering in the drive.

Sebastian gave a low snarl. "Let me ask you, if you were being asked to raise yourself how would you feel?"

"I'm not even sure I understand the question when you word it that way," Thomas joked. "Let me ask you, you've observed her with Cordelia." He put a hand up to stop Sebastian's attempt to interrupt. "Don't deny it. We've all seen you studying her. It's clear to all of us, she's a lot like you but she's not you." He remained silent for a minute.

Sebastian could see his father standing with Ian and Lindsay.

"At this point, can you really think about destroying her?" Thomas asked, pulling the Rover to a stop.

Sebastian looked at his best friend, sick with consternation, his thoughts beyond sorting.

Thomas nodded with astute empathy. "Didn't think so." He opened his door. "We'll back you up." He saw his wife step out of the house. "You always have ours." Thomas left him sitting in the car to hug his wife.

Sebastian watched curiosity bloom on Rachna's face. He hadn't cleared any of the Hong Kong team to inform the others about the child. "Fuck all," he said out loud. He stepped out of the car to face his family.

His father stepped quickly to hug him. "Damn good to see you, boy." He looked past his son. "Where's Cordelia?"

Ian and Lindsay moved forward.

Sebastian waved his hand at the rest of the vehicles.

Seamus hopped out of a silver Rover and hurried around to help Cordelia out of the backseat. Sebastian returned the measured look she gave him. They both stayed in their own heads. Taking the little girl out of the car seat, Seamus handed her off to Cordelia.

Alonzo, Andre, and Park exited their vehicle and started walking toward the house.

"Oh my." Ian gasped following his brother's gaze to Cordelia and the child. "Is that—" He stopped, overwhelmed.

The little ebony-haired sprite met Sebastian's eyes for the briefest moment. He felt her measurement of him as he had every time she looked at him the last two days. *One of the reasons to keep my thoughts to myself.* He turned to his family. "Yes."

Cordelia covered the distance with Seamus at her side and Nadja on her hip. "Nadja," she said, "this is Sir Gerald." She looked at Sebastian's brother and his partner. "This is Ian and Lindsay. Gentlemen, this is Nadja."

Sebastian felt the energy moving between Cordelia and the girl but he stayed behind his wall.

Cordelia cocked her head listening to the child's thoughts. "Oh, it's complicated." She looked at Sebastian with puzzlement on her face. He felt the woman's thoughts brush his barrier. *How do I explain all of this?* he picked up after dropping his block.

You're asking me? he shot back at her.

"Fine, don't help," she sniped at him out loud. She looked at the group, which now included a beaming Rachna and Reynolds. The butler stood looking ruffled for the first time Sebastian could ever remember.

"Look." Sebastian gestured them all into the house. "We can hash this all out inside." He took a deep breath and moved to Cordelia's free side. He placed a hand on the small of her back, careful not to touch the child. His movement shook everyone free of their shock.

Lindsay spoke up. "Yes, yes, there are refreshments on the patio." He motioned to the frozen Reynolds. "Reynolds, have the staff unload the bags."

"Sebastian," Ian said, trying to keep his eyes from staring at the girl. "I spoke with Madame Mdivani's surgeon. Ujah will accompany Anthony here on Monday. Alonzo has arranged for a direct flight and we'll set him up in the London clinic as soon as he arrives."

Sebastian nodded at his brother and had a thought. "What day is today?"

"Tuesday," Ian offered with a puzzled look.

"It's been a busy couple of weeks." Sebastian caught the sense of someone else watching the group. He scanned the house and the trees surrounding the drive. Pinpointing the source, he peered to the south and caught a glimpse of burnished red fur. Just as quickly, he lost sight of her. *Elsa.*

"You can say that again," Cordelia said, leaving him wondering which thing.

"Obviously we're going to raise her," Ian said, enthusiasm filling his voice.

Sebastian leaned back into the leather chair interlacing his fingers across his midsection. The discussion had started shortly after they'd arrived and resumed every time they were alone.

His father sat at his desk with his patriarch face. At least Sebastian thought of it as the patriarch face as he only saw it when he or his brother was caught in some mischief. "There's no question we'll raise her." Sir Gerald steepled his fingers under his chin and he shot Sebastian a stern look. "The question is, what's our cover story? We need to keep her safe."

Sebastian leaned back and pressed his fingers against his eyes. "Shoot me." He groaned. "Dad, you're the better shot."

Sir Gerald brushed his irritation away with a wave of his hand. "You'll have to adopt her."

He sat straight up aghast at the suggestion. "You're mad! I've conceded to keeping her but I'll be buggered if I'm going to adopt her. What will people say?" He looked at his brother. "Why don't you and Lindsay adopt her?"

Ian gave him a look like he was one of his dim patients. "Even if we adopted her, we have to explain the resemblance." He thought a minute. "We could say we hired a surrogate."

"Then it's a cover story. Paying off someone to be on the birth certificate." Sir Gerald ticked things off on his fingers. "Much easier to say one of Sebastian's former lovers gave birth and left her with us." Sebastian saw his father shoot a side glance at him. "Once we've sold the story, nothing's to say you and Lindsay couldn't formally adopt her."

Sebastian stood up. *Enough already.* "Make up whatever story is the easiest to sell." He glared at this father. "You, stop trying to maneuver me into feeling some sort of, I don't know, connection, to the girl." He swung around to glare at his brother. "You, get on those files and figure out exactly what she is." Moving toward the study door, he looked over his shoulder. "I've got things to wrap up. Not the least of which is to get Anthony home." He shut the door firmly behind him and stormed through the house.

****

Sunshine streamed through the trees onto the little patio outside of the room set aside for Nadja. Next to Cordelia's suite in the south wing, it previously housed Lorena. *She'd be laughing her ass off over all of this.* The little girl sat in Lindsay's lap with a selection of colored pencils spread on the table to her left and a generous drawing pad. The author made a game of looping letters, giving each one its name while Nadja doodled.

Sitting back with a cup of tea, Cordelia loved the ease with which Lindsay had connected with the reserved child. *Next to Seamus, he's her favorite.*

Nadja looked up at her with a gentle nudge of her mind.

"Yes, I see. That looks like Elsa." Cordelia leaned in to examine the girl's squiggles.

Lindsay chuckled. "Or maybe Seamus."

The tiny sprite studied her drawing a moment. She added claws and then nodded.

"You're such a smart girl," Lindsay said.

Cordelia suddenly felt Sebastian's boiling frustration. "Uh oh," she said, standing up from the table. "Sir Gerald and Ian have been at him again."

She patted Nadja's shoulder when the girl looked at her, the question in her mind. "Don't you worry, little duck, he'll come round." She glanced at Lindsay. "I'd better see if I can talk him off the ledge."

Lindsay laughed. "Or push him and get it over with."

Cordelia chuffed and rolled her eyes.

"Nadja and I need to decide on colors." He winked at Cordelia. "Reynolds is determined to redecorate her room as befits a Cole heiress."

"He's loving this, isn't he?" Cordelia asked, sliding her chair to the table.

"Who knew he has a soft spot for children?" Lindsay shrugged.

Moving through the double doors, Cordelia hot-footed her way through the south wing to the foyer. She pushed out with her thoughts catching Sebastian's movement to the driveway. Bolting through the heavy main doors, she saw him stop at her mental touch.

He turned with a sour expression that matched his growling reflections.

Cordelia shook her head and smiled, picking up the conversation with Ian and Sir Gerald. "They mean well," she said, moving closer to him. She looped an arm through his and gestured toward his Rover parked farther down the driveway. "They're excited."

"They're mad," he said. She felt him loosen into her body as they strolled toward his car.

"Think about it this way: your father has all but given up the idea of grandchildren. Lindsay would have children in a heartbeat but Ian—"

Sebastian cut her off. "Works all the time."

She shrugged. "It's just not on his radar right now."

Cordelia felt the wry humor of his thoughts. *And he thinks I'm a hopeless case.* She couldn't help but agree. "Yes, exactly. And now here is this little girl to change all of that."

His frustration swelled again. "Goddamn it, Cord, I'm so tired of Vivienne Carlson's fallout. How long do we have to deal with the ripples of her mess?"

She leaned up against the wheel well of his silver Rover. "For the rest of our lives." She looked up at him and took his hands. Shifting topics, she said, "Anthony isn't going to be happy with my choice."

He sighed. His weariness drifted out toward her mind. "Were you supposed to let him die?"

"He believes we're monsters. If you had a choice, what would it have been?" she asked.

Sebastian thought a moment about waking up in Ian's lab after his first transition. He felt her tracing the swirl of his thoughts. He released one of her hands to lean against the car next to her. He gazed at his childhood home. "I'd rather live Cordelia." For the first time, he allowed himself to think his life worth the sacrifice. He squeezed her hand feeling her mind mingling with his own. "You made the only choice you could have. He'll live. That's what matters."

She followed his thoughts around to Nadja. Moving away from the car, she pushed him toward the driver's door. "You go get Anthony. I'll be here, we'll be here, when you get back. Nothing needs to be decided right away. That little girl is as much a victim of circumstance as you or I and she needs us."

He opened the door and turned to her. "I can't promise I'll ever be okay with any of this."

"There you go again, talking promises when I haven't asked you for any." She stood up on her toes and kissed him lightly. "Who says we'll let you have her? I'm pretty sure the queue starts and ends with your father."

"Insanity runs rampant in my family." Sebastian sighed as he got into the Rover. He looked at her. "You'll be here."

"Now who's asking for promises?" Cordelia shut the door firmly and waved him off. She lingered in his thoughts until the car passed through the iron gates. *Hurry your ass back.* She shot at him.

Consider it hurried. She smiled at feeling his response.

CHAPTER TWENTY-EIGHT

"Thanks for this, Dad." Cordelia hugged Enzo over the box of books.

"How could I refuse? You know, you could've purchased these here at much less expense." He smiled.

"Yes, but then I wouldn't have you." Cordelia beamed.

He gestured at the grand foyer of the Cole estate. "Your grandmother couldn't wait to come back."

Lucia Fiore whistled. "Hey now, can I help it if I like to travel?" She followed the echo of her trill upward to the fifteen-foot dome of Italian Frescoes. "Ah," she sighed. "Ben fatto, molto bello. This is such a beautiful house." The fierce grand dame clasped the grown woman to her chest. "We're glad to help."

Lindsay entered from the study with Sir Gerald. He reached both hands out to Cordelia's grandmother. "Benventuo, Signora Fiore, you're a most welcome guest. Reynolds will have your things placed in your rooms, not to worry. I'm happy you've returned."

Lucia pulled herself to her full five feet under the gaze of the handsome author. "Buonasera, Signor Lindsay, I'm glad to be back under better circumstances."

Sir Gerald's eyes twinkled at the matriarch as he bowed over her hand. "As always, the estate's beauty is improved by the presence of such a formidable woman."

Cordelia's grandmother waved his bow away. "Hmph, you've beguiled mia nipote. She never wants to return home after visiting you."

The English lord swept his arms open in welcome. "But my plan succeeds-- I've whisked you into our little kingdom along with her."

Lucia Fiore chortled. "You're an evil man, Signor Cole. I've got my eye on you." She looked around at Cordelia. "Where's your young man?"

Cordelia laughed at her nonna completely charmed by Sir Gerald. She shared a hooded look with the two Brits. "He's—"

Enzo cut her off. "Oh ho, he's on a tear is he? Not happy about this little girl I take it."

Clasping the shorter Italian over the shoulders, Sir Gerald led him into the study. "My dear Enzo, I see where Cordelia inherited her directness. Yes, my oldest son is struggling with all of this. Let's have a sip before tea, shall we?"

The distinguished author held an elbow out to Lucia. "Signora?"

The eagle-eyed woman waved him off. "I've told you, it's Lucia, per favore. I'd like to meet this bella bambina." She looked at Cordelia. "If that's all right?"

Cordelia nodded along with Lindsay. "Of course, Nonna, Lindsay and I will take you to her room." She looked for the box of books she'd had her father put together. Realizing Reynolds had whisked them away she asked, "How does he do that?"

"Between you and me, I think he's Batman." The dapper author offered Lucia his elbow again.

This time she accepted. "You mean the sour-faced butler?" She nodded her head in appreciation. "He's efficient," she said with respect.

"Enzo." Sir Gerald gestured. "Let's head to my study and give the child a chance to meet your mother. We can have a spot of tea."

Cordelia knew the mischievous lord meant scotch and narrowed her eyes at him.

"I'd love a cup of tea after the trip," her father said.

Before they disappeared through the sitting room, Sir Gerald gave Cordelia a look of pure innocence.

Lucia said, her voice bubbling with humor, "That man is up to no good."

"Don't you know it," Lindsay agreed.

The three took the south hallway to the guest wing. Cordelia thought about the first time she'd followed Reynolds to her suite. The memory brought with it a pang for Lorena. *She'd laugh this off and open a bottle.* She only half listened to Lindsay charming her grandmother. Reaching out with her mind, she detected the now familiar thrum of Nadja's thoughts.

The door to the nursery, as Cordelia thought of it, stood open. A soft, fresh breeze visited from the wide open French doors. The delicate scents of the garden floated along the sighing wind. Reynolds knelt near a bookshelf on the left wall surrounded by piles of picture books. Nadja sat cross-legged next to him solemnly studying the covers. She thought a minute then selected a book and handed it to the butler. He, in turn, placed it on the top shelf, title out.

Cordelia sensed the stodgy martinet's gentle patience for the girl and resisted the urge to hug the man.

In response to her emotional surge, Nadja looked up shyly at the trio. Pleasure for Cordelia and Lindsay radiated from her with an overtone of wary curiosity for the older woman.

Reynolds, not a whit discomfited by their witness to his librarian duties, stood. He bowed to Nadja. "We'll continue later, Miss." He nodded cordially at them as he passed.

Lindsay led Lucia deeper into the room and offered her a cushioned chair. "Nadja, this is Lucia Fiore. She's Cordelia's grandmother."

The tiny nymph remained silent, but her face showed interest.

Cordelia moved to sit next to her. "Do you understand *grandmother*?"

Nadja looked quizzically at Cordelia, her mind full of query.

Lucia, no mind reader, but sharp, leaned forward. "Cordelia's father, Enzo, is my child."

Lindsay sat in the other chair fascinated by the energy in the room. "Like Sir Gerald is Sebastian and Ian's father."

The little girl placed a small hand on Cordelia's knee, sharpening the woman's connection to her swirling thoughts. "Oy," Cordelia said out loud.

"What?" Arthur gave her a piercing gaze. His longing for her connection to the others was palpable.

"She's struggling with the concept because she doesn't know about families." She offered the two other adults a measured gaze. "How do we explain this?"

"Simply," the elder woman said as she gingerly lowered her bulk to the floor opposite of the little girl and Cordelia. She opened her arms inviting Nadja to her lap.

The taciturn child studied Lucia for a full minute. Cordelia felt her whirring concentration and then suddenly making a decision—Nadja crawled into Nonna's lap.

Lucia sighed with pleasure. Cordelia sensed her nostalgia for small children. "It's like this, Zucchera. You come from Sebastian, Sir Gerald's son." She looked at Cordelia. "She knows him, si?"

"She knows who he is." Cordelia offered a little grimace. "He's been avoiding everyone."

"Phht!" Lucia snorted.

Nadja scanned the books on the floor.

"What're you looking for, love?" Lindsay kneeled down into the stacks of books.

The little girl clambered from Lucia's lap into the circle of titles. She slid tomes off of each other searching for something. Finding it, she handed Cordelia a bright green book. *Are You My Mother?*

Breath catching at the familiar story, Cordelia remained quiet for a beat. She looked at her grandmother and Lindsay, helpless.

Lindsay's eyes welled as he cleared his throat. He offered an anguished shrug. *I don't know what to say either.*

Cordelia's grandmother gave a firm and stern nod.

A catch in her own throat, Cordelia met Nadja's frank gaze. Memories of her own mother's voice echoed in the archives of her head. *A mother bird sat on her egg. The egg jumped.* She rubbed her hand over the cover of the familiar, well-loved story. Sadness and longing choked her. "If you'd like. I'll do my best."

They lingered, frozen, staring at one another, thought threads trailing and twisting together.

Breaking the impasse, Nadja put her tiny hand on Cordelia's larger one. In response, Cordelia touched her forehead to the little girl's.

Cutting the silence, Lindsay clapped his hands and laughed through tears. "Wonderful!" He sobered briefly. "What're we going to tell Sebastian?"

****

Ian peered into his microscope. He switched out a slide and made some notes. A light rain tapped a soft rhythm on the bank of skylights. He switched to another slide. After a brief glance, he turned to his computer station to find one of the files they'd downloaded from Vivienne Carlson's computers. A soft giggle from the far corner drew his attention.

Elsa sat on the floor with Nadja. The large, sentient chimera slid wooden alphabet blocks across the floor to the little girl. Each time Nadja touched a block, the gentle creature signed the letter and then the color. Ian's excitement brimmed over when he discovered Elsa learning to read. Her silky, cinnamon fur shone combed smooth. The chimera's vanity tickled him. Nadja reached out to stroke Elsa's velvety knee. *She's good with her.*

Busto lay on a blanket in the corner snoring softly, the kittens heaped over him. There had been some ruckus until Elsa in her quiet way had commanded the hulking puppy into the corner. One of the kittens, a creamy blonde and white one that Elsa named Butter, walked over to chimera and clone to crawl into Elsa's lap. Nadja tensed briefly and then smoothed the kitten's fur with her tiny hand. She didn't know what to make of the animals but under Elsa and Cordelia's guidance slowly learned they were pleasant company. Busto's lolling tongue was a surefire trigger for the child's rare giggle.

Nadja touched a block. Elsa signed E then drew her pointer finger down her lips, *Red.* Ian stared when Nadja signed Elsa's name. Elsa chose the sign. One of the first she learned. A combination between pretty and E. Their small charge repeated the sign. Palm facing her forehead, fingers open, she drew her hand down in front of her face and closed it into the letter E. She pointed at Elsa. *E for Elsa.* Elsa ruffled Nadja's ebony bangs to show her approval.

Yes, Elsa nodded with her fist. The beautiful creature looked up to confirm Ian watched. Her telepathic communication was limited to Cordelia and she was able to read the others, but Elsa had developed an intuitive sense for Ian and what he was thinking. She signed a combination of the symbol for young using the letter N. Both hands tucked with her thumb dividing her fists, moving her hands gently in toward her chest. *Nadja.* She pointed at the girl.

Nadja signed Elsa's name, touching her soft fur, then repeated Elsa's sign for her own name and touched her chest. Elsa again ruffled the girl's hair and nodded.

Ian cleared the lump from his throat. All of the tests showed Nadja capable of speech with extraordinary cognitive skills, but her silence worried everyone. Lindsay, whom Nadja showed the most affection toward outside of Cordelia and Elsa, assured everyone in time she'd grow comfortable and things would click into place. Ian, frustrated, wanted to do more tests, but Lindsay put his foot down. Ian smiled. The love of his life had become quite the papa bear.

He rolled his head down to his chin in a few head circles and stretched his arms out before returning to his work. He studied Nadja's DNA signatures on one of his computer screens while he noted samples of blood cells from Elsa, Sebastian, and Cordelia. As Sebastian's clone, Nadja matched his altered DNA, but lacked the antibodies created by Arthur Carlson. Her blood cells showed closer similarity to Cordelia's. He believed she could donate an organ to Sebastian, but without exposure to the biotoxin, he didn't think she would shift. Of course, he couldn't say with certainty either Nadja or the Shaw's unborn baby wouldn't shift. *Time will tell.*

On his second screen, he scanned the interesting research into the DNA structures of certain fungi compared to the human DNA structure. Research into medicinal fungi discovered breakthroughs on the efficacy in the treatment of disease. Elsa's snort drew his attention away from his computer. Looking up, he smiled as Nadja climbed into Elsa's lap with a picture book. *Goodnight Moon* by the looks of the distinctive red and green cover. Running a generous finger over the entire illustration, the kind giant cued her tiny fledging to turn the pages. A favorite of Elsa's primers, she learned to read it in a flash with Cordelia's help.

The library of books the Fiores delivered made a regular trek between his laboratory and Nadja's room. Reynolds, also something of a papa bear, frequently rounded up the books and returned them to the shelves in the nursery.

Watching chimera nurture clone triggered an idea. He raced to his desk computer, fingers moving lightning quick. He brought up the original research linked to Sebastian's insertion. He brought up a different page on the other screen. Skimming the new article, he patted his pockets for his cell phone. "Where is my bloody phone?"

His search of the desk was interrupted by a distinct tapping. Turning to see the source, Elsa beat a rhythm on the corner of the board book. She nodded her head toward his work station. He saw his cell phone next to the keyboard at his work counter.

"Thanks, Elsa," he said. *She knows the lab better than I do some days.*

With a little nod, she returned her attention to the girl in her lap and the book.

He dialed a number and waited as it rang.

"This is Sebastian Cole. Leave a message and I'll return your call as soon as possible."

"Sebastian, listen, I know you're frustrated with ... well, all of us, but I think I might have a line on a way to fix it. To fix you, I mean."

Continued in *The Esau Transcendence*

###